THE FINAL CUT

THOMAS ULMER

Edited by
WILLIAM OPPERMAN

To my wife Janice, to which I owe much for her patience, knowledge as an RN, and computer skills throughout the arduous process.

CONTENTS

FOREWORD

With the masses of undocumented aliens crossing our borders every day, it was only a matter of time for unscrupulous doctors to take advantage of their healthy organs for financial gain. The harvesting of organs continued unchecked until one man whose wife became a victim took it upon himself to stop the slaughter.

CHAPTER ONE

The rain had stopped about fifteen minutes earlier. It was still dark outside, but there was a faint glow in the east that could be seen over the mangroves surrounding the small cove where he was anchored. As Gus lay there, the slight breeze was creating small ripples that slapped against the hull of his Bertram 33 Cruiser. There was quite a difference between this gentle breeze and the squall that gripped the boat last night and convinced him that his remaining time on earth was limited.

It was ironic. The squall that he was sure would kill him had saved his life. If it hadn't been for the rain with the lousy visibility, and the wind that had blown him off course, the other boat would have overtaken him, and its crew would have disposed of him in short order. As it was, they did manage to put a hole in him, but in a spot that just made him hurt and wouldn't kill him since he had managed to get the bleeding stopped. The bullet had gone through the fleshy part of his right side just above the belt, missing all the vital parts. A towel and pressure had stemmed the flow but left him weak from the loss of blood. He was in pretty good shape for an old fart of sixty but could have been in much better shape if he had kept up a more persistent regimen of exercise.

That was fine, but right now he'd have to lift anchor and look outside of his little cove. He got up carefully from the bunk so the bleeding wouldn't start again and steered for the head to perform his pressing morning ritual. Feeling very relieved, he headed for the cooler to attack that icy bottle of water. He guessed the temperature was at least 95°, with the humidity at about a sweltering 85%. There were two six-packs in the cooler, but beer doesn't relieve thirst like a long cool draft of water, and certainly wouldn't do much for his niggling headache.

He couldn't lift his right arm very far because of the burning pain in his side, so he'd worry about grooming when his life wasn't on the line. His Seiko said it was 4:35, and that meant at least another half-hour until sunrise. Out on deck, the sun was busy painting the clouds a pale pink, as usual. Normally this was his favorite time of day and had been ever since he came down to Miami in 1958. The surroundings were beginning to take on form, and he could hear the pelicans from their nests in the mangroves. The chicks were beginning to get vocal to let Mom know that their bellies were grumbling.

The anchor wouldn't come up. Damn! If it wasn't one thing it was another. When the wind had changed last night, he had just kicked the anchor overboard and secured the line to the nearest cleat in his haste to keep from getting blown out of his hiding place in the cove. The anchor was a small price to pay for finding shelter from the double threat of the storm and the killers chasing him. It had served its purpose, and he didn't think he'd have the strength to ease over the side, loosen it from the mangrove roots, and then climb back on board. He cut the line and grabbed a boat hook to ease his way out of the cove. No sense starting the engines in case the butchers had gotten blown onto the coast near enough to hear the noise. Gradually he pushed off toward the opening of the cove. Not an easy thing to do with a boat that weighed almost 23,000 pounds. It was his own damn fault; he didn't have to buy one that heavy. On the other hand, he would have kicked his behind for the rest of his life if he had turned down a deal that good, especially since he had just sold his other one for a tidy little profit.

———

The boat had belonged to a retired architect who had just bought it to cruise down the Intracoastal Waterway with his wife. Unfortunately, she had collapsed and died of a heart attack shortly after they had arrived in Fort Lauderdale. Her loss had knocked the wind out of his sails, and his interest in boat ownership lost its appeal at the same time. Gus just happened to be in the right spot at the right time. The architect went to the marina office when he returned from the hospital to see about selling his boat, and Gus overheard him ask the manager if he knew anyone looking for a good boat.

Without hesitation, Gus, who had admired the boat coming into the marina two days before, said to him, "I might be interested, what's your asking price?"

"I'll take one hundred thousand for an immediate *cash* purchase, right now."

Gus's toes curled up inside his sneakers. "Has she got gas or diesel?" he calmly asked.

"She has two 320-horse Cats on board with a 315-gallon gas tank," he replied.

"Would you mind if I took a little tour of her now?" Gus asked.

"Not at all. By the way, I'm Carl Masters, just call me Carl."

"And I'm Gus Farrell." They shook hands and headed out the door.

The boat was as clean as you could ever hope for, and with all the amenities of home. She had a well-appointed galley with range and oven, refrigerator, sink, and plenty of locker space. The cabin was completely outfitted in teak, had a stall shower, water closet, sink, and two staterooms: one with bunk beds and the other with a V-berth in the bow. We could live on this, Gus thought. That is if he could convince Anita.

Gus checked all the stowage areas looking for leakage just in case Carl had run aground and possibly damaged the hull integrity. Nothing. She was as sound as an "old" dollar bill. They went up to the flying bridge, and again, Gus was impressed. She had a beautiful shape from up there, with a beam of almost thirteen feet. Carl started the engines and said, "Cast off the lines if you want to give her a sea trial."

Gus was impressed with the way she handled with the deep-V hull.

He ran her full out and was hitting thirty knots when he headed back toward the marina.

"Sold," he said. He had checked out the price of this boat when he had first seen her and knew that she would easily bring 35,000-40,000 more than the asking price. He hated to take advantage of someone in pain, but Carl seemed anxious to close the deal.

———

A sudden noise and activity caught him by surprise. He broke out in a cold sweat as a blue heron, jabbering like a fishwife, broke for the safety of flight. When he managed to get himself under control and breathing again, he inched the boat forward with the boat hook until he could see past the branches to the Gulf.

Most of the night was gone, but the dawn hadn't cracked yet, so there were still shapes that he could not identify. One of the shapes turned out to be a crocodile, easily identified as it slithered into the water on the other side of the cove, scaring even more birds into flight. He had once seen a crocodile get up on all fours and run like a race-horse through a burned-out area of the Glades, so he well understood the birds' respect for them. Both the crocs and alligators could outrun a man for a short distance, so it was exceedingly smart to keep at least thirty feet between these overgrown lizards and yourself.

———

From his vantage point just behind the branches of the mangroves, he could see no other form of humanity. On the off chance that there was another cove nearby that might contain the boat he was trying to avoid, he very cautiously poled clear of the mangroves and into open water as his eyes continued to scan the shoreline.

At a point he judged to be approximately one hundred yards out from the mouth of the cove, he dropped the boat hook into the boat and sat down in the captain's chair. The pain was back twofold but he had no time to worry about it; the important thing was to get to a haven as soon as possible. He checked first for visitors, then the gas gauge, and found that he had only about four running hours of fuel left. Since he had fished the Cape Sable area for many years, he had a fairly good idea of where he was and figured he would be able to get to Martin's Fish Camp on the fuel he had left. He would then refuel and head southeast for one of the Keys. If he waited for the outgoing tide, he'd use less fuel getting there. On the other hand, he could head due east, pick up the Intracoastal Waterway and sneak into Kings Bay in south Miami. There was plenty of time to decide on his course of action, and there would be plenty of fuel to do either.

Most people would be lost in the Florida Bay area because there are at least three or four hundred islands. All of them look alike and, depending on the light, it's sometimes difficult to tell whether you're looking at an island or the mainland. What he didn't want to do was run out of gas and be forced to land on one of those islands. They're breeding grounds for mosquitoes big enough to carry off a key deer. He had found that out when he picked one to rest on for lunch while out fishing one day. He had steered for the island and at the right moment, cut the engine. It wasn't until the rumble of the motor died off that he heard the humming sound, and by then it was too late and too shallow to back out with the motor. He was engulfed in a cloud of mosquitoes that blocked enough light to make it appear to be twilight. They were stinging him everywhere, up his nose, in his ears, his eyes, and in his mouth. He had thrashed about, barely able to see, trying to find the boat hook to push away from the pain and get into deeper water where he could start the engine. It was quite a while before he was free of all of them. After all, they knew a good meal when they found one. The incident left an indelible mark in his memory, and he wasn't about to repeat it.

Before starting the engines, there was a damage assessment to be made. If one of the bullets, a 9mm judging from the size of the hole in his side, had found him, another may have found a vital area of the boat. The few other bullet holes he found were above the waterline and with a trajectory that led him to believe that they had caused no damage. He went to the control panel and flipped on the switch for the blower. With all those bullets flailing around in the bilge, a nicked gas line would have created enough fumes for a beautiful explosion as soon as the ignition was switched on.

He opened the engine access cover and lowered his head into the opening to sniff for fumes and make sure the blower was working. The engines were free of damage, as were the control cables. There was no gas odor but the strain of leaning that far over made him lightheaded. He had to sit back on the deck until his vision cleared. He guessed the dizziness stemmed from the loss of blood.

He kicked the access cover back over the opening, took another look around, and twisted the ignition key of each engine in turn. As usual, the twin Cats started immediately. Although he enjoyed sailing, sailboats made terrible fishing boats. When you're a resolute fisherman, you need a motor to maneuver the boat; after all, you can't handle a sailboat and a pissed-off tarpon at the same time.

The deep-throated roar was music to his ears as the boat jumped into action, planed out, and headed east. He cut back on the speed and synchronized the engines. He was good at it since he'd had them for a while and knew by the resonant sound on each that they were right. Although tempted to open them up to full blast and get going, he knew that with the fuel as low as it was, he wouldn't be going far with that high of a burn rate. He didn't have to watch the depth gauge since the tide had come in around four o'clock and was only just starting to ebb. He figured he had another hour and a half before the depth would be important. By then the sun would be up far enough to see the white sand channels coursing through the seagrass where the receding tides swept the floor clean. The channels were usually about three to six feet below the tops of the seagrass and crisscrossed each other so that you could weave your way through the grass when the tide was out.

He remembered when the grass was green, and the water didn't have a yellow tint to it, before the overzealous Corps of Engineers tried to please the greedy developers in southern Florida by draining off the Everglades, in the name of improvement.

The result left southern Florida with a maze of canals that almost totally stopped the natural flow of water from Lake Okeechobee, the largest freshwater lake in Florida, to the Florida Bay tucked in between the mainland and the string of keys off the southern tip of Florida. The grass that grew in the brackish water, nourished by the nutrients from the everglades, could not survive the saltwater incursion and died. Lack of oxygen enhanced the growth of algae and the algae killed off most of the fish. So far, they had managed to destroy 2,000 square miles of the wetlands. No telling how much more of the ecosystems will be destroyed before common sense wins out over greed if it ever does.

With a little time to kill and the boat purring along at a fair clip, he had time to see what he could scavenge from the galley to quench the spell of hypoglycemic nausea that he could feel creeping up on him. He set the compass to 85°; tied the wheel and went below. The galley was a mess. Everything that was loose last night was still loose but in a different spot, and mostly in pieces. His SCUBA tanks wound up at the bottom of the stairs. Good thing none of the bullets had found them or he might not have a boat left. He'd have to tend to it later. Right now, he'd have to find something to eat and get back up on the bridge before he ran over something or somebody. He found some hard salami, some baguettes, a bottle of mustard, a knife, and a can of ice-cold beer. He headed for the ladder feeling the clammy sweat break out from his effort and climbed the ladder only to find everything running as smooth as clockwork.

It's amazing what a little food can do for the constitution. He felt almost human again but found that he was still a little clammy; probably a slight fever from the two extra orifices he'd acquired. A first-aid kit was not a legal requirement by law, but it was a good idea to keep one on board. He had meant to get a first-aid kit for the boat but was never in the right place when he thought of it and was never able to think of it when he was in the right place, consequently no bandages or medication. The pain had eased up while he was eating, and he was comfortable.

The sun was climbing now, and he could feel the heat of it even though there was a cooling breeze from the forward motion. His captain's chair swiveled, but he could lock it in place to keep from twirling around in rough seas. It was locked now, and aside from perusing the horizon periodically for unwanted visitors, most of his attention was focused on the bottom of the bay that was becoming more visible as the sun climbed. His gaze dreamily dropped to the white sand channels coursing through the seagrass. He had to be careful not to fall asleep, an anomaly that had gradually overtaken him as he aged. Get the least bit comfortable and bang—the eyelids coasted to half-mast.

Good grief! As he passed over a particularly wide channel it looked as though the white sand ended. What it really was, were two of the biggest manta rays he'd ever seen. They each must have been at least ten feet from wing tip to wing tip and were flying just above the bottom. That woke him up! In the slow-motion, the wings appeared like those of a bird. One of them had one wing over the wing of the other, so together they looked to be as wide as the channel.

This was when he missed Anita the most. He never realized in his thirty-seven years of marriage to her how much more he had enjoyed everything when he could share them with her. Her death was the most devastating thing that had ever happened to him. He knew it would be a long time before he would become interested in anything because almost everything reminded him of her. He still found himself calling her name if something of interest caught his eye.

After the realization that there would be no answer, the tears would well up and force him to think of something less depressing. All the professionals told him that he would go through a period of denial, then a period of hating her for leaving him. He never felt any of those emotions. Not that the pros didn't know what they were talking about, but the only thing he felt was a very deep depression during which time suicide seemed like a reasonable alternative.

How can you hate someone who had no control over the maniacal group that had set out to deliberately slaughter her? It was after the depression that the fury set in. Not toward her, but the bastards that had killed her, and by God, they were not going to live one more day than he could prevent. If it took the rest of his life to avenge her death, then that was the direction his life would have to take. He had a good pension and a hell of a lot more time than they had. The little bump jarred him out of his reverie. He jumped up and pulled the throttle back to idle, and as he did, a searing pain shot through his side. Dizziness washed over him like a cloud and his hearing had a slight ring to it. He sat back down to keep from passing out from the pain. Gradually his sight cleared, the ringing in his ears stopped, and he remembered to look to the stern to see what the hell he'd run over. The only thing different was the cloud of muddy water directly behind him that was rapidly dissipating. So, now it was time to wake up and pay attention to the depth. That was the last time the tide would catch him napping!

With caution, he climbed up on the wheel console to get his bearings and look for the nearest channel. He could see that he'd come over a slight rise in the sea bottom that accounted for the "bump." He could also see that there were no other irregularities in the bottom as far as he could tell. There was a channel off to port about thirty yards, and there was another one, the one he was looking for, about forty yards to starboard that appeared to have better access and run out further. That's the one he'd go for.

The sun and the temperature were both climbing, and the bridge was getting hot. He took another look around and climbed down to the shade of the cabin. Taking advantage of the water bottle seemed appropriate, but he didn't want to drink too much. You never know what might happen; running out of gas; hitting a sunken boat and losing the propeller. Better to leave some water between the keel and the bottom and be safe, not sorry.

He slipped the transmission forward and kept the engines at idle speed. It gave him enough forward speed to ease over to the channel off the starboard bow. He wasn't worried about touching bottom again because it was mostly silt that had washed out of the glades over millions of years, and he was pretty sure the slowly moving water carried no large boulders with it. As he passed over the grass at the side of the channel, he eased the throttles forward and slowly picked up speed. He was lucky, the breeze he'd woken to this morning hadn't returned, and the water surface was like glass. The glare was as bad as it would get, and when the sun rose a little further, he'd have no trouble seeing the channel, unless the chop came back. The Polaroid sunglasses helped considerably.

———

According to his watch, it was 8:35. He had been traveling for almost three hours and, as close as he could figure it, had a little over a half-hour to go. He really had no business being here in the grass beds with a boat this size, but after all, he'd had no choice with those bastards chasing him and then getting caught in the storm. If he didn't get gas here, he'd wind up drifting into open water where they would surely find him. He liked the odds in his favor and that meant having weapons and surprise on his side.

About three points off the port bow was a thin ribbon of smoke trailing up into the clear morning sky. He knew instinctively that it was the smokehouse at Martin's fish camp. Old Cal smoked a good deal of the unwanted fish that were brought in by the fishermen. No refrigeration was needed for a while, and he could make a nice little profit off of what other people were willing to throw away. He also ate a lot of it.

You knew that you were at a professional fish camp as soon as you arrived. There was no doubt about the odor. In fact, if there were no breeze at all it could get downright overwhelming. One thing that was as distinctive as the smell was the number of cats milling around Cal's fish camp. They didn't allow too many fish scraps to lie around for very long, and they were really good with rats.

Most of Cal's business came from the day-trippers or weekenders that came down to rent one of Cal's thirty or so rowboats. He had them in all sizes with any size motor you thought you might need. They were used mostly for drift fishing out on the trout beds, which is without a doubt the most relaxing type of fishing you can do and still catch fish. Just put a live shrimp on a hook about eighteen inches below the float, with a small sinker just above it, and let the breeze push you over the seagrass. The islands and the mainland protect the bay, so the water is usually like glass. You never know what you'll pull up, but most of the time it's speckled trout; and what a treat they are!

––––––

The entrance road to the camp was easy to miss if you weren't paying attention. A mile south of the Monroe and Dade County borderline, and off to the left, was an unimproved road. The road led to two spits of land, shaped like a horseshoe, on the ends of which were Shark Point and Mosquito Point. They almost encompassed the little bay. His camp was about eight and a half miles from the main road and west of the apex of the two points so that he'd be able to get the prevailing breeze off the water instead of off the swamps. Locating the camp on the West Side of the bay was what Cal called mosquito control.

He had a few house trailers for the overnighters to rent for a modest fee, but they had seen better days and were known to have a roach or two in them. Cal's camp sat on the only high ground for miles around; high meaning three feet above the tide mark. His dad had bought this land back in the early forties to get away from the rat race and do some fishing. Trouble was, if there's a road, eventually someone will come down to see what's at the end of it. By the time someone did come down, he was so lonely that he offered to take the guys out on his boat just to have someone to talk to. They turned out to be pretty nice guys and one suggested that he start a small fishing camp where people like them could rent a boat and spend some quiet time. That's all it took. The word got out and the business started coming in despite the dirt road that the county later paved.

As Gus cautiously approached the dock area, he noticed that one of Cal's boats had sunk with the bow sticking up out of the water, and another one had been tossed up on the dock, right side up. Gus eased the boat up to the broad side of the outward dock as a teenager came running up to get the lines. Gus waved to him and threw the kid the end of the mooring line from the bow, waited for him to secure it, then cleated the other end. They repeated the procedure at the stern and then Gus stopped the engines. Just for drill, he checked the fuel tanks and found that he had enough to turn the boat around and that was about it.

Cal came sauntering down the dock with a beer in each hand and held one out to Gus. They'd been friends almost from the beginning, and this was their usual greeting.

"Looks like you caught a little of that blow last night, Cal. Any other damage?"

Cal sucked his teeth; took a swig of beer and said, "Naw, most of it was offshore. All it really did was clean the camp up a bit. All the loose trash went west, and three tourists probably went with it. At least they're missing. Those are the only boats that need tending to." He pointed a grizzled hand at the dock. "Looks as though you didn't fare too well, judging from the blood. What happened?"

"I'll tell you over breakfast, Cal, but first I think I need to clean this up a little. Have you got a first-aid kit handy?"

"I've got a pretty good one in the office, but I think you need more than a first-aid kit. Let's scoot into the clinic in Flamingo and see what they can do for you." Cal had one of those 1950 Ford pickups that looked heavy in the front end because it was too big for the rest of the truck. Ugly or not, if it had been running all these years, he'd take it.

On the way to the Clinic, Gus said, "Cal, I've been thinking about the tourists you said were missing. "How could anyone get lost? There's only one road down here, so surely someone would have seen them or their vehicle."

"True enough," said Cal. "However, they had already arrived, rented a thirty-eight-foot boat in Homestead, and headed out to Islamorada for some tarpon fishing. They were due back last night about the time that storm hit, and no one has heard from them yet. All the law officers around this area, including Sheriff Ben Harden from Everglades City, were asked by the Coast Guard to help in the search. The Coast Guard boats carry too much draft to be any good this close to shore, consequently the request."

"Do they know how many there were?"

"Three, according to the marina that called the Coast Guard."

What a coincidence, thought Gus. Tourists, renting a large boat like that in Homestead instead of going to Plantation, Islamorada, or Matecumbe Key for a real tarpon boat. Apparently, they needed power, speed, and protection for whatever they were after, and Gus had a pretty good idea what that was.

I better get out of Flamingo, Gus thought.

CHAPTER TWO

The clinic was a relatively large, square room on the ground floor at one end of the two-story Flamingo tourist center. There was no doctor there, but they did have a medic who had military service and was probably as good a patcher-upper as you'd find anywhere. He'd seen plenty of bullet holes and considered this as one of the least dangerous he'd come across.

"Not too bad. There's no evidence of infection. The entrance hole in your back is already starting to scab over, but the exit wound is a little ragged around the edges. I'm going to take a few stitches there. You won't like it much, but I'll give you some local anesthetic, so it won't cause too much discomfort. Remove your shirt and lie down on your back."

Without wasting another breath, he turned and pulled open a drawer in the stainless-steel cabinet. He pulled on a pair of gloves and reached back in for a hypodermic. After he'd loaded it from a little bottle in the glass portion of the cabinet, he got another larger bottle and some gauze pads to clean the areas where he'd be working and put them all on a stainless-steel tray. He gave Gus six injections around the open wound and said, "We'll give that time to numb up before cleaning the wound."

The medic was wearing a white medical jacket with a pair of olive-drab pants with patch pockets. He had a nametag above the left breast pocket spelling out "Hamlet."

Gus had retired from twenty years in the US Air Force and couldn't remember too many times when a medic considered the patient's comfort. His kindness prompted Gus to ask, "What's your first name?"

"Neil. What's yours?"

"Gus, Gus Farrell. I haven't seen you around here before. Are you new to this area?"

A smile pulled up the corners of Neil's mouth creating little fold lines below the rim of his glasses. "Not really, I was born here and just came back four months ago." He prodded around the wound and asked, "Do you feel that?"

"No, just a little pressure. Looks like it's safe to work on." Gus knew instinctively that he was in good hands and practically fell asleep while Neil worked.

Neil shook him and quietly said, "You'll have to roll over on your left side so I can work on your back."

Neil assisted him to make the turn then went to the cabinet again for more bandages and tape. He cleaned the wound, then smeared some ointment on the bandage and placed it over the rear orifice. He covered it with gauze pads, taped them in place, and said, "You can sit up now. Easy does it! They'll be tender for a while, so just get some rest for a couple of days. While you're sitting there, let me take your blood pressure."

Gus submitted to the procedure. When it was over, Neil said, "Well, it seems that you have another problem besides bullet holes, Gus. Your blood pressure is 180 over 96. Are you taking medication for it?"

"Didn't even realize I needed it until now," Gus said, looking a little shocked. "Can you do anything for it, Neil?"

"Let me see what I've got," he said, reaching for the cabinet door again. After a little rummaging around in the drawers, he said, "You're in luck! The doctor before me left some Atenolol sample tablets that expired last month, but they should still be good since they leave a little safety buffer on expiration dates. Take one of these once a day and get to a doctor for a check-up as soon as you can." He lowered his voice and added, "You don't need to mention to anybody that you got these from me, Gus. I'm not qualified, nor authorized to dispense medications without a license. Dr. Justin won't need them anymore since he was killed six months ago in a boating accident, and no one else has claimed his equipment or pharmaceuticals."

Gus stretched out his hand, and Neil laid a new packet, containing five tablets, in his hand then dropped the opened package alongside it.

"Oh, I nearly forgot. You'll need a tetanus and a penicillin shot just in case. There was a little inflammation around the front wound."

He used the same type of hypodermics as before, only smaller. He took a swipe on his shoulder with an alcohol pad and jabbed him twice.

"Neil, you're going to believe this is strange, but I need a favor from one old vet to another. Could you keep this wound under your hat for a couple of days, just till my wound heals and I can get out of town? I'll explain it all to you later, but for right now I'd prefer that no one knew I was here—or shot."

"No need to worry, Gus. I had no intention of informing anyone about your arrival or being shot from behind. With no apparent powder burns, I figured you weren't robbing anyone, just trying to get away. Besides, you scratch my back about the medications, and I'll scratch yours."

"Thanks, Neil. I won't forget this. Now I'd better get my tush out of town. Thanks for all the help, I feel better already. How much do I owe you?"

Neil handed Gus a plastic bag of gauze pads, alcohol, tape, and salve. "For dressing changes, and you better take these as well," he said, throwing in a pair of scissors. "Keep your money for now. Later you can help put me through medical school," he said, chuckling. Gus stuck his big paw out to Neil, and they shook hands like longtime buddies, regardless of their age difference.

Cal was waiting on a park bench in the shade of a coconut tree and saw Gus come out. He got up and met him at the car.

"Makes me queasy, Gus. It always has. I can't stand the smell of those medications."

"Don't much care for them myself, only I didn't have a choice."

They headed east until they came to the only gas station in town. It was an old Gulf Gas Station, identified by a rusty round sign on the roof over the pumps. After filling up and checking the oil, Cal slipped the surprisingly well-running truck into gear and crossed the Buttonwood Canal, heading for obscurity.

When they arrived at the fish camp, the teenager walked up to Gus and said, "I filled up both gas tanks, checked the engines, straightened up down below, and found an old anchor for her. If there's anything else I can do, just let me know."

"Well, I certainly appreciate it—."

"Jeff," said Cal. "His name is Jeff Bennett, and he's the best damn kid in the county!"

"Again, Jeff, I appreciate all you've done," Gus said as he handed him a five-hundred-dollar bill. "Keep anything left over after the bill."

Jeff looked shocked and said, "Gee thanks, Mr. Farrell. Thanks a lot." He turned and walked toward the office waving over his shoulder.

"Whatever you do, Cal, don't let him get away!"

"I won't. He's my sister's boy, and his parents just died in a plane crash. He doesn't have anyone else, and he loves it here. If you didn't notice, the two boats tossed around by the storm were cleaned and back on the surface of the water, without anyone telling him to do it."

"He'll be good company for you, Cal. Now let's have some lunch, and I'll fill you in on what's happening."

They headed to the small cafe attached to the camp store. Nothing fancy, but it had four tables and a counter for short orders. They sat at a table under a window, to get the breeze. A rather rotund black woman in her late forties, with remarkably beautiful features, came out from behind the counter, carrying a couple of menus and two glasses of ice water that she placed in front of them. After they had ordered, Cal leaned back, looked at Gus, and said, "Shoot."

The shadows were beginning to lengthen by the time he finished explaining the previous events to Cal, and he planned to be up all night navigating unfamiliar waters in his attempt to get to safety and back to the project he needed to finish.

"Well, Cal, I hate to ruin a good party, but I've got to get some sleep for my all-night cruise."

Cal said, "C'mon, I'll walk you out to the boat. From the sound of it, you'll need more than sleep. Hold on a minute." Cal walked back toward the office, went inside, and came out three minutes later.

"No sense being a cripple; take this."

Lying in the palm of his hand was a dark gray 9mm Ruger, a menacing-looking semi-automatic that held seventeen bullets, one in the chamber and sixteen in the clip. In the other hand, Cal was holding a box of Black Talons and another clip loaded with the same bullets. Under his arm was a rectangular red plastic box.

Cal said, "A lotta states are trying to outlaw the Black Talon because it opens up like a claw when it goes through you, so naturally they're worried about their use against lawmen. So, before that happened, I grabbed a good supply of them. That's the only kind of ammunition you'll find here. It's good for close work, so keep it on you at all times. Don't worry about returning it to me real soon. I have a revolver I can use." He handed the gun and its accessories to Gus. "This red box is the cleaning kit you'll need for it. Don't get saltwater on any of it, and don't forget to clean it after you use it. Your life may depend on it."

They both turned to look toward the office when the screen door slammed. Jeff was running towards them. "I just heard on the radio that they found the wreckage of the boat that the tourists were on. One of the Navy pilots spotted it on East Key in the Tortugas, but no sign of the tourists."

To Gus, it was like getting a last-minute reprieve.

Cal, as if reading his thoughts, brought him down to earth. "If they haven't found the bodies, there's no proof that they drowned. They could have been picked up by another boat or managed to get to one of the islands. If I were you, I'd stick to my original plan. That's the safest route. Come to think of it, they may not be the only group out looking for you."

"By God, you're right, Cal. That thought never even crossed my mind. Take care of yourself, and I'll see you next time I'm in town."

Gus climbed on board, opened the hatchway, and went below. Jeff had not only cleaned the cabin better than he kept it but had also restocked the larder with the items that had broken or were getting low. The place was spotless. Gus made a mental note to make sure Jeff wasn't forgotten at Christmas. He put the gun and its equipment into the drawer under his bunk, set his alarm clock for ten o'clock, lay down on top of the bunk, and promptly fell into a deep sleep.

The alarm clock scared him awake. He hated that damn alarm clock! He'd have to get a clock radio that would wake him up to classical music. It just wasn't necessary to start the day with a heart rate of 140. Well, anyway, it had certainly performed its function and achieved the desired result.

The moonlight lit everything up so well that no other light was needed. This would help him to navigate through the islands and find the Intracoastal Waterway, and the light would get stronger as the moon ascended. Good for navigating, but not good if others were looking for him.

Gus flipped on the blower switch and went to the locker under the forward starboard deck seat. He lifted the seat and took out a life jacket and a portable sealed-beam spotlight. He slipped into the life jacket and put the light on the dash within easy reach. Next, he went down into the cabin and took out the gun, the extra bullets, and the extra clip and put them on the dash in front of the wheel. After checking the gas tanks to make sure they were full, he turned on the running lights to check them and then turned them off again. He cranked both engines, set them on a fast idle, and stepped up onto the deck. He took off the stern line first and then went to remove the bow line. With the bow line off, he needed to get back on board fast, since there was now a light breeze blowing offshore and away from the dock.

Gus switched off the blower, slipped the transmission into forward, and gradually eased the boat onto an outward course through Rankin Bight. He set a course bearing to starboard just off of Otter Key, which appeared like a black mound on the water. He had about a mile and a quarter to go before he passed Mosquito Point. Once past Otter Key, he made a course adjustment of 49° to port, putting him on a course of 122°. He waited a sufficient time after passing Mosquito Point, then headed due east toward a pass between Big Key and Samphire Keys just over four-and-a-half miles away and not yet visible.

Once through the pass, he'd be in deeper water, and with an ebbing tide, he'd be able to move a little faster. From beginning to end, with the jogging back and forth to get around all the keys, the whole trip would be about sixty-eight miles to Kings Bay. His route would be relatively easy judging from the charts. He could head for the pass between the east end of Madeira Bay and the northern island of the Black Betsey Keys, take a straight shot southeast past the south end of Whale Back Key to the south end of Little Buttonwood Sound and pick up the Intracoastal Waterway from there to just outside Kings Bay. Once into the waterway, the route would be marked with buoys indicating the channel.

The moon was almost directly overhead, so he could see fairly well.

There was a long run between the Big Key pass and Madeira Bay, so he went below and put on a pot of strong coffee, made some sandwiches, took a big swig of water from the jug, made a head call, and headed topside. It was going to be a tiring night.

CHAPTER THREE

Anita had started to become depressed while she and Gus were stationed in Alaska with the US Air Force. The months of darkness; Gus's long hours at work; her inability to spend an appreciable amount of time outdoors due to the weather; and an unbearable loneliness, all took their toll. These things are symptomatic of a prevalent problem in localities with climates like Alaska, "Cabin Fever." Typically, most people feel a tinge of cabin fever and manage to put it aside, but when the tour in Alaska is three years long, some just can't adjust to it and have to be returned to the contiguous forty-eight States. A few were even taken out for psychotherapy.

In addition to the cabin fever, she felt that she was missing out on the one thing most women desire above all else, having babies. Her desire for motherhood had become almost an obsession with her. Instead of relieving the stress, when the doctor told her and Gus that she would never be able to have children, it started her on a slow spiral of depression.

The summers were her only salvation. The fishing was good, the weather was beautiful, and she enjoyed taking day trips with Gus to the native villages, the glaciers, and even to the Matanuska Valley for huge fresh vegetables. The sun was up twenty-four hours a day, and the fruit and vegetables kept growing steadily. It wasn't unusual to find strawberries as big as tennis balls, one-pound tomatoes, or fifteen-pound cabbages.

A camping vacation to Dawson, in the Yukon, was the highlight of their tour in Alaska. It almost made her forget her depression. Crossing the Yukon River on a small ferry was very exciting for her, and she reveled in it. The water had been so swift that the ferry had to run upstream, well past Dawson before cutting out into the muddy current, still racing full speed while carefully crossing to the other side. By the time they reached the other side, the current had washed them downstream, and they were level with the dock in Dawson. The captain had been very skillful in navigating the crossing. Years of practice in reading the current, judging the speed of the ferry and the distance required before pulling into the current, had gained him the skill of hitting the dock dead-on each time. Anita had stood on the bow smiling like a Cheshire cat for the entire crossing.

They set up their Apache trailer on the bank of the Klondike since it was the only open ground, or open rocks, set aside for camping. Good thing they didn't have to sleep on them. The water was clear, fast, and cold. Just about 300 yards downstream, the Klondike ran into the northward-flowing Yukon with such force that the clear water displaced the Yukon's muddy water almost halfway across.

After camp had been established, they decided to walk into the town on a sightseeing trip. They locked everything up, climbed the bank, and walked over to the boardwalk. There didn't appear to be one paved road or concrete sidewalk in town. The boardwalks only added to the quaintness of the place. Thanks to a lady who seemed to be very happy to see them, they obtained directions to the only grocery store in town. It appeared that they didn't get many visitors this far out, so the ones that came were welcomed like family. On the way to the store, Gus glanced up the embankment and was surprised again, this time to see the cabin of the poet Robert Service perched on top. They went in and discovered what must have been a luxury during that period, a cabin with a fireplace in a room that couldn't have been larger than a hundred square feet. Most of the population lived in tents and cooked over a campfire.

During their Dawson visit, they discovered an old prospector named Harry Lehman, who had traveled from London to Dawson in 1898 at the beginning of the gold rush. He was full of stories, told in a distinct British accent that captivated them both. He was living in a log cabin that listed to one side by about thirty degrees, had a smooth dirt floor, and was the replacement for the cabin that had fallen in 1932. His mine had also collapsed, but access to the bedrock was still possible toward the mouth of the mine. In fact, he dug out some of the dirt between the rocks, panned it, and came up with about a quarter ounce of gold dust for Anita. It made her day, and before they left, Gus slipped him a ten-dollar bill.

Anita seemed to be in a perpetual state of astonishment the whole time they were in Dawson. She was intrigued by the thirty-five-dollar gold nugget rings that were gold bands with a nugget about the size of a large wad of gum sitting on each of them. Gus loved to watch her eyes during moments like those. They held the wonderment you'd find in a small child.

The trip back to Anchorage was mostly uneventful except for the side trip they took after crossing back over the Yukon River. There was a dirt road heading north along the river, and so they drove up through the weeds to emerge again along the flat bank of the river directly across from the town of Dawson. Sitting there were five stern-wheeler boats that had been dragged up on the bank. They had seen them from across the river when they'd climbed the hill behind Dawson and wanted to see them up close. The boats had been used to resupply the miners since there was no other way to bring supplies into Dawson. When the mining petered out, they were of no use anymore. They were bleached from decades of intense sun and in various stages of decay, so it was dangerous to climb on them, but they did anyway. Later, and closer to the border of Alaska, they were shocked at having to pay sixty-five cents a gallon for gas in the town of Chicken. Their supply of gas, carried in four "Jerry-cans" on the luggage rack, had run out and there was no other choice. The fact that the new gas was in imperial gallons didn't reduce the sting.

The summer was soon over, and they faced another year on the Alaskan tour. As the daylight hours got shorter and shorter, Anita's depression deepened, and she became more withdrawn. Gus started taking days off to spend with her, during which he did all that was humanly possible to cheer her up. Despite the repeated doctors' visits, her condition remained the same except that now she had to visit a Gastroenterologist as well. She had developed stomach pains that doubled her up in agony. The Doctors could find nothing physically wrong and prescribed antacids to relieve her suffering. It seemed to come in spells and left her exhausted after each spell.

Anita's medical record was available to any doctor, nurse, medic, or records clerk who felt like reading it since it was kept in a central repository for records on the first floor of the four-story hospital. As a result, her medical doctor had received it as a matter of course when she had made an appointment with him. When he read that she was also seeing a psychologist, he assumed that she was imagining her stomach condition, or was looking for sympathy. He didn't spend too much time with her after that; just enough to keep her from bitching to the administration that she wasn't getting her share of attention. His contention was that if all these military dependents had to pay for their medical visits, you'd see a hell of a lot less of them. Most of these dependent wives stopped by the hospital when there was nothing good on the one channel of television that they also got free. He considered most of them to be just slightly above cretins, and not worth the effort of a highly educated doctor like himself.

Anita was delighted when the Alaskan assignment was over, and the day of departure had arrived. Their next assignment was to a base near Shreveport, Louisiana. It was a long trip in a car, but after considering that both of them would get travel expenses, a vacation on the way, and an opportunity to see parts of the country they had never seen before, they decided to drive down the Alaska-Canadian (ALCAN) Highway so they could spend time together. It was summer, and the flowers were blooming and, just perhaps, Anita would perk up a bit at the new adventure, as she did in Dawson. Besides they could visit Calgary during the Stampede and take little side trips through Yellowstone and the Grand Teton National Parks. It wouldn't add much to the journey, and they were in no hurry. One slight drawback was that the ALCAN Highway between Tok Junction, Alaska, and

Dawson Creek, British Columbia, was twelve hundred miles of dirt road.

Unfortunately, their car, which they had purchased in Alaska, didn't have air conditioning. This didn't seem too traumatic at the time, but once they got onto the dirt road, reality struck! Without air conditioning, they couldn't maintain positive air pressure inside the car, and without that pressure, every little crack in the door seals, around windows, and through the foot pedals would slowly allow in enough dust to build piles of it around each hole. What didn't settle in a pile would become airborne and swirl around fogging glasses, plugging noses, coating sunglasses, and the mirror. Everything had to be cleaned off regularly.

Gus was authorized to drive 350 miles a day for the entire trip. The direct route was from Anchorage to Shreveport, LA, but they planned to take their time, and if it ran over the allocated time, they could use leave time. The trip amounted to 4,550 miles.

Even though the ALCAN was regularly graded, Gus had never seen so many bottomless potholes. He could rarely drive over forty miles an hour without doing severe damage to the car. As a result, it took them nearly three weeks for the trip. They had five flat tires; the radiator came loose; the battery fell out, and the doors wouldn't stay closed. Their little adventure had cost them a car.

Their life together passed through the years without much change in their feelings for each other, or Anita's bouts with depression. Gradually Anita developed migraine headaches and muscle aches. It had seemed to start after a particularly bad case of flu. As a matter of fact, the low-grade fever she had with the flu never seemed to go away.

Gus was the perfect best friend, lover, and caregiver for Anita, but nothing changed. As much as she loved Gus, and wanted the best for him, she couldn't snap out of her depression and be the wife she wanted to be for him. She seemed to be so tired and irritable most of the time.

Finally, after a series of military assignments, the day arrived when Gus was eligible to retire. They had picked out a small cement block stucco house in South Miami to retire to, not because they had family in Miami, but because Gus wanted Anita to have as much sun as she could stand. The use of light boxes to overcome depression had helped Anita in Alaska, so Gus figured that they'd go one better and get light without the boxes. Their house had a myriad of windows throughout and was painted white both inside and out.

There were other advantages to settling in Miami. For one thing, there was always a breeze. even on the hottest of days, the nights were sure to bring the balmy breezes to cool everything off. Since they lived on a canal only about a mile and a half from the coast, they got full advantage of even the lightest of breezes. They spent as much time on their screened-in porch as possible for just that advantage. Another advantage was the accessibility of water. There were so many public boat ramps, marinas, and fish camps around that they hadn't had time to scout them all out.

The hospitals were not in short supply either, and Gus considered this a godsend to have them so close just in case one was needed. Anita's migraines were getting worse, and it bothered her to walk at times, due to sore joints, so knowing where she could be taken in an emergency eased the stress a little.

For about a year they took life easy, getting acclimated to the sub-tropical climate of Miami. They spent a lot of time exploring and going for long walks or bike rides on Old Cutler Road in the balmy evenings. They fished off the bridges or took the boat out for leisurely cruises while trolling for barracuda. Gus loved fishing for barracuda. They were great fighters and provided a lot of excitement, as well as a delicious meal. Some time back, a tourist planning to surprise her husband with a great fish dinner had purchased a barracuda from one of the charter boats at the downtown pier. Since she wasn't that fond of fish, she cooked it and served him the whole thing. After he had died, she was informed that the skin of a barracuda is poisonous and has to be removed before cooking and consumption. The State of Florida made it illegal to sell barracuda from that time on.

The bike rides were among their favorite pastimes. They lived in Cutler Ridge and had easy access to Old Cutler Road, the oldest road in South Florida. Their rides took them past the Parrot Jungle, Matheson Hammock Park, Alexander Gardens, the Deering Estate (Villa Vizcaya), and on up into Coconut Grove. At least two-thirds of the trip was in the shade of the mammoth banyan trees overhanging the roads. Sometimes they would make day trips and stop at the Parrot Jungle to eat breakfast while watching the parrots through the restaurant windows, then take a stroll through the gardens with the magnificent mammoth fig tree growing over the walkways. It was always a treat to watch the flamingos go through their marching act on the lawn, directed by their choreographer/trainer. Other times they would stop at Matheson Hammock to have lunch and read the paper under the trees filled with orchids. This was their special time together.

Dr. Benson, the Gastroenterologist at Homestead Air Force Base, could find nothing physically wrong with Anita either; however, he did recommend a visit to a psychotherapist because of, as he indicated to Gus, all the stress she was apparently unable to overcome. What he did not indicate to Gus was that she also had a few of the symptoms of chronic fatigue syndrome. Dr. Benson didn't know of a psychotherapist that he could honestly recommend, since he was relatively new to the area himself; however, he'd heard about one who was practicing at the Saint Agnes Hospital in Coral Gables just up the street. His nurse called and made an appointment for Anita the following week. The therapist's name was Dr. Angelo Cruz.

CHAPTER FOUR

The Saint Agnes Hospital looked like it had been built in the twenties with its long corridors, dark oaken doors inset from the hallway walls, dark red floor tile, and the arched ceilings supporting beautiful glass chandeliers. It had an ominous appearance when entered from the parking lot side. The dark feeling was soon dispelled when the lobby came into view. It was a spacious white cavern with multiple windows that reached from the floor to almost twenty feet high. The warming sun streamed through the glass. Big red pots were filled with palm trees, the furniture was white wicker with flowered upholstery, and flowers were arranged at the sitting areas each consisting of three couches bordering three sides of the large low table in the center. There appeared to be five of these groups, but it was hard to tell with all the palms around. On the wall opposite the massive front doors was the reception area with an unobtrusive counter, again in dark oak that ran across the front of it for about twenty feet. There was an elderly lady receptionist and a gray lady sitting behind the counter.

As Anita and Gus approached the counter, the receptionist smiled and said, "May I help you?"

Gus said, "My wife has an appointment with Dr. Cruz for 9:30."

Glancing at the appointment book in front of her, she said, "That would be Mrs. Anita Farrell, correct?"

"That's right!" replied Anita, just a little piqued at Gus for assuming he needed to speak for her.

Handing Anita a clipboard and a pen, the receptionist said, "Would you mind having a seat and filling out these forms for us. I'll let you know when the doctor can see you. The date is May 17."

They were the usual forms for a new patient, personal health history, insurance forms, consent forms, etc. There was only one other person in the lobby that Gus could see. Even though he was seated in one of the end groups of furniture, Gus could tell that he was elderly with cataracts, busy reading one of those large print books. Gus guided Anita to the couch in the middle of the group of furniture facing the receptionist. Gus grabbed a magazine while Anita filled out the forms.

Anita handed the receptionist the forms she had filled out and came back to sit beside Gus.

After about ten minutes, a nurse came to the side of the receptionist's desk and accepted the folder handed to her by the gray lady. Glancing at it, she announced, "Mrs. Farrell." She waited for Anita.

Gus started to get up, but Anita put her hand on his shoulder and said, "There's no need for you to come with me, sweetheart. I'll be right out."

Anita followed the nurse around the corner of the hall where they'd come in.

Gus never saw Anita again. He waited in the lobby for an hour and a half and then went to find the men's room. When he came back to the lobby, the receptionist and gray lady were gone and in their place was a young black orderly. He walked over to the orderly and said, "Excuse me, I was wondering if Mrs. Farrell has finished with Dr. Cruz yet?" The orderly looked at him as though he had a screw loose, and said, "There ain't no Dr. Cruz in this hospital!"

Gus didn't know how to respond. It was such a shock that he stuttered when he said, "Sh-Sh-She had an appointment at 9:30. Check your appointment book!"

"Look, Jack, I said there wa'nt no Dr. Cruz in this hospital, so then, how the hell could this Mrs. Farrell have an appointment wit em?"

"Let me see the appointment book," said Gus, maybe a little too gruffly.

"Kiss ma ass, ya old fart. And the next time yo calls me a liar, yo better have a gun in yo hand." He felt a certain sense of bravado with the counter between them.

If there had been a bystander, he would have seen the black kid come over the counter as if a 20mm cannon shell had propelled him. He never hit the ground. With Gus's fist clenched firmly to the front of the kid's jacket, he seemed to come around in an arc and hit the front of the counter with his back. He ended up bent over the top of the counter with Gus's face an inch from his. Very calmly, Gus said, "I have a powerful desire to break your back, so let's cut the crap. Tell me how to find this Dr. Cruz, now!"

"Honest to Gawd, mister. Ah doesn't know no Dr. Cruz, heah, or nowheres else. Yo don't have to take ma word fo it, yo can check the Doc's register, and yo *is* breakin' my back, lemme go."

"Show it to me, you creep. And if you try anything other than that, you'll have to get someone else to piss for you."

Gus pulled him to an upright position and let him slide down to the floor. Without letting go of him, Gus said, "Lead the way—" He glanced at his name tag. "—Leroy."

They went around to the little door at the left side of the reception counter, which Gus had not seen before, opened it, and went to the under-counter cabinet at the other end of the booth. He pulled out a dark blue book about a half-inch thick, labeled Practicing Physicians of Dade County, under which was the year, 2010, and handed it to Gus.

Gus went to the index and scanned the "C" section looking for Cruz. None were listed.

Frantically, Gus checked the in and out baskets, looking for the name Dr. Cruz. There was no evidence of that name anywhere. He headed down the hall looking for a door with a Dr. Cruz nameplate. No luck. He checked the other hallways with the same result.

When he returned to the reception area, Leroy was watching him with saucer eyes. "What's the name of the receptionist that was working here?" he asked, scowling. The orderly backed up to the wall before answering.

"Yo ain't goin to believe me, but we don't have no receptionist heah."

"Then who the hell did you relieve when you came on duty?"

"Eddy! He's another orderly works heah. But he gone for the day." A siren could be heard in the distance, but neither Gus nor Leroy heard it until it stopped right in front of the hospital. In Miami, you get immune to the sound of sirens. Gus's head turned toward Leroy, and he said, "You called the cops, didn't you, you little puke? Well, that's one call you're going to wish you hadn't made!"

Two uniformed officers walked up the sidewalk and through the front doors. "Who was it that called for the police?"

"Ah did, officer." Leroy piped up.

"What's the problem—son?" The temptation to say "boy" was almost too strong to overcome. However, the dressing down from the captain on human relations was still imprinted in his brain.

Pointing to Gus, Leroy squeaked, "This old fart attack me and like to nearly broke ma back."

The officer's head jerked up from his notebook, and you could see his muscles tense through his shirtsleeves. "And I'm going to break your fuckin head if you don't show some respect, boy."

Turning to Gus, the officer said, "Is that true, sir?"

Gus nodded yes and looked square at Leroy. You could see the vibration of Leroy's body. It was almost too much for him, especially after hearing the tone of the officer's voice and then having this geriatric muscleman scowling at him. He felt light-headed and just slightly nauseous. He wished Eddy was here. Eddy protected him from bullies like these.

The officer said, "I need to get some information. Could I have your name, sir?"

Gus filled him in on all the identification and address information he needed. When that was over, the officer asked, "What happened?"

"My wife had an appointment with Dr. Cruz here at 9:30 today. I haven't seen her since. And this little creep, pointing at Leroy, says there's no Dr. Cruz at this hospital."

The other officer, the stout one, said, "Have you called home? Sometimes they wander off."

"No," replied Gus. "She wouldn't do that. She knew I was waiting for her."

"Nevertheless," he said, "it would save us a lot of time and effort if you gave it a shot."

Gus turned to Leroy, safely behind the counter, and said, "Give me your phone."

Leroy looked at the officer, and the officer jerked his head toward Gus. "Give it to him."

Gus let the phone ring ten times so that she'd have a chance to come in from the yard if she was out there. "No answer," he said to no one in particular.

"Well," said the first officer, "go down to the Cutler Ridge Police Station in twenty-four hours and file a missing person report."

"What do you mean, twenty-four hours. She's missing now!"

"I'm aware of that, sir, but we're here on a disturbance call. If you have a problem, you'll have to file that report. Then, and only then, will someone be assigned to work on it."

"Thanks for the advice," said Gus, sarcastically.

The officer turned to Leroy and said, "Do you *really* want to press charges against Mr. Farrell? You can see how distraught he is over this incident, and I'm sure he wouldn't have acted that way in any other circumstance."

Hearing this, Gus's eyes jerked sharply at Leroy with an unmistakable threat in them.

Leroy wasn't the brightest of people, but he knew that if he pressed charges his life would definitely take a downturn.

"No, suh, ah guess ah don't."

The officer wrote something on his tablet, made a mock salute to Gus and both of them walked out the door.

Gus turned to Leroy and asked, "How do I get in touch with Eddy?"

———

The day arrived with the sun just peeking out under the cloud layer, and then it turned overcast with dark scudding clouds. The directions

Leroy had given him brought him into a maze of dilapidated shacks just south of the Rickenbacker Causeway and east of the Dixie Highway. They all looked alike, and most of them had no numbers on them. One of the houses in this block had a number, so he could count up from there until he came to the house that should have been the right one.

He parked in the street and locked the car doors. When he knocked on the screen door, it rattled and looked as though it was about to depart from its hinges. A little old black man came to the door and looked at Gus. "Wadda yo wan?"

I'm sorry to bother you, but I'm looking for Eddy Kraven. Could you tell me where he lives?"

"Don't live nowheres! Used to live two doors down but got run over by a truck yesti'dy afternoon on his way to go bridge fishing. It were a hit-and-run, and no one seen it, if you really want to see him, they tell me the viewin' is next Tuesday at the Belvoir Funeral home over on 37th Avenue."

"Oh, I'm sorry to hear of it," replied Gus.

"Don't be. He was the meanest son-of-a-bitch on the face of the earth. No one is goin' to miss em."

"Did he live with his family?" asked Gus.

"Naw. He lived alone, and I never seen anyone come to visit either."

Gus thanked the old man and walked back to his car. Now what, Gus wondered. Most doctors have a private practice somewhere and are on the staff of a hospital, or hospitals, he thought. He pulled out onto the empty street and headed south on Route One.

Gus passed his street and continued down US-I to the Cutler Ridge Police station. He hated this, primarily because he didn't think it would do any good. He told the desk officer what he wanted to do and was escorted into a small office where a policewoman was sitting behind a desk. She stood as the escort made the introductions and he was asked to sit down in the chair in front of her. Her name was Sgt. Samantha Cross; she was finishing up some paperwork and asked him if he'd mind waiting for a bit.

This policewoman wasn't unattractive at all, so the wait wouldn't be too uncomfortable. She had natural blonde hair, which she kept short to expose her slender neck. He judged her to be about forty-five years old, about 130 pounds, five-foot six, blue eyes, fair skin (slightly tanned), and either a widow or divorcee, judging from the lack of rings and ring marks. She had some little crow's feet at the corner of her eyes that didn't detract from her beauty at all.

Finally, she looked up, smiled, and asked, "What can I do for you, Mr. Farrell?"

"I'd like to report a missing person."

"Certainly, if you wouldn't mind answering a few questions for me."

After about forty-five minutes, Gus stood up and said, "Thank you very much, Sgt. Cross. Would it be all right to call every day to find out the status of the investigation?"

"You're very welcome, Mr. Farrell. However, it won't be necessary. We'll call you as soon as we learn anything."

Gus said, "I'd appreciate a message if I'm not home at the time."

"We'll leave a message, Mr. Farrell, don't worry."

"Thanks again, and I'll see you," Gus said as he turned and walked out of her office.

"You're welcome and I...I hope so."

Gus was having one of his slow days, and it didn't occur to him until he was heading out of the parking lot what exactly she had said, and how she had said it.

As usual, Ivan, the neighbor's beautiful pure white Samoyed, was waiting in his driveway to greet Gus whenever he came home. Gus usually gave Ivan a dog biscuit when he came home because he loved Ivan and truly felt sorry for him. The woman who owned Ivan was a divorced psychologist who lived alone and was determined to drown either her problems or herself in booze. As a consequence, Ivan didn't get regular meals, if any at all, so Gus would always try to have something for him to eat. Ivan responded by keeping a close eye on Gus's property, sometimes to the chagrin of the mailman, garbage collector, meter reader, or paperboy.

When Gus pulled into the circular drive, Ivan trotted over and sat on the grass beside the driver's door. Gus, thinking about the empty house he'd have to face, didn't get out immediately, so Ivan reminded him that a friend was waiting for him by giving him one low "Woof." If

Gus was too slow, Ivan would repeat this bark about every three minutes.

Reawakened, Gus smiled and opened the door to a flurry of dog love. With a dog biscuit in his mouth, Ivan would follow Gus to the front door and lie on the stoop to eat while he guarded his best friend.

Gus grabbed the phone book, a cold bottle of Millers Draft, and sat down at the kitchen table. The yellow pages showed three physicians by the name of Dr. Angelo Cruz. One was an ENT Physician, another was a Dermatologist, and the third was a Plastic Surgeon. There were other doctors by the name of Cruz, but they had the wrong first name, and none of them were psychotherapists. In fact, since the Cuban incursion, there were Cruz's everywhere.

There wasn't much in the refrigerator, but one was able to scrounge a sandwich out of it. He ate the sandwich, finished off the beer, cleaned the table, and headed for Homestead Air Force Base. Ivan stood guard.

CHAPTER FIVE

Dr. Benson was in with another patient, so Gus grabbed a magazine and sat in the corner of the waiting room. One of the articles in the magazine dealt with the high rate of missing persons in South Florida, Texas, Arizona, and southern California. It seems that the "Porno" industry was still in the filthy business of "using" illegal immigrants for "snuff" movies, where the victim was viciously murdered during the sex act as it was filmed. After the victim was killed, the body would be hauled out into the Everglades for the alligators, or to the desert for the buzzards and coyotes. The animals would take care of any remaining traces. No one would ever report a missing illegal immigrant. Most of them were young kids, and none of them would have been exposed to a doctor or dentist, so of course, there would be no dental or medical records to reference.

"Mr. Farrell, Dr. Benson will see you now," said a medic while maintaining a stoic appearance.

The hallway looked identical to almost all military hospitals; it was lined with doors on either side with plastic record-holders attached to the wall just outside of each door, and a few armless steel chairs against the walls.

Dr. Benson's door was open and inviting.

Gus announced his presence with a single knuckle rap on the door and stepped into the office at the invitation, "Come in."

"Thank you for seeing me without an appointment, Dr. Benson." He was older than Gus remembered him from the first visit, somewhere in his early fifties with salt-and-pepper hair. Must be one of the contract doctors the military was hiring to offset the recruitment problem they were having, thought Gus.

"That's quite all right. What can I do for you?" Gathering up his courage, Gus explained the circumstances of Anita's' disappearance after her appointment with Dr. Cruz.

"Again," Dr. Benson said, "What can I do for you?"

Gus looked at him for a moment, then said, "I don't know. I was hoping that you might be able to give me some idea of how to track down this Dr. Cruz that you suggested to my wife."

Dr. Benson's eyebrows arched, and he said, "He's no longer practicing at Saint Agnes Hospital?"

Gus gave a deep sigh. "I'm not sure he ever did. It seems that the people who appeared to know of him no longer work there or have died."

"Well! First things first. The name 'Cruz' is, as you know, a very common name. It could be the correct name or a derivation of another name. He could have graduated from a reputable medical school somewhere in the western world; or a not-so-reputable school, perhaps like you might find in the Dominican Republic; or he may not be a graduate or a doctor. What is his full name?"

"Dr. Angelo Cruz is the only information I was given," Gus said despairingly.

"Then you wouldn't know if he had any friends or family anywhere, would you?"

"I don't know anything about him. I've never even seen him or heard his name before."

"Well, don't be too dejected, I have a reporter friend at the Herald who owes me one. I'll see if he can scratch around and get a line on your Dr. Angelo Cruz. Let me have your number, and I'll call you if he comes up with something."

Gus obliged with his name and number on a little yellow post-it, thanked the doctor, and headed for the parking lot. He felt a little pang of nostalgia as he walked to his car, accompanied by the roar of two F4 Phantom fighters taking off on a training mission. Compared to the seven B52's warming up at the end of the runway on Guam three times a day, it was like hearing a little breeze. Until the one designated standby aircraft returned to its hangar and the other six took off for the bombing raid into Vietnam, there was no sense even trying to talk. Gus, who was unfortunate enough to live one and a half blocks from the warm-up area, got the full brunt of each mission departure.

———

Gus opened the door of his car and stepped back to avoid the gush of 130° air that was coming out. He rolled down the driver's window and went to the passenger side to lower the window there, then got in and started the engine. The next step was to turn the air conditioner up to full blast. He sat there for a few minutes trying to decide what to do next while the steering wheel cooled enough to touch.

The obvious course of action was to try to locate Dr. Cruz or someone who knew him or knew of him. He'd have to be methodical in his search to save time and get to Anita as soon as possible. He reasoned that to do this, he'd have to divide Miami into a grid pattern and search each block of the grid individually, sort of like an archeological dig. On the way home Gus stopped at a grocery store to replenish his stock and pick up a Miami map. He took his goods into the house and put them away, then got back in the car and drove to the nearest library.

Gus asked for all the phone books in Dade County, got them, and found an unoccupied table that he could spread out on. Gus took out his map of Miami and spread it out flat on the table. He started outlining a grid at the northern boundary of Dade County with a yellow marker and placed a number in the center of each block with a green marker. Jesus, Miami is a lot bigger than it looks on a state map! After outlining thirty-eight blocks, he took a scratch pad out of his briefcase and numbered each page: one page for each block.

He opened the first phone book to Clinics and started writing the names and addresses of each clinic, hospital, or medical facility in Miami on the page corresponding to the block where the address was located. It took longer than he thought, and when he stepped out of the library, he was surprised to find that the sun had gone down. Nothing more I can do tonight, he thought, might as well get some rest. He stopped at a fast-food place and got a hamburger because he was too tired to fix dinner.

Gus woke up later than he planned to. He got dressed fast and called the police to see if they had found out anything. He asked the person who answered the phone if Sgt. Cross was available. It was her day off. He'd check back with her later.

The sun was brilliant this morning, and there was not a cloud in the sky, Gus noticed. It was going to be a scorcher today. A quick run over to IHOP for a stack of flapjacks and that should hold him for a while. He returned to the house, patted Ivan on the head, and went back to his map.

ʹGus took each address on his list and numbered it to give himself a route. No sense in backtracking. A couple of minutes now could save him hours later. Eventually, Gus had a route for each of the thirty-eight blocks. Some of the address lists spilled over to two and three pages. The course of this investigation was going to take too long! That was fairly evident, but there just wasn't any other way.

He'd start in block one bordered on the north and south by Routes 821 and 826 and sandwiched between Palm Springs North and 37th Avenue. Then he'd work his way east to block three; drop down to block six and head west to block four; drop down to block seven, and so forth, in a zigzag pattern.

Gus continued this search for four days, stopping at least once a day to call Sgt. Cross for an update. He was becoming a pain in the ass to her, and he knew it, but he just couldn't stop. She was extremely patient with him and would go to great lengths to help him find her, mainly because she knew how much he loved his wife and she had always been a sentimentalist. Anyway, she was beginning to like him, with his gruff manner and kind heart.

On average, it was taking two days per sector, and that was certainly unacceptable. According to the density of the list for sector three, the search would take over three days, meaning that the total search time would be in the neighborhood of three months. He'd have to work longer each day and change his approach. He had been leaving his name and phone number at each clinic with the request for anyone to call him if they knew of Dr. Cruz. He had to try something different. Instead of asking if a Dr. Cruz was practicing there, he'd just try to make an appointment with him, and either be rejected immediately or get an appointment. Gus stopped at a print shop on the way home that evening and ordered one thousand personal cards with his phone number on them. He'd pass them out at each clinic and see what happened.

Each day passed into another until the end of the nineteenth day when Gus hit pay dirt. There was a message on the answering machine. The voice was that of a man. If you want to meet Dr. Cruz, call 955-7438 at 11:00 sharp tonight, let it ring twice and hang up. We'll contact you.

Payday thought Gus. Gus could hardly wait to call Sgt. Cross to get her help on this. He dialed her number at work and was told she was not on duty that evening. They wouldn't give him her home phone number for obvious reasons, so he had no way to contact her. Damn, damn, damn! Of all nights for this to happen and she's off. There wasn't enough time to drag another inspector into this, so he'd have to go it alone.

At precisely 11 o'clock Gus pushed the last tone button on the phone. He let it ring twice and then hung up, as instructed. As he waited, his nervousness almost overwhelmed him.

When the phone rang, it caught him by surprise and scared the living daylights out of him. Gus answered with a tentative "Hello."

"Don't say anything until I tell you to." said a voice on the other end. "Go to Bakers Haulover and meet me on the north side of the cut, where the end of the old A1A bridge was."

Gus asked, timidly, "How will I know you?"

"You won't! I'll know you. Be there at midnight." The phone went dead.

My God thought Gus, that's a long way to go from here!

Gus pulled out his map and thought, the fastest way to get there is up Interstate 95 to Route 826, then East to A1A. It would go north further than necessary, but it was faster than going up Miami Beach through Surfside and Bal Harbor. Grabbing his jacket and the 9mm Ruger from the front closet, Gus dashed to the car, nearly tripping over Ivan, and headed across Eureka Drive to West Dade Expressway. He'd go up the East/West Expressway and link up to I-95.

There were no longer any streetlights on this part of the old bridge approach ever since the new bridge went in sometime in the fifties. A hurricane had moved the whole solid concrete bridge sideways three feet. The "new" rusty steel bridge stands a little further inland but a bit too far away to provide any useful light. Gus pulled onto a paved part of the abutment, turned out the lights, and got out of the car.

He walked over to the edge of the cut where the north end of Biscayne Bay fills and empties, according to the tide. The current was toward the sea now, moving down at least a five-degree decline, and he remembered how hard it was for the twin-engine cabin cruisers and fishing boats to get through, either in a flood or ebb tide, even with both engines at full throttle.

He didn't hear anything, but suddenly he was bathed in bright light. He shielded his eyes and turned toward the source, stepping to the side as he did so. The lights suddenly went out, and he heard a car door close.

"What exactly are you looking for, Mr. Farrell?"

"Dr. Cruz!" Gus replied.

"I gathered that from your request for an appointment." As he spoke, he was slowly moving toward Gus until he was within reach. "What exactly is your complaint, Mr. Farrell?"

Gus had not moved from the sea wall overlooking the swift current below and wanted to see this guy's face when he told him what he really wanted. He moved slightly to allow the faint light behind him to fall on the man's face. Gus glanced toward the car and, in the faint light, could make out the easily recognizable Mercedes ring decoration on the hood. The same ring he'd seen hundreds of times on the top of the corporate office building on the Kurfuerstendamm in Berlin.

Ignoring his question, Gus said, "Am I to assume that you are Dr. Cruz?"

"You can assume anything you like, but you'd be wrong about that. My name is Garson, Frederick Garson, and I represent Dr. Cruz."

Even with the low light level, Gus could see that this guy had money and didn't mind spending it on clothes and cars. He appeared to be in his early forties, with a swarthy complexion, black hair, stocky build, and a dark blue or black suit. It was hard to tell in this light.

"If you don't mind my asking, how do you represent Dr. Cruz?"

"I am his attorney, and he is considering litigation against you for harassment by spreading your cards all over the place and asking questions at all the clinics. I have come to warn you to desist or face the consequences."

Gus didn't believe him; for one thing, his face didn't fit the clothes or the language. He appeared to be a monkey in a tux even though he was fluent with the buzzwords used by most ambulance chasers. Why not a meeting in the middle of the day, instead of the middle of the night?

Gus could see the man's demeanor changing in his facial expression. This guy isn't here to warn anybody; he's more sinister than that, Gus thought.

No sooner had Gus had those thoughts than the monkey lunged at him. Gus had taught judo for years and was ready for any overt move this guy might make. He sidestepped the lunge and assisted the forward momentum by placing his hand on the back of the monkey's head and pulling. He went off the sea wall like a torpedo and landed headfirst six feet below in the swirling current.

The majority of the swift current is under the surface, like an undertow, and he never surfaced for as far as Gus could see in the faint light. His body would travel under the surface for probably a half-mile, but even after he surfaced the current would continue relentlessly carrying him out to sea. Not a pretty way to die, but that's exactly what he planned for Gus, so there was not an ounce of pity, and certainly no regret.

Gus walked over to the Mercedes, pulled out his shirttail, and covered the door handle while he got the door open. The jerk had even left his keys in the ignition. He used his shirttail to open the console and found some napkins in it. He took out a few of them and used them to snoop into the glove compartment. He found what he was looking for and was mildly surprised. According to the registration, the car belonged to one Frederick A. Garson. There were several old registrations in the same envelope with the same information on them, so he took the oldest one and put the rest back.

He pushed the latch release for the trunk lid and heard it pop open. He made sure that there were no inadvertent fingerprints left behind and eased out of the car, slamming the door behind him. He walked around to the trunk and opened the lid. There were what appeared to be four black plastic body bags stacked neatly on the shelf at the front end of the trunk. There was nothing else that looked suspicious, so he closed the trunk lid.

He couldn't dispose of the car by driving it into the channel, because of the guard rail at the end of the road, so he got into his car and headed home, leaving it for the car thieves or cops. After all, no one knew that he had ever been there.

CHAPTER SIX

Gus got up too early for the amount of sleep he'd had during the night, but he couldn't wait to see if there was anything in the paper about his little incident. Ivan was waiting for him to open the door, so Gus had to pat him on the head and tell him what a great guard dog he was. Ivan was satisfied with that and let Gus get the paper without any further demands.

Gus read the paper from front to back but could find nothing about a disappearance, or any bodies that had washed up on shore. He was mildly surprised to find out that it was Friday. He had been so focused on the search for Cruz that he had lost track of time. One thing he knew for sure though was that he had narrowed down the area of the search to what he had already covered. Somewhere along the way, Cruz had gotten wind of him and had sent his dogs out for the kill. So, Cruz was involved with one of the clinics in North Miami as well, or possibly all of them. In any event, he couldn't see any future in continuing to investigate the rest of the clinics on his lists. Gus put a paper clip on them and stowed them in the lower desk drawer. He put a paper clip on the ones that he had covered already, put them in his map, closed it and called Sgt. Cross.

"Well, Mr. Farrell, so nice to hear from you again."

"Good morning, Sgt. Cross, the feeling is mutual. I've got to see you. Will you be in for a while?"

"Yes, I'll be here all day."

"Great, I'll be right there. I have something important to tell you."

When Gus came through the door to the police station, he could see that Sgt. Cross was talking to someone in her office. It irritated Gus that he had to wait for this other person to vacate her office, even though he was another policeman.

As soon as the other officer left, Gus hurriedly occupied the doorway, knocking gently on the frame.

"Is it OK to see you now?"

"Yes, of course. Please come in and have a seat. What's so important?"

While he'd been waiting, Gus considered what he was preparing to tell her and had second thoughts. After all, she was a police officer who would be listening to his admission of killing another person. He didn't know if that was such a hot idea, at least not yet.

"I just wanted to bring you up to date on what I've surmised, and what I know so far. Maybe if we compared notes, it might reveal something."

"Go ahead, but I've got to warn you, I don't have many 'notes' so far."

"Well, let's see what falls out. First of all, I think someone is covering up tracks. The receptionist, the nurse, and the gray lady at the St. Agnes Hospital, all of whom we actually saw, have disappeared with no trace. A truck killed the black orderly that Leroy said he relieved, the following morning. There's no link left that ties anyone to the people we saw at the hospital."

"Wait a minute, Gus. Oh, I'm sorry. Do you mind if I call you Gus?"

"No, not at all, in fact, I wish you would."

"Good, in that case, you may call me Sam."

"I like that," Gus said.

"I just remembered that there was a police report, made about two weeks ago, which frankly I hadn't connected to the nurse in your case. One of the airboat operators reported finding a body dressed in a nurse's uniform out in the Everglades, not far from Shark Valley. It was a gruesome report. Needless to say, there wasn't much left of her to go on. The alligators found her first, and it seems that her head and hands were missing, in addition to most of the body. There were no other forms of identification on the body. The coroner was able to establish the time of death to be about two weeks ago. If you have time, I'd like to see if there's an update to her case."

"Please do," said Gus. "I have no place to go."

Sam was gone for about ten minutes, and Gus was getting anxious. Finally, she came into her office reading some papers in her hand.

"This is really peculiar," she said, sitting down at her desk.

Leaning forward Gus said, "What's peculiar?"

Looking over the top of her glasses and through her eyebrows, she said, "This lady wasn't just killed. According to the autopsy report, her stomach and chest cavities were opened by a scalpel, and both her kidneys are missing, along with her liver."

"My God!" exclaimed Gus. He sat there contemplating what Sam had just said, then asked, "What else is there?"

"Well, she had heart disease and judging from her lungs it was probably from smoking, She was in her late forties, was only slightly overweight and was probably five foot, six inches tall."

"Is there a summary of the autopsy?"

"Yes, there is! The pathologist made the comment that it appears this lady was harvested."

"What does he mean, harvested?"

"Well, Gus, it just means that this lady was killed for her body parts. There are a lot of rich people with failing organs who will pay anything for a healthy replacement, and unfortunately, a lot of doctors who want to get richer. Most of the organs go to South America where the drug money is abundant and where networks have been established to transport the harvest to the recipients. We've known about it for some time but haven't had the resources to do much about it. Within the last year, we've heard about the cargo (meaning body parts) being distributed in the United States. It's hard to know who is legitimate and who isn't anymore.

"Miami is a lucrative market for body parts because of all the illegal immigrants. Just like the Mexican border. The victim is kidnapped and held until blood typing can be done, usually within a couple of days since most of them have their own labs and technicians. They match up the buyers' requirements with the victims, and then arrange for a mule; that's the person transporting the organ to the customer, plane tickets and travel money for bribing customs officers. No mule ever comes back! That way there's no trace back to the harvester."

Gus was astounded! He had never heard of anything this gross before, and it sickened him. Gus reached over to Sam's desk and pulled out a tissue to wipe his forehead. He was sweating and hadn't realized it until it dripped off his nose.

"Gus, I know what you must be feeling, but please don't assume that Anita was pulled into this ring. We can't assume anything until we've ruled out all the other possibilities."

Gus said, "I'm not giving up on anything, Sam. I just need to try to put this all into perspective and see what I can come up with."

"Well, don't think you're alone in this, Gus. I plan to work with you in your investigation and between the two of us I'm sure we'll come up with something. Now, tell me how you're planning on proceeding."

Gus seemed to calm down considerably and then began to bring Sam up to date.

"OK, I'm pretty sure that this Dr. Cruz has connections all over town. He was allegedly practicing at the St. Agnes Hospital in the Gables, and then when I started to hand out my phone number in the northeast section of Miami, I must have hit a nerve because I had a response last night."

"What do you mean, a response?"

Gus felt that he could trust Sam not to turn him in, so he threw caution to the wind and decided to tell her what happened.

"I got home relatively late last night, and there was a phone message for me to call a number, let it ring twice and then hang up. I did that, after trying to get in touch with you, and I had a call-back to meet someone on the north end of the old A1A Bridge at Bakers Haulover."

"Oh my God, Gus! I wish I had been here; I'd have insisted that you stay away from there. You're obviously all right, but what happened?"

Gus retraced the events of the night before, including the toss into the drink, and the Mercedes.

"Wait a minute, Gus." Sam looked through her Rolodex, picked up the phone and dialed a number. She apparently reached the number she was after and said, "Could I speak to Lt. Guerry, please?"

She waited for a few minutes, then said, "Rod, this is Sam, have you got a report on finding a Mercedes at the north end of the old Bakers Haulover Bridge? Well, could you have a patrol car check that area for an abandoned Mercedes? Just a second, Rod."

Gus was holding a registration card in front of her nose. She took the card and said, "The car belongs to a Mr. Frederick A. Garson," then rattled off the information on the card. "OK, Rod, I'll be waiting, and thanks.

"That was Rod Guerry at the North Beach Police Department. He'll get back to me as soon as they check that area. He has a car in the area so it shouldn't take too long."

It seemed to take an eternity, but eventually, the phone rang, and Sam picked it up. "This is Sgt. Samantha Cross; can I help you?"

She thanked the other party and hung up.

"There's no trace of a Mercedes anywhere near the old bridge, Gus."

"I didn't think there would be, since the keys were still in it, and it is a quick turn-around for thieves. Anyway, since that's out of the way, perhaps you'd care to have some lunch with me?"

Sam handed the registration card back to Gus and said, "That sounds lovely. Could I have a few minutes to wash up?"

"Take as long as you like since, as I said...."

Sam smiled and said, "I know, you have no place else to go, right?"

Sam excused herself and disappeared around the corner of her office door. She was gone longer than Gus expected her to be, but he said nothing when she came back.

"Sorry I took so long, Gus. Are you ready to go?"

Jasper's was one of those trendy little restaurants, heavy on brass and green Formica, with just the right touch of oak and etched beveled glass. It was attached to the Cutler Ridge Shopping Center, which made it handy, and the food wasn't bad either. Since Sam was still on duty, they didn't get much time to talk. All they had time to do was eat and get Sam back to the station. Before she opened the car door, Gus placed his hand on her arm and said, "Perhaps if you're free tomorrow night, you would let me take you out for a real meal."

"Yes, I am free, and I'd enjoy that."

"Good I'll pick you up at seven if you tell me where to do that."

Sam scribbled her home address and phone number on the back of her business card and handed it to Gus.

"You be careful, Gus. They know where to find you by now."

"Don't worry, Sam. I can take care of myself."

The sun was almost straight up when Gus pulled into his driveway. It must have been 95° because not even his air conditioner could overcome the sticky heat. The vinyl seats in his car were so hot they were releasing some gas into the air that had a foul odor. That must be the yellow gunk that kept accumulating on the inside of his windows. Next time he'd get cloth seats for sure!

Ivan didn't even get up from his guard position under the oak tree in the front yard. He just looked at Gus, wagged his tail and stayed put. When Gus went into the house, there was a faint odor, sort of like fertilizer, but he couldn't be sure. The skin crawled on his neck, and he stood stock-still to listen. The only sound he heard was the refrigerator running. He stepped out of his shoes, removed the Ruger from his belt and cautiously checked out all the rooms.

Nothing. Maybe he was getting paranoid. He replaced the gun, put his shoes back on and went out to the kitchen. Gus got the dog dish he'd bought with Ivan's name on it, filled it with ice water, and set it on the front porch. This time Ivan did get up to investigate. He looked like he was ready to pass out as he walked across the grass. Gus thought it's too hot in Florida for a dog like Ivan.

Gus got a beer and sat down at the kitchen table with the lists of the clinics he'd covered in North Miami. It was time to take stock again.

He'd gotten a call last night. If he'd hit a nerve earlier, they wouldn't have waited to come after him. So the logical assumption is that Thursday's search had turned up the clinic he was looking for. The clinics he'd visited on Thursday were in sector nine, which included

Miami Shores and Little River. He decided to take a run-up to Little River, since it was the closest, and check out the clinics again to see if he'd missed something before it got dark.

Ivan's bowl was empty, and he was back under the tree again, looking a little peaked. Gus took the bowl into the house and filled it up again for Ivan.

The clinics were grouped together on the southern end of this sector. His plan was to drive behind each one and see if Cruz was egocentric enough to have his name on a parking slot. He was able to check out four clinics before it got too dark to see anymore. He headed back to South Miami.

Gus was beginning to get tired and frustrated at his lack of real progress, and after a skimpy meal of leftovers he locked up the house and went to bed.

———

Gus woke up at 1:30 sweating like a horse. There was just no breeze at all, and he knew he'd never get back to sleep in this oven. He got up and pulled on a pair of shorts and a T-shirt, slipped his boat shoes on, and grabbed his keys. Gus kept his car in the garage because there were several teenage vandals in the neighborhood who roamed the area at night looking for anything they could mindlessly destroy.

He pushed the door switch and got into the car while the garage door opener did its duty. He backed out of the garage and noticed Ivan still under the tree. He didn't move a muscle, and Gus thought that that was peculiar, but thought no more about it. Ivan must have been worn out.

Gus drove over to Old Cutler Road, turned north, then right at 144th Street. Kings Bay Marina was the closest boat slip he could find that was still reasonable; they treated him pretty good there, and he was satisfied. The *Anita* was resting gently on her lines. He went aboard, opened the hatch, then went below and opened a few of the windows to let that little breeze get in. It wasn't cooling off, so he got the sleeping bag out of the locker, went up top and threw it on the deck, unrolled it and lay down. He was lucky; the mosquitoes weren't that bad tonight. He was asleep within minutes.

He was awakened suddenly and could still hear the rolling blast. Something had blown up, but he couldn't determine where. He lay down again and tried to get back to his dream, but now the sirens were wailing, somewhere to the southwest. There were gas lines throughout the area, and he imagined that someone's stove had become a rocket.

The sun, shining in his face, woke him up. There were others up and busy with preparations for their all-day fishing trips. He could smell bacon, and his stomach growled to remind him that he had been neglecting it. He rolled up his sleeping bag, stowed it back in the locker, closed the windows and hatch cover, locked up and jumped onto the dock.

The activity on his street was unbelievable. He'd never seen so many fire trucks, ambulances and police cars compressed into such a small area before. This must be ground zero for the sound of the explosion that woke him up last night. A uniformed police officer stopped him about two blocks from his house and told him to turn around, that this area was closed due to an explosion.

When Gus pressed him by asking, "What happened?" The officer told him just to turn around and go back to the detour.

Gus wasn't that easily put off. "Officer, I live up there, and I want to know what blew up!"

The Officer took a long look at Gus and said, in a more compassionate voice, "A house on the corner blew up and took half of another one with it. You can pull off on the shoulder over there, pointing behind Gus, and check with Detective Addison at the scene. He'll answer your questions."

"Thanks," Gus said and put the car in reverse.

When he approached to within a block of his house, the blood drained from his face at the realization that the center of all the attention had been his house.

CHAPTER SEVEN

Gus was feeling dizzy and felt like his knees would give way. He sat down on the grass for a few minutes to regain his senses. He wasn't feeling any better, so he lay out on the grass with his arm over his forehead to shield the sun. Eventually, the dizziness stopped, and he was beginning to feel human again. He rolled over on his side and curled up to get his knee on the ground, then managed to stand up.

Gus walked over to the knot of policemen standing in the middle of a group of their cruisers and asked the first one he came to, "Excuse me, could you tell me which officer is Detective Addison?"

The cop turned his pimply chin toward Gus, jabbed it upward and said, "That guy in the blue jacket over there."

Gus headed toward the man in his late forties wearing tan pants and a blue jacket that said CRPD in yellow lettering across the back. It was obviously too hot to be wearing a jacket because he was sweating profusely. He probably needed to wear the jacket as part of his public relations obligation. He was also probably a member of a Disaster Investigation Team or some such group.

"Excuse me," Gus said to the back of the man's balding head. "Could you tell me what happened here? I was the owner of this house."

Ignoring Gus's question, the officer turned and said, "You're Gus Farrell?"

Gus said, "That's right."

"Well, Mr. Farrell, without a thorough investigation, we're not sure. What we do know for sure is that it wasn't a gas explosion. None of the gas pipes are ruptured, and we've cut off the gas to both of these houses."

Gus's head jerked up, and he asked, "Both houses?"

"I'm sorry, I assumed you knew. The lady next door was killed when the explosion occurred. It took out about half of her house including the bedroom she was sleeping in."

Gus didn't react to the officer's statement because if the truth were known, he didn't think much of his neighbor, because of her treatment of Ivan, her late-night carousing, and perpetual drunken state.

"Mr. Farrell, I'm Detective Chuck Addison, and I've been assigned to this case. Could you tell me why you weren't killed in this explosion?"

"I was on my boat over at Kings Bay Marina."

"OK, well, later on, I'd like for you to come over to the police station and answer some questions for me. Would you be able to do that?"

"Sure, I'll be over later this morning. Oh, Officer Addison, could you tell me if a white dog was hanging around this morning?"

"Was he your dog, Mr. Farrell?"

"No, he belonged to the lady that was killed. He just thought he lived here."

"There was a white dog here, but he wasn't hanging around. He was lying dead under that tree. We're almost sure he was poisoned, but the lab results aren't back yet. I'm sorry!"

Gus's mind started racing like an engine without a governor. They were getting close, and only luck had saved him. He would not be put on the defensive again! From now on he would be the one in pursuit.

"Do you have a place to stay, Mr. Farrell?"

"Oh, yes, thank you. I'll give you the address when I come in later this morning."

"Good, because we'll need to be in touch with you during this ongoing investigation."

Gus asked, "Do you suppose that I could go into the remains of my house and retrieve something?"

"Sorry, Mr. Farrell, the crime lab is going over it, and they don't like company. I'll get in touch with you...on second thought, you check back with me." He fished around in his wallet and came out with a business card. Handing it to Gus, he said, "You'll be a little hard to get in touch with now, so check back with me tomorrow and I'll let you know when you can get back in. Right now, though, you'd better get something to eat and rest up a little. Then I'll see you in a couple of hours, OK?"

"OK," Gus responded.

Gus walked back to his car and drove over to the Dixie Highway to find a phone.

"Cutler Ridge Police Department. This is Sgt. Cross; how may I help you?"

"Hello Sam, this is Gus."

"Oh, Gus. I heard what happened. Are you hurt?"

"No, I'm OK. I was over on my boat. It woke me up when it happened, but I didn't realize that it was my house. Listen, could I talk with you? I'm coming over to talk with Detective Addison later this morning, but I'd like to see you when we're done, OK?"

"Sure Gus, I can take a long lunch break. Just stick your head in my office when you're ready."

"OK, I'll see you later."

The first thing Gus had to do was get some clothes. He only had one change of clothes on the boat, and nothing else. Good thing he had his money and cards with him when it happened. Otherwise, he'd have had a lot of running around to do to get everything reinstated. He drove up to the Kendall Mall and bought all the necessities plus a jacket. The gun tucked into his belt was beginning to feel conspicuous, and he needed something that would do a better job of hiding it. He bought pants, shirts, shoes, socks, and belts and carried all the bags out to the car.

Gus was on Eureka Drive and almost back to where the house was before it dawned on him that the house was no longer there. Damn short-term memory! He hadn't lost much time though and continued over to the marina. He unloaded his goods and took a shower in the matchbox of a shower stall.

Gus was a little embarrassed wearing clothes with fold wrinkles showing, but it couldn't be helped. His iron went up with the house.

The new shoes were pinching a little as he walked up to the police station. He went in and found Detective Addison.

"Hello again, Mr. Farrell. You look like you're feeling better than you looked this morning."

"I am, thanks," Gus said. "Have you found out what happened yet?"

"Not yet, the crime lab has finished up and are busy, as we speak, analyzing all the samples. We think, at first glance, that it was Plastique, but we'll know for sure shortly."

Detective Addison leaned back in his swivel chair, stuck his thumbs into his belt, and sighed. "Mr. Farrell, do you have any idea why anyone would try to kill you?"

The words hit Gus like a shock wave. Of course, that's what has been happening, but that's the first time it was ever put into words. The thought was discomforting, to say the least.

"I think I might have an idea, Detective Addison," said Gus.

"Chuck, just call me Chuck. What idea is that?"

After bringing Chuck up to date, he asked, "Has there been any word yet on the missing person report on my wife?"

"Not yet, but it is an active investigation. We're slightly under-manned due to budget cuts, but people are working on it. Now, could you tell me where you're staying?"

"Slip twenty-three at Kings Bay Marina."

"OK, Gus. It's all right to call you Gus, isn't it?" Chuck asked as he stood up, extending his hand.

"Perfectly all right. Thanks, Chuck, I'll see you later."

Sam's office was three doors down from Chuck's on the opposite side of the hall. When he stuck his head around the corner, Sam was looking directly at him, smiling.

"Hi, Sam, are you ready?"

"Sure am! I've been waiting for you!"

There was a nice little restaurant not too far away, out on Krome Avenue near the strawberry fields, and since Gus was driving, he headed for it.

"What did you want to see me about, Gus?"

"Several things. First, I just wanted to see you again, Sam; and second, to see if anyone has come up with anything yet."

Gus parked in front of the restaurant, and they found a nice window seat in the rear where they wouldn't be disturbed. They ordered and then Sam said, "I'm flattered, Gus. I am! I haven't been getting much attention since my husband was killed. Not the right kind of attention, if you know what I mean. I guess it's all right to tell you that I've been looking forward to seeing you again as well. As for the second part, Lt. Guerry phoned me late yesterday to say that there was a body found washed up on John Lloyd Beach, just north of Dania. It was a man who had identification describing a Frederick A. Garson, the same man whose registration card you showed me."

They ate in silence while watching the giant mobile sprinklers inch their way through the fields. Finally, Gus broke the silence when he said, "If they don't tie him to me, I can continue with my investigation." Gus took her hand in his and said, "Thanks for the info, Sam, you've been a big help, and I appreciate it."

"Anything I can do to help, Gus. All you have to do is ask. Now, I'd better get back to work."

Gus dropped Sam off at the police station and then headed for an army/navy store over in Perrine. He needed to do some more shopping.

There was no one in the store besides the slovenly clerk who was preoccupied reading a comic book.

Gus got a shopping cart and went up and down the aisles, loading the cart as he went. When he was satisfied, he paid the clerk and dropped an extra ten in his hand, saying "I might need some other things later. Maybe you could steer me in the right direction." He put the goods in the trunk of his car and then headed for the marina. Handling the money reminded him that he had to contact the insurance company about the house soon. In fact, there were a lot of things he had to do, but the interest just wasn't there.

Gus checked the boat over before attempting to board it. If anyone had been there, they hadn't left any traces that he could see, but he had to make sure no one got on board that he didn't know about. He hauled his goods below and stowed them, then spent the rest of the afternoon preparing the security for his new home.

Feeling confident that he'd covered all the necessary avenues for entry to his boat, Gus took a shower, got dressed in fresh wrinkled clothes and drove to the Kendall Radio Shack. There were a few things he still needed to get for his little foray into Mr. Garson's house. He threw the bag into the back seat and made his next stop at a hardware store for tools, then to a camera store where he picked up a miniature camera with a flash, 400 ASA film, and a black carrying case.

He carried all the booty onto the boat to sort and store where he could find everything in a hurry. Gus got dressed in his new black rubber-soled shoes and black socks; black pants; black turtleneck shirt, and black knit cap. A quick glance in the mirror assured him that he'd achieved the effect he was after. He was black except for his hands and face, which he'd take care of in short order.

Gus made a pot of coffee and a couple of sandwiches; got the thermos out, washed it in boiling water and filled it with the coffee. He put the sandwiches into a brown bag and set all of it on the galley table. The next stop was the head, both to take care of business and to paint his face with camouflage grease paint. He stretched the knit cap over the edge of the grease paint and unrolled the turtleneck to cover most of the exposed skin on his neck. He turned out the light to see the effect. It worked! The only thing he could see in the ambient light was the skin of his hands and the whites of his eyes.

Gus drove past the address on the registration card to get the layout of the house. It was a beige Spanish style, two-story house with a red barrel tile hip-roof sitting in the middle of the block, with other two-story houses adjacent to it, on both sides. There was a huge fruit tree on either side of it, and across the street were empty lots. Gus continued down the street and around the corner to see what he could of the back of the house. There was an alley that ran behind the house, but there were so many large trees in the back yards of the other houses, that he couldn't get a good look. He went completely around the block and then realized that there were no other cars parked on the street in front of the houses. His car would look too conspicuous if he parked there or in the alley, so he retraced his route again and finally found cars on the avenue two blocks from where he needed to go. He found an open spot and backed in, turning off the lights as he did so.

Gus walked back up the avenue one block past the street he was interested in and turned up the street. When he reached what he assumed was about the middle of the block, he turned into the empty lot and worked his way through the scrub oak, palmettos, and tall weeds until he could see the houses across the street. There was a light on in the house to the left of the Garson house, but it appeared to be far back in the house and shouldn't be a problem.

He found a hidden spot where he could lean against a tree and still see the whole front of Garson's house. He sat down and spread his thermos and binoculars out in front of him. A quick scan of the house showed no activity at all. He kept watch on the house until twelve-thirty. Only two cars had driven by, and there were no pedestrians at all. There had been no activity in or around the Garson house since he'd arrived.

Gus pulled on his black driving gloves and picked up his goods, leaving the thermos. He didn't need to carry anything not immediately useful. He carefully checked the street for activity, and there was none. Someone might be out holding a leash while waiting for their pet to mess someone's yard up. He walked to the edge of the woods, waited for a second, and then darted across the street to get between the fruit tree and the left side of the house. He cautiously moved around to the rear of the house and found the back door. The top half of the door was glass panes, and the bottom was paneled. Gus could find no alarm system attached, but he was taking no unnecessary chances. He pulled out his glass cutter and duct tape and then scored as large a circle in the top pane as he could. Next, he pulled off enough duct tape to cover the circle and securely taped it to the window. With the bottom of the glass cutter, he tapped the circle gently. Nothing happened and he had to tap it again. The circle broke loose, and he pulled the tape off with the circle of glass attached. He reached through the hole in the glass and felt along the top edge of the door. Nothing!

He repeated the hole-in-the-glass trick on the lower pane next to the doorknob, reached in and threw the deadbolt, then turned the inside knob. The door came open slowly. He was ready to run in case there was a motion-sensing alarm. There wasn't. He shouldn't have been worried; the police were notoriously slow to respond to residential burglar alarms. They always had an excuse, like court appearances, budget cuts, responding to accidents, etc., etc. Almost everything had a higher priority than house burglary.

Nothing jumped out at him, and soon as he was completely inside, he stopped and listened. He could hear a clock pendulum clicking. Garson had only been dead for two days, so there was nothing unusual about that. The door opened into a narrow hallway, lined with coat hooks. There were doors at both ends and both were shut. Since the hallway was across the rear of the right side of the house, he figured that the kitchen would be to his left. There was very little ambient light coming from, he supposed, a streetlight a block away.

He took many small steps to keep from kicking anything that might be in the hall and ambled toward the door on his left. He eased the door open slowly and checked for light. There was a light on somewhere because he could make out distinct forms in the kitchen, including a rather large island. He closed the hall door and started towards the open door leading to the dining room. Again, he stopped to listen for activity. Nothing, just that incessant click, click, click of the pendulum that must be coming from the living room. He continued into the living room and noticed the nightlight, located on the wall near the floor to his right. It was between a grandfather clock and him. He also noticed a door at the rear of the room. Probably a den or office of some sort. He continued to that door and opened it slowly, listening for any unusual sounds. It wasn't locked, so he let himself in and turned on his penlight. It was a very functional office, and everything was where you would expect to see it. He went to the desk and pried open the locked center drawer. Nothing in there, so he tried the drawers to his right. The top one contained a leather organizer that was zippered shut. He opened it and turned to June 6.

The only entry on that date was "Take care of Farrell!" Bingo! He leafed through the pages from January to June and stopped to read entries occasionally. His eyes bugged out at what he saw. This was exactly what he was looking for. He continued to check the rest of the drawers and found a package wrapped in brown paper in the bottom left drawer. He laid it on top of the desk and putting the penlight in his mouth tore open a corner of the package. My God, it was a bundle of hundred-dollar bills; and a rather hefty bundle at that.

Gus dropped his booty on the kitchen counter and returned to the living room looking for the stairs to the second story. They weren't hard to find. The second story was just bedrooms and a bathroom opening into the hallway. He assumed that the master bedroom would be on the same side as the den, in the front of the house. Right again! There was nothing spectacular about this particular bedroom at first glance. He rummaged through the dresser and found only the normal items.

The closet, however, proved to be a windfall. At the rear of the overhead shelf, he found two small bundles of paper each wrapped with a rubber band. They were earlier versions of the organizer downstairs and covered the two years preceding the one he had already found. He replaced everything he'd moved, picked up what he was taking and headed for the back door. On second thought, the holes in the windows of the hall door would speak volumes. He had to make it look like a burglary. No sense making it obvious that he had been the one to break in. He went through the drawers in the kitchen, looking for a couple of towels, found a metal meat tenderizing hammer, which he kept, and found the towels in an alcove used for a pantry.

He laid the equipment on the kitchen counter and went back into the den. This time he opened drawers and made it look as though someone had rifled the desk by dropping some of the contents on the floor. He also knocked over a floor lamp and then went back into the kitchen. He placed everything within reach of the rear door and then using the towels to muffle the noise, broke out the rest of the window in the door. He put the towels and hammer back where he'd found them and made his escape through the open door with his pilfered items.

CHAPTER EIGHT

Gus awoke with the boat bumping the dock to the rhythm of the gentle swells. He found the sun to be well up on the horizon. It was coming through a window on the port side, bathing his legs and warming his bare feet. The new watch on his wrist indicated 8:32. He hadn't gotten back until 2:15 and had been too tired to check his booty.

Now he had things to do and needed to get busy. He got up, started the coffee perking, and performed his morning ritual in the necessary room. That first cup of black coffee was like a shot of adrenaline to his system. He took the second cup to the table and retrieved his booty from the night's adventure, then put it on the table beside the coffee. He moved the bundles of day planners aside and pulled the bundle of hundred-dollar bills over in front of him. He removed the outside wrapper and lined up the bundles in stacks of equal height and volume. Each bundle was wrapped with a plain one-inch-wide band of brown paper, on which was marked $10,000. There were ten bundles in four of his five stacks.

Gus had been painfully honest all his life, and the thought of having all this money caused him to break out in a nervous sweat. He sat there looking at the money in amazement until a thought crossed his mind; they blew up my house and were responsible for the disappearance of my wife, so why in hell should I feel guilty. At that moment, his mind was made up. This money would replace what was lost and also finance his investigation. What he needed to do immediately was find several banks where he could spread out the deposits under bogus names. This was just to ensure that his deposits wouldn't be flagged in federal bank computer searches for illegal deposits. When push comes to shove, they could lock up his bank accounts and deny access. He'd make sure they had a tough time finding them. Earlier, there was so much drug money coming into South Florida that it wasn't unusual for banks to accept deposits brought to them in brown paper grocery bags. After George's task force had changed the undeclared deposit limit to $10K, it had become increasingly harder to deposit huge sums. The answer for a while had been to buy up all the real estate available. That worked for the short term but eventually drove up the price of real estate, and it became increasingly harder to find anything that wasn't inflated beyond realism. Next, they tried buying up the banks or opening new ones. To this day, you'll find at least one bank per block along the Dixie Highway. This, fortunately, worked in Gus's favor since it gave him a multitude of choices for deposits. He just had to divvy up the money into small parcels under $10K and keep good records.

Gus went to the locker and brought back his overnight bag. He stuffed all but one of the bundles into the bag and then got busy unscrewing the decking of the V-berth to get to the hatch cover over the bilge. Since it was Sunday, he couldn't do anything about deposits until tomorrow. In the meantime, the money had to be hidden. Gus got a large plastic bag, put the overnight bag inside, and stored it in the bilge.

After the money had been stored, the hatch, decking, and mattress replaced, Gus got out the phone book and his calculator and started making a list of the banks along the Dixie Highway from Coral Gables to Homestead. It dawned on him that to stay under the 10K limit; it would take almost fifty banks for the $450,000. His list only included twelve banks and he was running out of banks, so that plan was a wash. He'd just have to keep the money in the bag.

The rest of the day was a wash as well, so Gus took the bundle of money he'd kept back, opened it up, and counted out five one-hundred-dollar bills. The rest of the package went into the locker behind the toilet paper. He set his security traps, and this time headed for the Cutler Ridge Shopping Center. He needed more clothes, an iron and ironing board, more comfortable shoes, and some food.

Gus loaded all the new purchases into the car and headed up the Dixie Highway toward his favorite restaurant. He and Anita had eaten at the Pumpernickel Deli almost every Sunday morning since they arrived in Miami. They had mature and pleasant waitresses who dressed in immaculate white uniforms and efficiently served hot and delicious food.

As usual, Gus suffered a bout of nostalgia when he thought about Anita. It was hard not to think about her; his waitress's name was Anita. He hurried through the meal and got back to Kings Bay faster than necessary. It was time to face the fact that Anita would never be found and would be lost to him forever.

There were public phones at the marina office, and after Gus had gotten through his security shield, he stowed his gear, grabbed the card with Sam's phone number and strolled over to the phone that was in the shadows. He dialed her number, and she picked up on the second ring.

"Hello."

"Sam, this is Gus. What have you been up to?"

"Oh, nothing. Just waiting by the phone hoping to hear from you all day. Are you all right?"

"Sure. Are you angry about something?"

"Not really. You certainly have a good excuse for forgetting our date last night."

"I'm sorry; we had a date last night?"

"At seven o'clock. Remember this phrase, 'Good; I'll pick you up at seven if you tell me where to do that'?"

"Oh, my God, you're right. I'm sorry. I just got so preoccupied that it slipped my mind."

"Well, it's not too late now, Gus!"

"You're right about that, Sam, but I've already eaten. Have you?"

"Yes, however, we could find a nice little lounge and have a drink, if you'd like?"

"I'd like!"

"Good and I know of a very nice place that's not too far from where you are."

"That's a deal, but I still need to know where to find you, Sam."

She gave him directions to her house in Coral Gables, just west of Tropical Park. It took Gus about twenty minutes to get there. She was waiting on the screened porch, looking like a million bucks.

He told her so.

"You're too kind," she said, a little smile playing on her lips.

"No, just honest," replied Gus. "Now, where is this 'nice little lounge'?"

"Just go down to 56th Street, then left to Red Road south, then left on Sunset Road."

Gus pulled into the parking lot of the Tropical Breeze Lounge and parked at the side in the shadows. He got out, walked around to her door, and opened it for her.

"That was very gentlemanly of you, Gus, and I appreciated it, but for future reference, I don't expect you to do that for me every time we stop; I'm not incapable of opening my door and will do so in the future. I always thought it was silly to expect the gentleman to waste time helping women out of a car when there's a door handle on the inside."

"Thanks for clearing that up, young lady; it's just a habit I picked up as a knight in King Arthur's Court."

The lounge was a surprise. Gus thought it would be one of those garish gin mills with loud music and smoke so thick you couldn't breathe. Instead, it was very tastefully decorated with saddle-tan leather seating and subtle lighting. The bar, trimmed in red leather along the front, was heavily mirrored with unseen indirect green neon lighting. The effect was very pleasant, particularly with a piano player at the end, playing mood music.

There was a row of booths along the right side, open to the dance floor. Gus steered Sam toward the next-to-last booth. After they were seated the waiter headed over in their direction.

"Good evening, folks, how might I help you?"

He was a swarthy, dark-haired man who appeared to be in his early forties, with black hair plastered to his scalp.

As pre-arranged, Gus said, "The lady will have a vodka gimlet, and I'll have a black Russian."

"Excellent, sir," he said, as he turned to leave.

Looking at Sam across the table, Gus took her hand and said, "I feel really at ease with you, Sam, and I don't think I've told you how much I appreciate what you've been doing for me."

"No thanks necessary, Gus, it's been a pleasure, and if there's anything else I can do for you, just let me know. As a matter of fact, I could iron those new shirts you just bought; I know how busy you are with your investigation!"

"That would be a big help, Sam, and would make me feel a lot less conspicuous and more like a human again."

"Done," Sam said. "We'll stop by your place and pick them up before you take me home." They sat there, getting to know the details of each other's lives for three hours.

Gus pulled into his reserved parking slot at the marina just after midnight.

"Why don't you come on board and see the only home I have left while I dig out the shirts?"

"I'd love to," Sam said.

Gus, as usual, went through the alarms he'd rigged and disconnected them, then opened the cabin door. "Come in. Would you like a drink?" Gus asked as she came through the door.

"No, thanks, Gus, if I had one more drink I might fall overboard. As a matter of fact, I'd like to see your bathroom."

"No problem," Gus said, pointing to the forward port side door. Gus started rummaging through the locker where he'd stowed the shirts, found them, and put them in a shopping bag for Sam.

That strange sucking sound of the toilet was a clear indication that Sam had finished her business and was coming out of the head.

"How would you like some bacon and eggs, Sam, since it is morning?"

"That's an excellent idea, Gus, but wouldn't they be better served in bed later in the morning?"

"Now, why didn't I think of that?" Gus chuckled.

They undressed in silence, in the dim light from the marina security lights, and Gus pulled down the blanket and top sheet. He wished he'd had the foresight to put clean sheets on the bunk. If he had, though, it would have looked planned instead of the unexpected pleasure unfolding.

Sam dropped her bra and panties, sat down, and rolled into the V-berth. Not a very favorable view for Sam, but a beautiful view for Gus. He didn't say anything but was in awe of her beauty. She had a full figure, but not too full for her height, and she smelled so good his head started reeling.

Gus crawled into the berth beside her and put his arm under her neck and kissed her ever so gently while snuggling up tight against her. He couldn't believe her skin was so smooth and soft.

———

Gus prepared two plates with bacon, eggs, and toast and put them on a tray with coffee, marmalade, napkins, and silverware. He very carefully opened the accordion door to the V-berth. She was still in the same position as when he had gotten up earlier, lying on her back, stark naked, and breathing shallowly with a small smile on her lips. He leaned over and kissed her lips very gently and became aroused again.

Sam opened her eyes and whispered, "Good morning, sweetheart."

Gus said, "Good morning, beautiful, are you hungry yet?"

"You betcha," she said.

After they had eaten, Gus put the trays back in the galley and did the quickstep back to the bunk, where they "slept" in for the rest of the morning.

CHAPTER NINE

Both needed showers when they finally awoke at 1:30. And being the consummate gentleman, Gus told Sam to take her shower first. Gus busied himself changing the sheets and opening the deck hatch to air the cabin out while Sam was taking her shower. Gus got ready to step into the shower and had dropped his robe in a chair just when Sam stepped out. By this time, neither one of them was bashful, having spent the last twelve hours completely naked. The admiration was mutual, and they just stood there looking at each other's bodies, Sam's nipples were already hard from the cold shower and now stood straight out. Sam reached down and took Gus's hand and led him back to the V-berth.

By 5:00 the sun had heated the cabin to an uncomfortable temperature and the breeze had disappeared. Gus woke up to something lightly scratching his chest. He opened his eyes to find Sam facing him on her side with her head resting on her hand and the other hand stroking his chest. She was looking him over with a little smile and a look of contentment on her face. "Surely you don't want another round, do you?" Gus asked.

Sam said, "You know what they say, you can never get enough of a good thing."

Gus lifted one eyebrow and said, "Maybe not, but you can't get it all at once either. Let's take another shower and get dressed. We can think about this 'good thing' later and enjoy it much more. Right now, I have to get rejuvenated. Let's go get some food before you wear me out."

"I guess you've never dated a nymphomaniac before, have you?"

Gus slapped her on the butt and said, "No, and I still haven't!"

Sam squealed and said: "OK, why don't you take your shower first this time and I'll pretend to do housework."

"You don't have to do anything," Gus said. "Just do what you want."

"You know what I want to do," Sam said.

Gus quick-stepped to the shower and turned the water on. After getting dressed and setting up the entry devices, they got into the car and Gus said: "What would you say to eating a big steak, Sam?"

Sam smiled and said: "That's exactly what I need, perhaps a Black Angus. There's one out near the airport." Sam gave directions to the restaurant, and they took the freeway west toward the airport.

There were several restaurants in the area including one that was supposed to resemble a French chateau, replete with French and German monoplanes, biplanes, and triplanes in all states of disrepair and attitudes scattered around the farmhouse buildings.

The Black Angus, however, was nothing more than a building with a sign out front holding up a huge pair of horns. After they were seated and had given their drink orders, they both sat back and looked at each other.

Gus said, "Sam, this may come as a surprise to you but the more I'm with you, the more I want to be with you."

"I'm glad to hear that, Gus, because I wanted to let you know that I've been having feelings along those lines myself. Let me further say that I want you near me all the time and suggest the possibility of you moving in with me. There's plenty of room and I wouldn't interfere with your investigation or say anything about your coming and going when you need to."

"You're right, Sam, that was a surprise. I had no idea you felt that way about me. I'd love to move in with you, but with the understanding that if you change your mind somewhere down the road, all you have to do is ask me to leave."

"That goes without saying, dear, but I'm going to work hard to see that it never happens, because you are now my man and I love you."

They hadn't spent too much time eating their steaks when Sam said, "I want you to take us home, Gus!"

Sam's house was a two-bedroom structure which was similar to the one Gus had lived in as a boy. It even had the barrel tile on the roof, cathedral ceiling and hardwood floors, and a porta cochere. This type of house was solid as a rock and withstood the hurricanes with no thought of worry. Gus's childhood home included a large rubber tree in the front yard, close enough to cause real damage if it came apart during the storm. The only foliage in Sam's yard was oleander and a few gardenia bushes, which, he later found out, were for the scent on balmy summer nights.

Sam pointed out where the bedroom was, and then the bathroom, as if it were hard to find. She said: "Since it's a workday for me tomorrow and I'm a little tired, it might be a good idea to go to bed."

"Oh, crap! Pardon my outburst, Sam, but I have to go to the boat again. There's something I have to collect." In his interest in this newfound virility, he had completely forgotten about the money.

"Well, I'll go with you then, I wouldn't be able to sleep while you're out anyway."

"Are you sure? I'll be back in a jiffy." Gus was a little worried about involving Sam in a felony when it wasn't absolutely necessary.

Sam gave Gus a quizzical look and said, "You don't really think you're going to get rid of me now that I've found you, do you?"

"That's not what I meant, Sam, but I can see you're not going to be deterred, so let's go."

As Gus pulled into the marina, Sam asked, "What's so important that it can't wait until morning?"

Gus smiled and said, "You'll see in a minute, Sam."

Gus stepped over the gunwale and reached back to give Sam a hand, then turned his attention immediately to disarming the alarms. That finished, he reached into his toolbox to grab a screwdriver and then headed into the cabin to start work.

He removed all the bedding and the decking of the bunk then turned to Sam and asked, "Is there anyone around, Sam?"

Sam stuck her head up out of the cabin and said, "Not that I can see."

Gus reached down and removed the bilge cover, laid it aside, and pulled out the plastic bag containing his overnight bag. He replaced the hatch cover, decking, and bedding; then handed the plastic bag to Sam and closed and locked the cabin.

Sam said, "Do you always keep your luggage in a plastic bag under your bed?"

"Not when it's just luggage, but when it's more important than that, I like to keep it dry and hidden for safety's sake."

They stepped onto the deck and Gus reset the alarms, then helped Sam onto the dock.

When they arrived back at the house, Sam was visibly squirming in her seat with curiosity about the contents of the plastic bag.

Gus opened the car door, stepped out, and looked around for anything suspicious. Seeing nothing out of the ordinary, he then went around to Sam's door and opened it for her. She stepped out and handed the bag to Gus.

They went into the house and Sam said, "Don't do anything yet, wait till I take a pee, I don't want to miss anything, and I can't hold it any longer."

Gus said, "There's no hurry, take your time."

Gus closed all the blinds, waited for Sam to finish, then almost closed the door so the light in the bathroom would provide enough light to see. The house was dark except for the bathroom light. He cleared off the dining room table and pulled the overnight bag out of the plastic bag, opened it, and poured the cash onto the table.

Sam's gasp was enough to indicate that she had had no idea what the bag had contained.

"Pardon my French," she said, "but where the hell did you get all that?"

"I got that from the animals that killed my wife," Gus said.

Sam lifted one eyebrow and said, "How do you know she's dead?"

Gus paused and said, "There was more than enough time to know that she wasn't coming home again, and then there was the affair at the hospital, the threats from the guy I dumped into Bakers Haulover, and my house turning into a roman candle. There was nothing wrong with her mind and I know she would have found me if she'd been able to. So, in my mind, she's dead!"

"I think I can help you out with that problem, Gus. When they built this house, someone had the foresight to install a hatch in the floor, there in the dining room under the rug. It beats getting down on all fours and crawling into the access port in the foundation, through all the spiders, scorpions, and snakes."

After moving the chairs, table, and rug, the hatch was in plain view, with a small loop handle built in flush with the floor. Gus removed it and peered into the pitch-black hole.

"You wouldn't happen to have a flashlight, would you?" Gus asked.

"One moment, sir," said Sam. She got up off her knees and headed into the kitchen, returning with a small light. "I hope this is sufficient, it's the only one I have."

"It will do nicely," said Gus, peering into the now illuminated hole.

Gus was surprised to find that the ground was approximately two and a half feet from the finished floor. "This will also do nicely!"

Gus pushed the money back into the overnight bag and placed it into the plastic bag, tying a knot in the top. He then dropped the bag into the hole and replaced the hatch. They both moved the rug back where it was, then the table and chairs.

Gus said, "Well, we better hit the hay." And they did.

The alarm went off at six, scaring them both. No one can go back to sleep after a wake-up like that. Sam headed for the kitchen and Gus headed for the john. After a few minutes, the smell of coffee permeated the house and Gus stepped out of the shower, brushed his teeth, slipped into a pair of shorts, and followed the scent. He slipped up behind her as she was preparing bacon and eggs, ran his hands down her haunches, and got all excited again. He leaned over and kissed her on the side of her neck when what he really wanted to do was to be totally inside her, a physical and psychological part of her. He actually ached for her.

Sam said, "If you keep this up, I'm going to call in sick because I won't be able to leave you. Sit down and eat."

Gus said, "Why don't you. That's a good idea, then we can get settled in, get groceries, run errands, and find other things to do, maybe."

"See, now you've gone and talked me into it, but we're going to eat this breakfast first, and then I'm taking a shower."

They couldn't take their eyes off each other all through breakfast. Finally, Sam got up and went to the bathroom. Gus cleared the table and washed the dishes, then went to find something else to wear.

It was a nice day, slightly overcast with a barely perceptible breeze, but it was lost on Sam and Gus who were so enamored with each other, they hadn't noticed anything outside of their rapture.

Gus suggested they try an old market that his mother used to take him to when he was a kid. "It's called Shells," he said. "It was located on 7th Avenue and was similar to an open market since all the sides were open. However, it did have an enormous hard roof that protected the shoppers when one of those thunderstorms, so prevalent in South Florida, came to visit. It's a little trip, but from what I remember, it's worth it."

It was definitely worth it, Sam thought, once they got there. Everything was so well displayed, and the produce and meat departments were excellent.

"I can see that we're going to spend too much money here," Sam said.

"Apparently, we don't have to worry about that, do we?" Gus reminded her.

"Oh, right! I'd forgotten for a minute."

They continued to load the cart until it wouldn't hold anymore and then got in line for check-out.

Unseen by both Gus and Sam, a man dressed in tan pants and a flowered sports shirt was watching them, while pretending to shop about two aisles away. He picked up a cantaloupe, pressed his thumb into the end of it, as though checking for ripeness, then laid it down and shifted the lump on his side under his shirt. He had a sharply pointed nose with a pencil-line mustache under it and slicked back hair as if he was trying to look like a successful actor from the thirties. He had been following them since they left the marina last night and knew where they lived, that they spent a lot of time in bed and that she was playing hooky from the police department today. He pulled out a cell phone, made a call, and returned it to his pocket.

Gus was surprised at the total but said nothing and paid in cash with a smile on his face while Sam and the bagger filled the cart. They were heading toward Sam's car, three aisles from the store when a car careened around the end of the aisle and headed straight for them while accelerating. Gus's first reaction was to get Sam out of the way by pushing her between two cars, shoving the heavy cart straight at the oncoming car, then jumping on the hood of the nearest car. The impact of the cart hitting the grill of the car was like an explosion, throwing groceries in a forty-foot arc.

Gus hit the hood he dove for and rolled over in time to catch a glimpse of the driver. He appeared weirdly out of style and Gus knew he would be able to easily pick him out of a lineup.

The car didn't even pause; instead, the driver continued to accelerate through the parking lot and out onto the street, through a red light, and up to 7th Avenue.

Gus had seen enough to recognize the car as a dark green Oldsmobile sedan with Florida plates on it but couldn't recognize the year.

Gus went to see if Sam was all right and found her fuming. She said, "If I ever catch that son-of-a-bitch, he'll wish he was dead."

Gus was surprised at her language since he couldn't remember hearing her use any cuss words except *hell* since they met.

Regaining his composure, Gus said, "Are you hurt, Sam?"

"No, just my feelings. Are you all right, Gus?"

"No problem, Sam, but we better get under cover, fast." Quickly walking to and entering the store, Sam and Gus were faced by the manager who stopped them, asking if either of them had been hurt.

Gus said, "No, but we lost a lot of groceries."

Probably fearing that the store would be sued, the manager said, "Please, don't worry, I'm having the clerk look for your receipt, and when we find it, we will completely restore your order and deliver it to you, no charge, if you'll just give us your names and address."

Gus gave him the obligatory information and said, "Thank you. I think we'll be leaving now."

Turning to Sam, Gus said, "What now Ms. Police Officer, are we going to report this and spend the afternoon filling out paperwork, or chalk it up as an indicator that I'm getting close?"

Sam said, "What I'm worried about is that you may very well wind up getting too close to it and dying in the process. I certainly don't want that to happen, so let's forget this one, eh?"

"OK, Sam. Now let's go home, I want to check you all over for scratches, contusions, bruises, and the like—naked of course!"

"There's nothing subtle about you, is there, you horny cuss? So, what are we waiting for?"

After a remarkably close scrutiny of Sam's naked anatomy, Gus was satisfied that she hadn't suffered an inordinate loss of skin tissue and was not in too much pain, so they got down to business.

CHAPTER TEN

One of the older districts in Miami, called "Little River," is located in northeast Miami, about a mile from Biscayne Bay, and bisected by NE 2nd Avenue at 79th Street, which continues over the 79th Street Bridge onto the North Bay Causeway to Miami Beach. The Little River Community Center had a lot of the amenities popular with the older generation such as shuffleboard courts, picnic tables, and benches out in the shade of a multitude of palm trees. Inside were tables and chairs, for the card players of the group, and bathrooms along one side of the building. Community Centers were very popular with the residents before the advent of television because they could come together to talk, relax, and enjoy the balmy breezes scented with gardenias and honeysuckle.

This beautiful community center had now degenerated into the perfect location for the sale of drugs, prostitution, and anything money could buy. Although the thugs, murderers, and pimps could barely tolerate them, the homosexual segment maintained a strong presence at the center because they were talented in procurement. If anyone needed a hand weapon, assault weapon, missiles, or little boys, they could provide anything needed, including white slavery victims. This array of misfits didn't worry about the police bothering them, because the street cops were afraid to come near the area, and some unknown entity was greasing the palms of the ones in charge.

There was one group that kept a low profile, knew everyone, and kept to themselves. This group was known as MI's (Murder Incorporated). Their services centered on contractual killings, kidnappings, rapes, or anything that couldn't, or wouldn't, be provided by anyone else.

Almost all the members had prison records that stretched back over many, many years. Enrique Gonzalez, a five-foot-five Cuban, was a member of this sordid group. Although a recent entry into the American community, he was very experienced in the practice of murder, Cuban style.

Going east, 79th Street crosses over Biscayne Boulevard which has a small bridge a couple of blocks south, over the Little River meandering beneath. Lining both banks of the river were large houses built in the thirties and forties. Each had its own seawalls with private docks and yachts. Most of these houses were surrounded by steel fences that fanned out over the seawall to prevent access from the sides. For privacy, tropical shrubbery, such as traveler palms, pygmy bamboo, hibiscus, pampas grass, and many other tropical bushes, completely encased the fences around the periphery of each house, providing an impenetrable wall.

The house at 624 NE 77th Street was not too different from the other two-story houses in the area with one exception: There was a two-story building connected to the main house by an enclosed seventy-five-foot walkway. There were no windows in the connecting walkway, the outbuilding, or the three-car garage on the opposite side of the house. There was a large single gate at the entrance which led to a curving drive lined with foliage, hiding the house from the road. The gate itself had two rotary TV cameras mounted to the sides with floodlights, activated by motion sensors, to illuminate the area. At the left side of the gate entrance stood a small sentry box, approximately forty feet square, containing a man with a micro-Uzi machine gun which he kept in plain sight.

Moored to the dock in the back of the house was a 44-foot Regal Commodore cruiser, facing east toward Belle Meade Island at the shore of Biscayne Bay. The boat was a relatively fast luxury cruiser, yet small enough to be able to traverse the rather shallow river. The sweeping lines made the cruiser appear to be moving even while still moored to the dock.

The main house was built with the Spanish influence common to many South Florida houses: red barrel tile roofing, and arched windows guarded by bars on the lower windows. The annex was plain with shingle roofing and no visible outside entrances aside from the entrance inside the walkway also guarded by another surly micro-Uzi-armed Latin. Thick foliage had been planted completely around the base of the annex and continued down into the back yard and across to the other side of the yard in a wide arc, intersected by a flagstone walkway from the patio to the dock. The patio was tiled in flagstone with a rather large rectangular swimming pool in the center.

Inside the three-inch-thick annex door, at the end of the walkway, was a tiled hallway leading to the other side of the building. The left side of the hallway contained a small office, with connecting door to a dining area and kitchen, a restroom, and a stairway at the end. On the right side of the hallway was a stairway that led to the upper floor, a laboratory, and another restroom at the end. At the top of the stairway was a series of chain-link cages on both sides of the hallway containing cots, washbasins, and toilets. An additional restroom was at the back.

Two of the cages held men that appeared to be from South America or one of the countries in between the US and South America. Both were approximately twenty-five to thirty-five years old and wearing shabby clothes and no shoes. Between the two men was a young woman in her early twenties, also barefoot, with her hands tied behind her and a wide strip of duct tape over her mouth. Her features were possibly Cuban or Puerto Rican. None of the three spoke English or had immigration papers. A guard sporting another micro-Uzi sat on a small stool at the head of the stairwell.

Across the back end of the annex office stood a three-panel oriental screen, which one would assume was probably used for privacy while changing clothes. However, behind the screen was a blank wall and, under close inspection, a very small ridge could be seen around a six-by-two-and-one-half-foot rectangle. None of the workers at the annex knew of the existence of the rectangle except for one person—*Dr. Angelo Cruz*. He'd had the panel installed by the contractor when the annex was built. If the need arose, he could walk through the thin wall on the inside.

The area was very popular with the rich and semi-rich of the 30s and 40s social groups, rubbing elbows with the Mafia who frequented the gambling casino on Biscayne Boulevard. The customers were guarded, and watched, by armed Mafia soldiers on the hidden walkways above them that surrounded the periphery of the gambling tables. The casino's demise came at the end of a string of murders which coincided with Al Capone's departure to his new residence in prison. His home, on one of the Sunset Islands in Biscayne Bay, guarded by a ten-foot wall, still stands.

Carlos was a little worried. He knew that that guy, Gus, had seen him while he was attempting to run over him and the cop at Shells, and if Dr. Cruz even suspected that he'd been compromised, he'd be wearing an anklet with a concrete block charm and decorating the barrier reef. He would have to get rid of his beautiful dark green Oldsmobile as his first priority, then worry about how to get another car without raising suspicion about the change. Time was the problem. A faked illness and a doctor's visit should provide enough time to look over the used car lots along Biscayne Boulevard but getting rid of the Oldsmobile would take a little more planning.

Then he remembered a chop shop down on Dixie Highway that wasn't too particular where you got the car. One of his acquaintances had successfully used them to dump a stolen car once. But first, he had to find a replacement.

Four used car lots later he found a "cherry" white '61, Super 88 Oldsmobile with a four-barrel carburetor. It had a maroon velour interior that was clean as a pin, and the motor had been reconditioned recently, which is why the dealer had it. He couldn't afford what it cost for the repair and had to get rid of it. Carlos finagled a deal with the proprietor, signed the papers, got a temporary license, and drove away.

The next morning, Carlos made a phone call at a local drug store and then drove his green Old's south on US-1 to the chop shop, almost into Homestead, parked around back and went in through a steel overhead door. Trying to get his eyes adjusted to the dark depths of the garage, he didn't see the figure approach him from the side. "Ya lookin' fer sump'n?" Carlos turned his head and was confronted by a slightly built man approximately forty-five years of age, standing near five foot four inches tall, wearing a filthy pair of blue coveralls and an equally filthy cloth cap on his balding head, and holding a ball-peen hammer.

Carlos said, "I'm looking for Rodolfo."

The little man looked toward the northwest end of the building to a small room, presumably the office, and said "Look in thar."

Carlos tried to appear casual as he walked over to the "office." He was a bit nervous, because there were another four people in the garage, and all of them were staring at him. He knocked on the office door and heard a quiet "Come." Once inside, the overhead fluorescent lights were almost too bright.

"Are you Rodolfo?" Carlos asked.

Ignoring the question, he said, "You have a dark green Old's?"

"Yes, it's parked out back."

"Let's take a look at it." Abruptly he came up out of his chair and started through the door, with Carlos following, nervously.

Rodolfo walked around it, checked the tires, and looked at Carlos who tossed him the keys.

"How long have you had it?" he asked.

"I bought it new twelve years ago," Carlos said.

Rodolfo started the engine and looked at Carlos. "Where did the scratches on the grill and hood come from?"

Carlos smiled and said he'd run into a grocery cart.

Rodolfo said, "I'll give you sixteen hundred for it."

Carlos said, "That would be fine. Are you going to chop it today?"

"What the hell do you mean by that?" Rodolfo said.

"Well, I thought you knew that I can't have it on the road anymore. It's got to be demolished as soon as possible."

"In that case," Rodolfo said, "you can give me a thousand to get rid of it."

"A thousand," Carlos said incredulously. "I can't afford that! I thought you could buy it for scrap metal and get rid of it."

"I either get a thousand, or you'll have to explain to the cops why it's sitting on Dixie Highway without an engine and your fingerprints all over it."

Gerardo, the ball-peen bearing grease monkey (according to the smeared name tag), stiffened, turned, and moved almost imperceptibly toward Carlos.

"Well, I don't have it on me, so I'll have to go get it."

"You're not leaving that thing on my property while you go scrounge up some money, at least not without collateral." Rodolfo said through clenched teeth. "I sure as hell don't need the cops asking questions about it. Give me your wallet!"

Carlos looked as though Gerardo had hit him on the head with the ball-peen hammer. "What do you need with my wallet?" Carlos stammered.

"Keep it as collateral so I have something to show the cops if you don't come back, and believe me, if you're not back in forty-eight hours, I'll call the cops myself."

"I don't even know where I can get that much, for Christ's sake, especially without my wallet!"

"That's your problem, not mine," responded Rodolfo. "Now get going, you're burning time."

Carlos handed Rodolfo his wallet and scooted across Dixie Highway to the bus stop.

CHAPTER ELEVEN

Gus woke up feeling like he'd run a marathon and was pleased with the sensation. The sun was up and Sam, according to her breathing, was still asleep. He lay there for a few minutes, soaking up the sun and enjoying the breeze coming first through the gardenias and then through the open window, carrying their scent over their bed and then disappearing through the door to dissipate somewhere in the house. How much better, he wondered, can it get?

He rolled toward Sam and began to scratch her back lightly with his fingernails. The regularity of her breathing changed. "Is that you, Gus?" she said.

Gus smacked her on the butt and said: "Just who the hell would it be if it wasn't me?"

Sam replied, "Maybe the milkman, or the meter-reader, or...."

Gus finished for her, saying, "Or maybe a crazed lunatic, or rapist, or...."

Sam rolled over and grabbed Gus around the shoulders, almost squeezing the wind out of him, saying "I love you, Gus, with all my heart! Perhaps you'd like to examine me again, just in case."

"As a matter of fact; just in case, I think that would be a good idea as a precautionary measure."

Sam flung the light sheet off, rolled over on her back, and spread out her arms and legs. "Have at it, Stud. I'm all yours!"

"I know it, Sam, and I'm going to keep it that way! Now spread your legs a little wider."

————

"What shall we do for recreation, today, Sam, since it's Sunday?"

Smiling, Sam said, "You'll probably think I'm crazy, but I'd like to go boating." With a twinkle in her eye, she said, "Do you know where we can rent a boat?"

"No," Gus said, "But I think I know of one we can use that's not too far from here, providing it hasn't sunk."

The marina was busier than usual since it's the favorite day for the clientele to get their families out of their hectic routines and on the water. According to the battery-operated weather station sitting on his instrument panel, the temperature was eighty-three degrees. Too bad the darn thing didn't have a wind monitor, but he assumed that the wind was only about five or six knots: hardly a ripple on the water of the sheltered inlet. He turned on his weather radio.

The Publix grocery store café on South Dixie Highway had provided them a very cute picnic basket which Gus stowed in the cabin. He then placed the beer and wine in the refrigerator and got it started.

Up top, Sam was busy cleaning some mildew off of the seats, so Gus grabbed the glass cleaner and a couple of paper towels and cleaned the windshield, wiped down the dash and instruments, and started the blower. After about five minutes, Gus started the engines and set them to idle to warm up while they finished cleaning and stowing.

Sam loosed the dock lines and climbed on board while Gus turned off the blower and slipped the throttle forward into idle. The boat eased out of the slip, and Gus turned toward the fuel dock to top off the tanks. That done, Gus headed out toward the lagoon in idle, since this was a no-wake zone for the manatees. It was still relatively early, but the cranes, pelicans, egrets, and all other forms of birdlife were busy filling their stomachs with the baby mullet and needlefish, then resting or feeding their chicks in the mangrove thickets along the sides of the lagoon.

Gus eased the boat to port enough to make a nice arc toward Paradise Point and raised the rpm to 200. Rounding Paradise Point, Gus advanced the throttle to twenty mph and headed south.

"You couldn't have asked for a nicer day, even if you'd planned it, could you?" asked Sam, holding on to Gus's arm.

Gus smiled and said, "Not hardly, Sam."

Moving in closer to Gus, Sam looked into his face and with a serious tone to her voice, asked, "Where are you taking me, Gus?"

"We're just going on a nice leisurely cruise to enjoy the day, that's all!"

"Oh. You won't be angry if I ask you something, will you?"

"I promise," Gus said.

"If it's to be just a leisurely cruise, why are there so many guns and ammunition in the forward locker?"

"That's just insurance. I've been caught with my pants down too often, and I don't plan on letting it happen again, at least not unarmed. I don't expect anything to happen but just in case it does, I'll be ready."

"You don't expect anything to happen today, do you?" asked Sam.

"Sam, I don't ever expect anything to happen, I just want to be ready if it does!" Gus got out the chart for South Biscayne Bay that covered Miami through Homestead and busied himself looking for channels.

Gus eased the boat over to 140° to bypass Arsenicker Key and get into the Intracoastal Waterway channel.

"I'm sorry, Gus. I didn't mean to upset you, and it's none of my business what you need to do, or what you need to do it."

"Oh, Sam, I'm not upset. I just feel guilty about dragging you into this, and I had a pang of guilt when you asked about the weapons." Placing his arm around her shoulder, he squeezed her hard and kissed her cheek. She, in turn, put her arms around his waist and her head on his shoulder and gave a deep sigh. They stood like this for what must have been half an hour.

"Are you hungry yet, Sam?"

"As a matter of fact, I'm getting a little hypoglycemic."

"Soon to be remedied, my dear. There's a country club on Key Largo, and they have an excellent dining room, so I've been told. Wait a minute! We do have a picnic basket in the galley. I just remembered!"

"Oh yeah, that's right! You find a nice place to anchor, and I'll set up lunch for us," Sam laughed, thinking of their approach to old age.

Gus said, "There's a hole in the deck back toward the rear, and it serves as a mounting hole for the fishing chair. There's a table in the locker with a pipe support, and it fits nicely into the fishing chair mount. The leaves of the table unfold and lock into place, and there are two folding chairs in the other locker."

Gus, while watching the depth gauge, slowly eased the boat to within a half-mile of the shoreline, dropped the anchor in six feet of water, and shut down the motors. Silence engulfed them with the loss of the soft rumble of the engines.

Lunch was delicious and long. Both Sam and Gus found their eyelids going to half-mast and mutually agreed to take a nap. It didn't take long to fall asleep with the soft lapping waves hitting the hull. They were on the lee side of Key Largo and were sheltered by the island from the breeze off the ocean on the other side of the island, so there was very little motion on the surface.

A young couple in an eighteen-foot Glastron, leaving the country club docks, woke them up with their bow wave. Gus swore under his breath, thinking they could have given them a wider berth to prevent the bow wave. It seemed that courtesy was a thing of the past, anymore.

"What are you mumbling about?" Sam said.

"I was just considering how inconsiderate some people are," Gus replied.

"They probably saw what looked like an empty boat and didn't consider that there was anyone aboard."

"Hey, aren't we getting nautical with that 'aboard' stuff," Gus laughed. "Come here and get your 'come-uppins.'" Their naked bodies intertwined.

Gus said, "If you want to troll for barracuda on the way back, I'll set up a rod and reel for you."

"Listen," she said. "I don't want to fish, I don't want to look through binoculars, I don't want to take a nap, and I don't want to get a suntan. All I want to do is hold you."

"I was hoping you'd say that." Gus smiled and gave her a tender kiss on the tip of her nose.

"The tide is running out so the return trip will take a little longer," Gus said as he reversed his former course, allowing for the slower speed.

They were approaching Paradise Point, and Gus said, "One of the duties of the first mate is to make the boat ship-shape at the end of the cruise, you know?"

"I assume that 'ship-shape' means to clean up the mess and put everything back where it came from. Is that right, Captain?"

"You're pretty sharp for a cop, lady," Gus smiled.

"I'm pretty strong for a woman as well, smarty. So you'd better be careful," she laughed.

They curved around Paradise Point and dropped the speed to idle again. The boat handled well, even at idle, which Gus was thankful for. The addition of the tabs on the stern had made a considerable differ-ence in the handling. Having two engines was also useful for turning when docking. They eased into the slip, and Sam threw the lines on the dock and climbed over to secure them, with Gus's tutoring. Gus set the alarms, closed up, and joined Sam on the dock.

Gus said, "Do you feel like a hot meal, or would you rather go home and finish the picnic basket, Sam?"

"I'd rather go home. After today I don't even care if I eat. That's not to say that I wouldn't cook something up for you, though, if you want a hot meal."

"OK, Missy, home it is," said Gus.

Gus got the picnic basket out of the trunk while Sam went ahead to open the front door.

"Oh no!" Sam cried. "The door is broken!"

Gus slammed the trunk lid and rushed to Sam, who was almost in tears.

Someone had pried open the door, breaking the jamb in the process. Gus placed Sam behind him and slowly opened the door and stepped in. The place was in shambles! Furniture was cut open; chairs were ripped apart; bedrooms were torn apart and ripped open; closets emptied with the contents thrown out; toilet tank lids on the floors, and the access hatch to the attic thrown off. The dining room table was upside down with one leg broken off, and the chairs were thrown across the room. The kitchen cabinets had been dumped on the floor. The oven door was broken, and the refrigerator doors were open, its contents defrosted; the washer and dryer turned over with a water hose broken, flooding the laundry room. Sam broke down, sobbing hysterically. Gus tried to soothe her but was unsuccessful.

CHAPTER TWELVE

Gus's eyes scanned the chaos and focused on the dining room rug, which had escaped undamaged, as had all the other rugs and carpets. He eased Sam away after she stopped crying, bent over, and took hold of one corner of the rug and pulled it aside. The hatch door was unscathed. Both of them dropped to their knees, and Gus lifted the hatch handle and pulled it open. It was pitch black in the hole, so Sam got up and looked for the flashlight amongst the clutter and found it against the wall. Returning, she handed the light to Gus who immediately held it over the hole.

"It's there!" he almost shouted, as Sam dropped down to look. They couldn't believe their good luck and sat there on their heels smiling at each other.

Gus said, "Looks like they just destroyed their own property with all this insurance we've got!"

"What are we going to do now, Gus?"

Thinking back to what happened to his house, Gus said, "We're going to look for explosives that they might have planted and then we're going to a hotel."

Sam said, "I'll turn off the water in the laundry room while you do that."

Gus's quick scan was sufficient to determine that there were no explosives, and he yelled to Sam, "Don't bother looking for a tooth-brush; we'll stop and pick up anything you need."

There was a new chain motel over on Treasure Island which was never too busy since it was on the causeway and off the beaten track, so that's where Gus headed. Gus parked at the entrance and went in to register while Sam got everything ship-shape in the car.

Gus parked around to the rear, out of sight, took the few bags that they had packed, and headed up to the third-floor room overlooking the North side of Biscayne Bay. Sam put the toiletries that they had purchased at Walgreens in the bathroom.

"I guess we can't eat the rest of our picnic because I left it in the kitchen," Sam said.

"Well, we passed the Flame restaurant on the way over here, if that appeals to you?"

"Mister, as hungry as I am, I'd eat at Walmart."

They got up with the sun and had the breakfast bar in the lobby. Gus said, "I guess the first thing to do is make a home again."

"There's a shopping mall over on 27th Avenue where we can get some furniture and appliances. Maybe we can talk them into taking out the broken stuff when they deliver it."

"Always thinking of the angles, aren't you Sam? I'm glad you're on my side. We'd better get some money out of the bag before we go in or they'll think we robbed a bank."

"You did! You robbed the crooks that have been robbing everyone else, so in effect, you got their bank."

"You could say that. Now, we better get going."

Sam pulled out her cell phone and called in sick.

After all the furniture and appliances were selected, the sales clerk was given directions to the house and time to be there, and Gus drove over to the nearest Publix store for restocking the larder that had been demolished. No sense going back to Shells because they were probably still watching for them there.

Gus got the 9mm Ruger from the trunk, slipped a clip into it and stuck it in his belt. They wouldn't walk away from another encounter with him, he thought, remembering that the clip was loaded with Black Talons.

They stowed the groceries and moved all the broken furniture out on the lawn to make way for the new stuff. While Sam cleaned up, Gus put the money bag back in the plastic bag and replaced it in the hole under the dining room rug. Chances were that if they missed it the first time, they'd miss it again. Only the next time, if they found the hole, they'd also find a big surprise. Gus was going to rig a shotgun in the hole with a trip wire, and another trip wire to one of his grenades, mounted under the table. These boys played rough, and he had to reciprocate in kind.

The delivery took longer than they thought; the washer and dryer had to be installed as well as the stove and refrigerator. The damaged appliances also had to be on the truck. Gus gave each of the three men a fifty-dollar tip, mainly because they didn't complain the whole time.

Both Sam and Gus were too tired to go out to eat, and Gus didn't have the traps set up yet, so they both agreed to have a peanut-butter sandwich and go to bed.

Sam got up early, made coffee, and brought breakfast to Gus who was still snoring.

"Wake up, sunshine," Sam whispered into Gus's ear. "Wake up and smell the coffee. I can't keep taking the day off. I have to go to work sometime, and I've already eaten, so take your time, and I'll call you later."

Gus rolled over and said, "Have I ever told you how much I appreciate you?"

"Many times, lover, but I haven't heard it too often. Now let go of my leg, or I'll have to get back in bed."

Gus didn't really like breakfast in bed but couldn't bring himself to tell either Anita or Sam because it was a woman thing, and they thought it was a nice thing to do for their man, so he pretended to enjoy it for their sakes. So, as soon as Sam was out the door, Gus got out of bed, took the tray, and went to the dining room table to eat. While drinking his coffee, Gus started thinking how he'd explain to the investigators, after he killed someone, why a grenade went off in his house. Maybe he could think of a subtler way to stop them. In any event, he'd have to see the pimply kid at the Army/Navy store again.

Pimples looked the same as he did on Gus's last visit, only now he smelled twice as high. Probably hadn't had a bath since the last time either. Gus acknowledged that he was there by a nod of the head as he reached for a cart.

"Got some new stuff in since you were here last time if you're interested." Pimples sneered.

"Let's see what you've got."

Pimples smiled, exposing the rotten teeth in the front of his mouth, and said, "Ain't nuthin like you was lookin for last time but you might like it. I know I do."

He led Gus to the other side of the store in the side aisle and pointed to a display of bows and arrows, with all the paraphernalia that goes with them, and gave Gus another smile.

Gus thought how in the hell is this going to help him.

Pimples walked away dejected because Gus hadn't shown any expression at all, and Pimples took it for rejection.

The longer Gus stood there looking at the display, the faster a plan was formulating. Bows and arrows don't make noise, and they are very effective. Maybe two bows, with the arrows to go with them, would be easier to deal with. No bloody bodies and the arrows plugged the holes. Visions of Bakers Haulover came into his head as the plan started to become more feasible.

Gus checked the model number he wanted and looked under the display counter for the same model in boxes. There were three. He picked up two of them and put them in the cart along with four packs of the meanest-looking arrows he'd ever seen.

When Gus got to the counter, Pimple's god-awful smile came back as he looked into the basket and saw the bows.

"Do ya need a glove or quiver to go with those?" he asked.

"No, just what I've got," Gus replied.

Pimples rang it up, and Gus paid up, thinking, it's not my money, or at least it wasn't my money.

Gus stopped at Home Depot and picked up C-Clamps, flat black spray paint, clothespins, an assortment of springs, wooden wedges, and eye hooks. There was a tackle shop on the way home, and Gus ran in to get some thirty-pound monofilament fishing line, a roll of 100-pound leader wire, some large swivels, and a box of large fishing hooks.

It was still fairly early when Gus got home, so he took his toolbox and the booty he'd just purchased and crawled down into the hole in the dining room with an extension light and his drill and went to work. He strung the bow and attached two of the C-clamps, eight inches apart, to the bottom of a floor joist about twenty feet from the access hole and mounted the bow to the handles of the C-clamps with the steel leader. The bow was aimed directly below the access hole in the floor. The other bow he mounted ninety degrees from the first and pointed it slightly lower for when he bent over to pick up the bag. Gus then installed the eye hooks on the bottom of the joists in a semi-circle about six feet from the hole over to the trigger he'd constructed from the wedges, clothespins, and springs. He finished the other bow in the same manner and then went to work threading and attaching the fishing hooks along the steel leader wire about a foot apart.

The theory was that each arrow would pick up the cable as it sped toward the intruder, sort of like the old military aircraft barriers that used fifty-pound link chains instead of steel cables. Two chains were laid out facing forward and then attached to each end of the barrier which, when contacted by the aircraft, would pick up more and more chain to slow the aircraft. Gus's arrangement used the same principle only instead of chain links—fishhooks. Since it wasn't attached at the hole end, it would wrap around him like a whip, and the more he struggled, the deeper the hooks would dig in. Since the arrow would be embedded in him and attached to the steel wire, he wouldn't be able to remove any of it.

Gus had a sudden epiphany—he had a mean streak!

Gus used an old piece of rusty pipe he found in the sand and laid it two feet from the bag. Taking the monofilament line, he ran it through the eye hooks back to the bows and attached it loosely to the triggers. Next, he attached the monofilament lines to an eye hook that he'd screwed into the bottom of the satchel for both bows. Picking up the pipe, Gus filled it with the loose sand to give it weight and laid it over the lines again and buried them from the bag out to where they came out from under the pipe. Next, Gus took out the spray paint and coated the lines and hooks, and anything that was shiny, with flat black paint.

After measuring the distance between the bowstring and the trigger, Gus made two steel wire lanyards to attach to the triggers. Setting the arrows carefully into the string, he then pulled the string until it was taut and attached the lanyards to the triggers. He had set the bag slightly off-center to allow room to get out and make sure whoever reached for it would lean in the right direction. He tied the lines to the triggers very carefully, made sure that nothing was easy to see, and crawled back to the hole, giving a wide berth to the lines.

Gus put his tools away and restored order to the house, then put his feet up on the coffee table to watch the news and wait for Sam to come home.

"Gus, Gus." Sam was shaking his shoulder to wake him up, and it sounded urgent. Coming out of a deep sleep takes a while, but eventually, Gus woke up, stretched, and said, "What's up, sweetie?"

"Someone in a white car followed me all the way home from Cutler Ridge. I lost him at the end of the street."

"Did you recognize him, or her?"

"No, he was too far behind to get a look. I tried to lose him by slowing down just before a couple of lights and just squeaking through, but he must have run the lights."

"Well, they know where we live anyway, so there's not much sense trying to hide from them. I'll start 'carrying' all the time, and you have your service revolver, which you'll need to haul around with you even when you're not in uniform. By the way, don't go down in the hole for any reason. It's booby-trapped and will kill you if you try. I took enough money out to operate on before I set the traps, so there's no need to go down there anyway. Whoever it was is probably just trying to learn your routine, so take a different route to and from work from now on."

CHAPTER THIRTEEN

The glistening white Learjet 85 sat on the tarmac with both engines idling and the gangway in the open position. No one appeared to be around, and there was no crew in the cockpit. The clock on the hangar wall said that it was 11:50 p.m. and Barry Ingram, the pilot, was fidgeting in a seat by the open gangway door while Sonny Rice, the copilot, was preparing a cup of coffee for the flight ahead of them. "Do you want a cup of coffee, Barry?"

"No, it keeps me awake," Barry replied. "Where the hell do you suppose they are? We won't make our departure if they don't get their asses in gear."

"Maybe they stopped for a beer."

Before they could say anything else, headlights swept the length of the plane as a shiny black Mercedes pulled up at the gangway, and two men in black got out; one of them with a box, that looked to be about seventy-five pounds, with "Human Organ" printed on the side. He set the box on a rear seat, wrapped a seat belt around it and then plugged it into a cigarette lighter and turned on a switch in the back. The pilot waited until they were seated and then closed the gangway door.

The driver of the Mercedes pulled the chocks from the plane's wheels, stowed them in the belly of the plane then returned to the car and drove away.

The pilot sat down in his seat, strapped on his seatbelt, started the checklist, and said, "Get me clearance to taxi, will you?"

Sonny fingered the mike key and asked the tower for taxi instructions then relayed it to the pilot. "Cleared to taxi to runway 08L."

Barry finished the checklist with Sonny's help, stowed the clipboard, and pushed the throttles forward. The roar of the Pratt & Whitney PW307B turbofan engines, fondly referred to as the Bombardier, increased as the throttles moved forward, and the plane moved in concert with the roar.

They had to get in a relatively long line awaiting takeoff but eventually reached the end of the runway and requested takeoff instructions.

"Cleared for takeoff on runway 08L, take up heading of one ten at Angels three-zero," came from the tower.

The men in black had snapped on their seatbelts and checked the Glock 9mms in their holsters under their left arms, dropped their seatbacks, and prepared to take a nap. The cooler, securely stowed on the seat by the seatbelt, was humming contentedly.

The engines, with over 12,000 pounds of thrust, pressed them into their seats as the plane lunged down the runway and lifted off. It seemed to them that the plane was going straight up until it gained altitude and leveled off. It would be almost eight and a half hours until they got there, so they loosened their seatbelts and got comfortable.

———

Eduardo Serrano, wearing a white tailored suit with a tan Panama hat, and shoes to match, stood at the large plate glass airport window overlooking the tarmac and runway lights, squinting to block out the reflection of the overhead fluorescent lights behind him in the terminal. He knew he was early but was anxious to get the delivery and be back at the clinic before his wealthy client expired and the money disappeared. The money meant nothing to his client, but it meant the world to him. It meant that he could continue to live in luxury and maintain the lifestyle much as he had been doing since he lost his medical license. If his client died, he'd get nothing.

Looking at his watch, which said 5:15, he turned and walked out to his white Mercedes and drove back toward the Sao Paulo airport access road. There were several warehouses located in the southwest corner of the airport and spaced far enough apart that it afforded a modicum of privacy for each. These were private hangars and Eduardo owned hangar two, purchased during his more affluent years as a surgeon. He pulled onto the peripheral road and drove out to the front of his hangar.

By now the sun was coming up, and there was no need to get a light. He nervously rechecked his watch, which now said 5:40, and he started to pace back and forth until he heard the powerful engines of the Learjet taxiing around the trees at the end of the tarmac. It pulled up to within thirty feet of the hangar and the engines stopped. Nothing happened for a few minutes. Then the access door opened, and the gangway folded out. Sonny stuck his head out of the door and said, "Good morning."

Eduardo said, "It always amazes me that you can get here so fast. Get the box into the car, quick."

Thiago, the shorter of the two men in black, stuck his head out of the door and came down the gangway carrying the seventy-five-pound box with "Human Organ" printed on the side and slid it into the trunk. He pushed the cord through the back seat and handed it to Gustavo to plug into the cigarette lighter.

"You didn't open it, did you?"

"No, sir. Of course not! I like to get paid as well."

"You'll get paid when I get paid, as you well know," said Eduardo. "Now get in the car."

Eduardo pulled onto the Helios Smidt (SP-019) Highway and headed south to the BR 116 road (Pres. Dutra) into Sao Paulo eighteen miles away. Thiago sat up front, riding shotgun while Gustavo sat in the back seat balancing the cooler on the seat beside him. Both Thiago and Gustavo were professionals and knew better than to doze off, or they might never recover from it.

Eduardo flipped open his cell phone and pushed a speed-dial number, waited for a few seconds, and then said, "Get him ready, we're on the way!"

Turning south, then southeast onto Av. Dr. Arnaldo, Eduardo drove a short distance then made a right turn into the one-way street, R. Silvio Sacramento. Number 118 was Eduardo's private clinic, but he didn't have a license to operate it, so he hired Dr. Bernardo Fagundes to keep the clinic in his name and operate it as though it was his. It didn't interfere with Bernardo's lucrative drug sales, and he assisted in the operations, along with Dr. André Silveira, who had accidentally killed one of his patients and never reported it. Another member of this elite team was Bruna Tozzi, a nurse in her fifties who had once killed her patient with an overdose, then covered it up.

Eduardo kept a dossier on all his help with the evidence to hang them all if the authorities got hold of them. It was like having insurance. None of them could leave without Eduardo's blessing. This included four orderlies and three nurses who had prison records and were anything but model citizens. All of them were housed on the second floor, each with their own room and freedom to come and go as they pleased.

A suite of rooms occupied the third floor in the rear of the twenty-eight-room brick building. Four of them were set up as hospital ICU rooms. Each had all the latest medical equipment and surrounded the nurses' station where each room was open for viewing. The room on the far left had some activity going on that included preparation to receive a patient.

A gurney was wheeled from one of the guest rooms in the middle of the floor only a few doors down the hall from ICU. On the gurney was a man with gray hair, who appeared to be in his late sixties. He was pushed into the hallway and down to the opposite end of the hall, through swinging doors, into a room approximately twenty by twenty-five feet in size. This room contained a full operating room with surgical tables, respirators, large overhead lights, instrument cabinets and carts, and a narrow operating table. Off to one side was a small scrub room.

At almost the same time as the patient arrived in the OR, Eduardo pulled into the garage downstairs. One of the luxuries Eduardo afforded himself was an elevator from the first floor to the third. This eliminated raising his blood pressure by climbing the stairs before an operation.

The staff in the OR removed the man from the gurney and carefully laid him on the operating table, then attached a respirator over his nose and mouth and covered his chest with an amber disinfectant. Then they placed a sheet over his whole body, with a hole just over his chest. Next, they put a large paper shield, with a flap over the hole in the sheet. One nurse was inserting an IV in his arm while another was counting instruments and sponges.

"When you wake up, Senor Mendes, you will feel just like a teenager." Eduardo nodded to the nurse as he pushed the cooler to her, and she pushed a buzzer on the wall. Dr. André Silveira appeared in the scrub room, as if on cue. Both André and Eduardo scrubbed while the nurse extracted the heart from the triple-bagged package, each bag containing a solution to prevent contamination, packed in a dry ice surround, from the cooler and prepared it for transplant.

An orderly helped the two doctors with their gowns, gloves, and masks and they emerged from the scrub room with their hands up as if being robbed. André nodded to the nurse who picked up a hypodermic and injected a clear fluid into the IV line. The nurse who counted the instruments checked the gauges on the respirator and nodded to the doctor.

———

Two months later Alessandro Mendes set his martini on the coffee table and sighed with satisfaction. He couldn't believe his good luck. Taking anti-rejection pills for the rest of his life was a small price to pay for his new heart. It certainly beat the alternative. He felt so much better now that it would probably only be a couple more weeks before he could go back to his bank and family in Rio.

He had transferred the $500,000 into Eduardo's bank with a wire transfer and was free and clear for the rest of his life. Only a couple of follow-ups and he could go home. He didn't know where the heart came from and Eduardo wouldn't tell him, which was understandable, he guessed. The heart was beating strong and felt like it would last forever.

CHAPTER FOURTEEN

The heart had been beating strong in Fidenciov's chest as well just over two months ago when he crossed the Rio Grande on a dead run into Texas. It was beating what felt like twice as fast as normal, not so much from exertion, but from fear that he'd get caught. He'd been running for what seemed like an hour when, in the faint light of dawn, he saw a road on the other side of a barbed-wire fence. He climbed the fence and started walking toward the east and shortly saw a gas station. He cautiously approached the station looking for any form of police. None were in sight, so he pushed the door open and went inside.

A balding fat little man asked if he could help him.

"I'd like some water, please."

The clerk pointed to the cooler in the back and said, "The cold water's over there."

Thank God, he'd had enough foresight to change some pesos into dollars before he'd started this journey. He set the bottle of water and a pack of peanut butter crackers on the counter and pulled out his wallet.

"That'll be two dollars and a quarter." Fidenciov handed him three dollars and got his change.

On his way out the door, he waited until a gentleman wearing a suit went through the door first, then just outside the man turned to Fidenciov and said, "I notice there are no cars in the lot but mine, so does this mean you're walking?"

"Yes, sir. My car broke down two days ago, and I couldn't get another in time," he said in broken English.

"Sorry to hear that. Well, I'm heading to Miami, and I'd be glad to give you a lift. In fact, there's a job available where I'm going, if you're interested."

Fidenciov gratefully accepted, and they became friends as they talked in Spanish. The man said there was a job on a boat that paid pretty well and came with room and board in Miami. He told Fidenciov about the job, and Fidenciov could hardly contain himself.

The man was driving a Hummer, and it didn't ride that well, but at least Fidenciov was on his way, and he could put up with a little discomfort for a while.

Two days later the man in the suit, who came to be known as Cordaro by Fidenciov, drove the Hummer through the gate at 624 NE 77th Street, wound around the drive, and pulled into the garage. The garage doors closed immediately.

"You look like you could use a meal and a bathroom," said Cordaro.

"Yes sir, I could."

"Well, you go wash up, and I'll get the cook to whip something up for you, maybe like a steak and salad. Would you like a steak?"

"Yes sir, I would."

"Well take those stairs," he said, pointing to the stairs in the kitchen, "Go to the next floor, and there's a room for you in the first door on the left. I'll go tell the cook to fix you a steak and salad. Come down here when you're finished, and you can eat in the kitchen."

After Fidenciov had left, Cordero nodded to the cook and went to report in.

Fidenciov ate with gusto, finishing the meal in record time. They'd been driving all day, and it was late evening, so there was reason to feel sleepy. He could hardly keep his eyes open.

———

Opening his eyes in the bright light was hard. He had a headache and couldn't raise his head. He couldn't lift his arms or his feet either. As a matter of fact, he was cold. It finally dawned on him that he was lying on a table with no clothes on and with just a sheet covering him. His left arm was pulled out to the side, and someone was sticking a hypodermic needle in it. Fidenciov was able to roll his eyes far enough in the other direction to see that his other arm was also stretched out to the side and there was an IV inserted into a vein with the bottle hanging above.

"What the hell is going on?" Fidenciov asked.

A man in a white smock and wearing a mask over his nose and mouth said:

"It seems that you have ingested something that didn't agree with you and we're trying to find out what it was so that we can treat you."

"Then why am I tied down?"

"You had a violent reaction to whatever it was, and we didn't want you to hurt yourself."

"Then untie me, I'm not thrashing around now," Fidenciov said sternly.

"Don't worry about it. It's just a precaution. We'll release you soon."

A nurse, who until now was out of sight, stepped into the light and injected something into Fidenciov's IV line, and disappeared again.

Fidenciov's eyelids started getting heavy, and he had no desire to talk any more. The last thing he remembered was the lights going out and the man in the mask saying, "Get his blood type and then throw him in the can."

———

When Fidenciov woke up again, he was lying on a hard cot supported by chains fastened to the wall, and he was covered with a blanket that made him sweat. Throwing back the cover, he discovered that he was wearing a pair of white coveralls and had no shoes or socks on. He sat up slowly to protect his aching head and realized he had no underwear on either.

He looked around and found that he was seated in a cell that was composed of cyclone fencing, from floor to ceiling, with a gate in it. It had a washbasin, toilet, table, and chair with a pair of slippers under the cot. Then, he realized that he wasn't alone. Three other people in the room were also in cells. He asked the man in the closest cell, "What the hell are we doing here?"

Before he could answer, the guard, whose presence Fidenciov hadn't detected yet, yelled, "No talking!"

The other prisoner backed away and sat down on the edge of his cot, looking at the floor.

About an hour had passed when a door opened at the end of the hall. A man with a gun came out pushing a cart with trays on it. He gave one tray to each of the occupied cells by shoving them under the gates, which were about six inches above the floor. Along with the trays came a roll of toilet paper and a plastic cup and spoon. Fidenciov picked up the tray and other things and placed them on the table. He sat down and began to eat, realized what the cup was for, and went to the sink to fill it with water.

The food looked like last night's leftovers. There was half a pork chop, green beans, a boiled potato, and nothing else.

Obviously, this couldn't be the new job Cordaro promised. He wondered what the hell he'd gotten himself into. He jerked his head toward the guard, to ask him if he could speak to Cordaro, and caught himself just in time. No sense bringing the wrath of the guard down on his head.

There were two fluorescent lights in the hallway between the cells and one incandescent bulb at the guard post near the end of the hall. While he was pondering his fate, the fluorescent lights went out. The guard barked in broken English.

"Lay down!"

———

Carlos couldn't have been happier with his new (to him) Oldsmobile. It had a four-barrel carburetor and would get up and go like a bat out of hell when he goosed it. It was worth all the effort he had to go through to get the dealer to let him have it when he had no wallet. He had to borrow the money from Manolo, one of the guards whom Carlos had known for years, to pay off Rodolfo.

He had been in his "new" car when he followed the Cutler Ridge cop home, to see what her routine was. It turned out that she must have spotted him because she never went back the same way again. He followed her for a few days to make sure and kept the distance between them further and further apart so she wouldn't spot him again. Of course, having a white car that stood out like a beacon didn't help much either. She probably didn't spot him again, but it became apparent to Carlos that it was futile to consider an ambush and he'd have to find another way. She was the secondary target, anyway.

———

Something warm and wet was brushing against Gus's ear lobe. He opened his eyes and found Sam leaning over the couch, breathing into his ear.

"Hi, lover. What would you like to do for dinner tonight?"

"Let's run over to Morrison's. You can't miss with them, and I'm hungry. Is that all right?"

"You've got a deal, sweetie. Just let me change, and I'll be right with you."

Even at Gus's age, a little thing like getting your ear licked caused little twinges in the right places, and his thoughts turned to dessert before he even got off the couch.

As usual, there was a long line at Morrison's, and as they were walking to the end, a white car pulled into the parking lot across the street. Sam was staring at it and finally said, "That car looks like the car that has followed me home several times."

"Stay in line, Sam. I'm going around to the back and see if I can get a look at him."

"You be careful, Gus. Don't let him see you."

Keeping the line between him and the car across the street, Gus slipped around the back of the building next door and came out further down the street to the rear of the white car. Gus could see whoever it was wearing a hat and looking down in his lap and not looking in the mirror. Gus took a deep breath and ran across the street right after a car passed and entered a small alley. From there he skirted around the building to get a view of him from the other side, only much closer.

"Son-of-a-bitch," Gus almost shouted, "it's Mr. Zoot-Suit himself. The bastard that tried to run us over at Shells."

At this point, Gus had to control himself to keep from going over and dragging the son-of-a-bitch out of the car and rearranging his face. What Gus needed was information, like who did he work for and where? The next question was, how could he arrange to wind up following the Zoot instead of the other way around? Gus returned to Sam the way he'd come and found her just outside of the door. He told Sam what he'd found out and told her to go ahead and eat while he rounded up another car and a mannequin. Reacting to the quizzical look on her face, Gus only said, "I'll clarify it later." Then he was gone.

Gus found a car rental place further down Dixie Highway and rented the most inconspicuous car he could find, then went to a men's store and bargained with the clerk to rent a mannequin. The clerk was afraid of being fired, so Gus eased his pain with five $100 bills and a guarantee that he'd return the damn thing in a couple of hours. The clerk became less reluctant and picked out a model that resembled the back of Gus's head and shoulders. Gus even bought a shirt that was nothing like the one he was wearing. He then took off his shirt and put it on the mannequin and put the new one on himself.

Gus parked the rental next to his own car and transferred the dummy into the front seat and put on the seat belt. He found Sam finishing her dinner, so he grabbed a piece of pie and a cup of coffee and sat with her until they were finished. He had told her the plan. She was to drive the car home with the dummy and stay in the car until she was sure the Zoot had gone, then lay the dummy down and go in the house. Gus was going to follow the Zoot. It was already dark, so following him would present no problem.

All Sam had to do was sneak out into the car, out of sight of "Zoot," drive out of the parking lot, being as obvious as possible without creating suspicion, and go home with her dummy. Sam parked in the driveway, and her phone rang. Gus said, "He's leaving now and so am I, so go on into the house, and I'll call you as soon as I can to keep you informed."

"OK, Gus, but you stay far enough back to avoid him. I don't want you getting shot."

"Neither do I, sweets, I'll be talking to you."

Zoot headed north with Gus following behind him by two blocks. It wasn't hard to follow him since he was driving a white car that was bright as a beacon under the streetlights. When he reached 79th Street, he turned right heading east, where there were even more and brighter sodium streetlights, which made him even more visible, so Gus dropped back a little further.

Gus followed him through Little River and over to Biscayne Boulevard where he turned right again. He went over the bridge and slowed for a turn to the left onto 77th Street. Gus was hanging back but knew where he had turned, then almost missed him when he made an almost immediate turn to the left onto a driveway. Gus was still on 77th Street, so he made a quick turn to the right, then left on 76th Street. He went to the end of the block, turned around, and came back to park at the curb with his lights off. He could see the taillights waiting at what appeared to be a large gate from between the houses. There were lights on that pretty much lit up the area in front of the car. Gus left his car on 76th Street facing back toward Biscayne Boulevard and got out quietly. There were houses with relatively large yards between the Streets, but they had space between them that was nothing but grass. Gus kept close to the house that should have been in a straight line back to where the car had gone, hoping that there were no dogs around. He could see a large gate with a sentry box and an armed guard. There were lights above the entrance on either side and from the light inside the sentry box he could also see that the guard was carrying an automatic gun, probably an Uzi, judging from the size of it.

The house appeared to have a tall fence around it that was covered in foliage like a jungle. He could see no break between the houses where he could get into the yard on that side of the street, so he returned to the car and drove out to Biscayne Boulevard and turned north looking for some access to the river from the north side. Just over the bridge, he turned right on 78th Street which only lasted one block, then turned north to 79th Street. He parked at the turn and got out again quietly and walked back between the houses. Not leaving the safety of the bushes, he could see a beautiful boat moored across the river and a path leading up from the dock to the patio behind the house. To the left, he could see another building that had no windows. Both buildings were two stories.

Gus could see that to get a good look at the property, he was going to have to rent a boat and come down the river and take pictures. He couldn't use his boat because they knew what it looked like, and it was too big anyway. He couldn't come back to where he was across the street either and risk getting arrested. He took the rental car back to the lot, dropped the key in the box, and hailed a cab.

Sam was waiting for him with a pot of coffee and wearing a thin nighty, both pretty hot!

He told her what he'd been doing and that he was going to rent a boat in Little River and make the trip with a camera.

"Did they have a guard on the boat, Gus?"

"It was too dark to tell, but I'd assume they would have."

"Maybe you should get a boat with a cabin, and then you could take pictures without being seen."

"That's what I was going to do, dearest. Maybe something with a little cuddy cabin; then there's the problem of steering in the cockpit while taking pictures in the cabin."

"Never fear, my dear, I'm now suddenly working on a case in Little River, and I'll be having lunch there, so I'll be in the area and available to steer for you," Sam said. "In fact, I'll get lunch for two and bring it to the boat. Sort of like a little picnic."

"Sounds great, Sam. Let me get the boat first, and then I'll call to let you know where it is."

CHAPTER FIFTEEN

Bart's Boats was a small sales office just north of the bridge on 82nd Street, over Little River. He had one dock with an assortment of boats tethered to it and a one-room office without air conditioning. Bart, who must have weighed at least two hundred and fifty pounds, was sitting on a chair that you couldn't see. He looked up with a grin, rose, and stuck out his big paw for a shake.

"Welcome friend," he said, "what can I do for you?" and immediately sat down in front of the floor fan, roaring in the corner.

"I'm looking for a small boat to rent, preferably with a cuddy cabin and a working motor," Gus said.

Bart's eyebrows went up, and he said, "I have one that just might suit you. Let's take a look at it."

Bart waddled down to the dock and stopped at the fourth boat to port. He pointed at a Grady White that looked as though it had survived a few hurricanes, with paint peeling off in places, and said, "Will that do for you? It doesn't look like much, but the motor is in top shape, and it doesn't leak."

Gus knelt down, pulled the line, and got over on the deck. He worked his way along the boat to the cockpit and jumped down. He opened the cabin door and went below to see if the windows were adequate. Everything looked in pretty good shape, considering the way the outside looked. It had medium-sized windows with clear glass, although slightly buggy with cobwebs. Gus went up top and asked Bart if he had the key.

Bart reached in his pocket and picked a key from a jumbled handful of keys and tossed it to Gus. "You might need to choke it a bit," he said. "It's been sitting idle for a while."

Gus started the exhaust fan in the motor compartment and looked around. It didn't appear to have dry rot, and the paint inside wasn't peeling, so he went back to the console and inserted the key, pulled out the choke and set the throttle to half, then turned the key. It turned over three times and then roared to life which caught even Bart by surprise. Gus shoved the choke back in and throttled back to a soft rumble.

"Well," Gus said, "this just might do, depending on the price, of course."

Bart shifted from one foot to the other and said, "Would seventy-five a day be too much?" When he looked at Gus's face, he added, "Plus gas of course."

"Seventy-five a day is fine if you can guarantee me that everything works."

"I swear that you won't have any trouble with it. In fact, if you have a problem, you can deduct the problem from your final bill, how's that?"

"All right, I'll take it," Gus said. "Now where do I get gas?"

"Right here," Bart said, pointing to a pump partially hidden by a sago palm. "Bring it back to the fuel dock and I'll gas it up for you."

Gus slipped the line off the cleat and put it in reverse. Bart secured the line at the fuel dock and began pumping the fuel while Gus called Sam and gave her the particulars. He stopped at full, and the meter read twenty-three dollars and fourteen cents.

Gus said, "Bart, you have to make a profit, so I'll pay for my own gas. Put that on my bill."

"Well, thank you, Mr. Farrell. It will certainly help."

———

"Wow," Sam said, facetiously, at first sight. "It's a beauty. I'll be proud to drive this anywhere."

"OK, Sam, it's just a rental and it'll do nicely for our purposes. Get off your high horse and let's get this thing underway."

"I was just teasing, sweetie. First, I'll get out of this cop uniform and then get the lines so you can get us out of here."

Sam took the bag she had brought and went below. In ten minutes, she was back wearing shorts, a halter top, and a pair of tennis shoes.

While Sam was changing, Gus turned on the exhaust fan and then checked his camera to make sure all was copacetic, and that the battery had kept its charge from last night. Everything was ship-shape with his camera, so he walked over and started the engine, turned his head, and caught a glimpse of Sam. He had an overwhelming urge to grab her and go below again but remembered that he was on a mission.

Sam dropped the lines in the boat and gave a slight shove off the dock so Gus could turn around. He idled past the docks and headed down the river.

"All right, Sam, just keep her in the channel and don't change the speed. Of course, you'll want to miss any boats coming the other way, so just give them a little leeway."

By now it was eleven o'clock and the sun was beating down and warming things up, so Gus opened the windows on both sides to get a little breeze and turned on the camera. He popped up in the wheel-house to get more of a breeze and his bearings. Sam was enjoying herself puttering along at four miles an hour. The depth gauge said eight and four-tenths feet which was plenty. He'd forgotten to ask what the draft was, but he assumed that it wasn't much more than two and a half feet, so they had plenty of room.

Sam kept to the center of the river going under the 82nd Street Bridge and, since there were no other boats on the river, stayed where she was under the 79th Street Bridge as well.

Gus was in the cabin cleaning the windows with an old towel he'd found in a drawer as they turned east. He turned the camera on and checked the range finder, then set it on the counter. By this time Sam was starting under the Biscayne Boulevard Bridge.

"You'll see a beautiful boat on the right, but don't look at it, Sam. Just keep looking forward so as not to draw attention. When you come to a fork, go to the right; you'll come to another bridge, and then stay on course until you get to the bay."

"Whatever you say, sweetie. I'm here for you no matter what the reason."

"That's nice to know," said Gus as he snapped picture after picture, both close-up and wide-angle, to make sure he got everything, including the registration number on the boat.

They circled Belle Meade Island and headed back up the river, again taking pictures, on both sides of the river this time. They pulled into the same slip at Bart's that they'd vacated earlier and moored.

Bart came out of his office and asked, "You're not through with it already, are you?"

"No, we'll be back a little after eight o'clock tonight, so I guess we'd better make sure the lights work."

"Oh, they work. I just tested them last Friday, and I have some spare bulbs you can have to take with you just in case."

"Great, will you be here tonight?"

"No, so come over to the office and I'll give you the bulbs now."

Gus went to get the bulbs while Sam changed back into her uniform and met them in the office.

"Let's go over to Pelican Harbor Park on the causeway to eat lunch," Gus said. "It'll be a whole lot cooler over there."

"Sounds wonderful," Sam said.

They found a picnic bench in the shade near the beach and there were oleander bushes between them and the road, so they had a semblance of privacy.

"You don't know how close you came to getting raped on the boat, Sam. I found it very hard—to keep my mind on what I was doing, that is."

Sam looked into his eyes and very seriously said, "The next time you find it very hard, I'd like to know about it."

Gus choked on a bite of sandwich and laughed. "I'd find it very hard to keep it from you!"

They both laughed and finished their lunch.

Sam asked, "What do you plan to do now; if I might ask?"

"Well, you're going back to work and I'm going to Walmart to get prints made from this memory chip. Then I'll meet you at home. Oh, by the way, see if you can find out who that boat is registered to," he added, handing her a sticky note with the registration number written on it. "That'll be a big help."

Gus drove Sam back to her car. They kissed and waved goodbye to each other, going their separate ways. He then stopped at the Walmart on 79th Street and asked for prints of all the pictures on the memory chip.

"Are you waiting for them?" the clerk asked.

"Yes, how long?" Gus asked.

"They should be done in thirty minutes."

"OK," Gus said, walking off. He went to the Sporting Goods section and asked for two boxes of 9mm shells. The clerk unlocked his cabinet and took two boxes of one hundred count shells and then relocked his cabinet.

Gus thought, this is one thing I didn't mention to Sam because she gets a little spooked, but the one thing I don't want to do is run out of ammo if things warm up.

Gus picked up the prints, paid for his purchases, and headed home, checking for a white car as he drove.

Gus dropped the prints and camera on the dining room table and headed for the refrigerator for a cold one. He sat down and started going through the prints, using a magnifying glass to pick out details. When he got to the end, he started over, this time spending more time with each print. He spent more time looking for an indication that there was anyone on the boat, such as a hand, shadow, smoke, gun barrel, etc., than any other aspect. Not finding anything to indicate there was anyone on board didn't necessarily mean that there wasn't. The only thing he found was a pair of legs on a chaise lounge behind the hedge that surrounded the pool and opened to the walkway leading to the boat. He'd get a better look when they made their cruise down the river tonight.

Sam came through the door carrying a plastic bag.

"Whatcha got there, sweetheart?" Gus asked.

"I thought you would be playing with the pictures and wouldn't want to go out, so I brought some chicken for dinner."

"Sounds great, Sam, because we have to leave about 7:30 for our river cruise. I'll clean off the table and get it ready."

"Did you find anything interesting in the pictures, Gus?"

"Well, there was no activity on the boat that I could see, and the only other thing I found was a pair of men's legs on a chaise lounge at the pool."

"Are you going to take more pictures tonight, Gus?"

"Well, I can't use the flash, and if I took them without the flash, you wouldn't be able to see anything, so we're just going to take a leisurely cruise to see what we can see when they have their lights on."

Suddenly Gus slapped the table, startling them both. "Good God, Sam, I just had an epiphany!"

"I hope it wasn't too painful, Gus."

"Not at all, but it just came to me that I have plenty of money and there are stores around here that sell night vision goggles and binoculars that would be ideal for what we're doing."

Sam smiled and said, "Does that mean we're going to Walmart before our cruise then?"

"You betcha," Gus chuckled.

Gus asked the clerk, a white-haired man in his mid-sixties, what the best-selling night vision units were, and without hesitation, he walked over to a locked cabinet and took out a box that he placed on the display case. The box said: "Night Owl Optics NexGen II 50mm Monocular."

The clerk cut the tape on the box and shoved it over to Gus.

Gus took the unit out of the box and looked it over. There was only one way to know if it worked, so Gus paid for it and got a double issue of batteries.

The clerk put them in for Gus and gave him the receipt.

"We're all set now, thank you," Gus said to the clerk, and they walked out.

They walked out to the car and Gus turned it on. There was a green picture with black highlights, and he handed it to Sam.

Sam pulled it up to her eye and exclaimed, "Wow, this looks like green daylight. We should be able to see everything with this."

"Now let's head for the boat," Gus said.

CHAPTER SIXTEEN

Gus went through the preparatory procedures while Sam got out the cushions and set them around for the both of them. She was determined to be comfortable this time.

While Sam was fiddling around with the mosquito repellant, Gus turned on the battery switch and got busy checking the running lights and anchor light, then cranked the engine.

"OK, Sam, you can loose the lines now, I'm ready."

As soon as the last line hit the deck, Gus dropped the throttle in reverse and idled back, pushed it forward, and idled out into the river.

Gus turned the helm over to Sam and then reached over and flipped the running lights switch to off. The only light they had then was the ambient light from the houses along the river.

Sam said, "Don't you think that's a little dangerous?"

"Only if you run into something," Gus chuckled. "Just watch what you're doing and there won't be any trouble—unless you give us a ticket, that is."

"Right now, in the dark, I'm predisposed to giving you something more personal."

"You can give it to me later. If you feel like fondling something, I can give you the night scope so you can see better."

"That's a good idea, hand it over."

Gus handed her the scope and sat down on one of her cushions.

"This thing lights up the whole night, Gus. What a wonderful invention."

"I'm glad you like it. However, I'll need it back in a few minutes and I don't want it to ruin your night vision when you're not using it. We don't need to collect a bridge."

They had gotten to the Biscayne Boulevard Bridge without incident, and since there was no need for Gus to hide, he positioned himself behind Sam and turned to the business at hand. He asked Sam to cut back on the throttle to three or four miles an hour; to prevent a bow wave which would certainly alert those on board, if there were any.

The picture on the scope was similar to looking at a negative image only this image was moving. Gus did a quick scan over the whole property and found nothing of interest, so he zoomed in on the boat. There was someone in the cabin, but it didn't appear that he was on guard because Gus could see a drink in his hand, and he was talking to someone Gus couldn't see. As he made the observations, he quietly repeated everything to Sam. She made no comment but was grateful that Gus included her in what he was looking at. It made her feel like she was part of a team doing investigative work. She had never felt closer to anyone before and suddenly blossomed into a rash of goose pimples from the emotion.

SNAP! Gus snapped his fingers near her ear and said quietly, "I don't know where you were but you're getting a little too close to 'Das Boot.'"

"Oh God, I'm sorry, Gus. I was daydreaming, but I'm back on the job now. You scared the poop out of me."

Gus said, "Don't worry about it. I can see into the house but no one's moving in there. There's a light on over at the other building and I can see movement through the hedge, probably a guard. I don't see or hear any dogs, and that's a relief."

"So, you think this whole exercise is a bust?"

"Absolutely not," Gus said. "I've learned quite a bit and plan on using the information. For instance, the owner, and this is an assumption, probably uses the boat in the evenings to conduct business and socialize. I won't know for sure until I've checked it out for a while, with your help, of course."

"Gus, when we get to the bay, why don't we spend some time out there and come back later? You might see more later, and frankly, I want to christen this boat in the bay because I can't wait."

Gus turned the night vision toward her face and could see that she was smoldering, which then turned him on.

When they got to the bay, Gus moved out of the channel and anchored in the shallows, and flipped on the anchor light, but before he got turned around, Sam had unzipped him and dropped to her knees.

Sam was right. While they were in idle on the way back, there appeared to be more activity. There were several people on the patio and the boat. Someone on the boat was holding a cell phone and waving his other hand around as though questioning the intelligence of the other party.

Gus zoomed in on the patio and scanned it from left to right. Just before he ran into the hedge, he caught sight of Zoot leaning forward talking to someone Gus couldn't see. It didn't matter. He just confirmed that he'd found the place that he had been looking for.

Zoot was the one who tried to kill them, had followed them home, and most probably was the one who had blown up his house and killed the dog. Gus felt like he owed Zoot quite a bit and he would definitely pay him off, in spades.

Gus turned to Sam and said, "We've just found the place I've been looking for and now it's time for action."

Sam looked lovingly into Gus's eyes and said, "Gus, why don't you turn over what you've learned so far to the police? Let them investigate this whole thing and bring charges if they find anything. I don't want you involved in anything that puts you in danger!"

"Maybe it slipped your mind, Sam, but I'm not trying to be a Good Samaritan. It's personal with me, especially after all that's happened, i.e., they killed my wife; they shot me; blew up my house and killed, essentially, my dog; they tried to kill us both, and they destroyed your house. Do you think they're going to quit even if I turn them into the police? I'm afraid I'm in it for the long run."

"No, I don't think they're going to quit. I just don't want you in the middle of this because I'm afraid of losing you. I'll tell you this though, you're not getting rid of me, and I am now your right-hand man. I have resources available to me that you don't, and I plan to use them. For instance, you asked me to find out who that boat is registered to in Little River."

"You found out already?"

"Yes. His name is Dr. Eduardo Serrano, Rio de Janeiro, Brazil."

"That's great, Sam. You didn't happen to check out who owns the house, did you?"

"Yes," Sam said. "Ditto."

"Great again," Gus said. "I didn't mention it before, Sam but there was something else on the patio that seemed out of place. It was what appeared to be a uniform flight jacket with stripes on the sleeve hanging on the back of a chair."

"Hey, now we're getting somewhere! What color was it?"

"Green! Just like everything else through the night goggles, Sam."

"Oh yeah, that's right, smarty-pants."

They idled back to the dock at Bart's and tied up. Gus took the key and slipped it into his pocket, then went below to close the windows while Sam gathered up the cushions and stowed them below.

"What do you say about getting a drink on the way home, Sam?"

"I thought you'd never ask. There's a place on Biscayne Boulevard that used to be a gambling spot in the thirties and now it's a market. Right next to it is a little bar that's kind of nice. Shall we try it?"

"Whatever you say, sweetheart."

When they arrived at the "Little Bar" next to the market, Gus was pleasantly surprised. The interior was decorated to resemble a Caribbean beach bar, with palm frond umbrellas over each table and Margaritaville-type music being played by four authentic-looking natives of the Caribbean Islands. There was even sand piled up in the corners on the concrete floor and huge plants and flowers everywhere. The owner had even gone to the extreme of keeping the temperature set in the low eighties. The bar ran the length of the room and there was a stage at the end which was occupied by the band. The ambiance was enhanced by the low lighting and the floral surrounds for each table, giving a modicum of privacy for each one. The dance floor was set discreetly off to the side of the band.

"Well, Sam you really know how to pick the bars. This is more like a nightclub. I'm impressed."

"I'm glad you're impressed, Gus. Let's have a couple of margaritas and go home so I can impress you some more."

"I don't know how you could impress me any more than you already have, Sam."

"Then I guess I'll just have to impress you with my dancing skills. Are you prepared for that?"

"I guess, but don't blame me for your flat toes afterward."

"You're such a romantic guy, Gus," Sam said as she pulled him out of his chair and toward the dance floor.

"I guess I was just born to be 'suave and deboner.'"

Sam laughed as they wrapped their arms around each other and moved toward the center of the dance floor. Sam was not surprised at his prowess on the floor since she had thought from the beginning that he was polished and also well-read. She had indeed pegged him right.

Gus, on the other hand, was surprised that Sam was as graceful as she was. He had thought that she might not be because, after all, she was a large woman, even though she had a really great body and certainly knew how to use it.

They danced until 10:00 and Sam said, "I have to go to work tomorrow, sweetheart, so I'd better get home and get some sleep."

The waiter had left the bill on the table and Gus glanced at it and threw down a twenty as they walked out.

The house hadn't been disturbed, so they both brushed their teeth and dropped into bed, but sleep came much later.

———

"What do you plan on doing today, sweetheart?" Sam said as she walked out of the bathroom.

"Thought I'd go fishing, after breakfast."

"Oh, are you going to take out your boat?"

"No, I'm going to fish from the bridge over Little River. I don't want to be too obvious with the boat, so I'll just walk the sea wall and the bridge to see what I can from there."

"They know what you look like, Gus!"

"I know, but I'm going to stop at Walmart again and pick out a big floppy hat to hide under. Besides, I don't plan to go too close. I'll be taking my binoculars in case something interesting turns up."

"In case it really gets interesting, you had better take your gun," Sam chided.

"I was planning on it, Sam. Plus a writing pad and pen, dry socks, my pocketknife, sunglasses, and suntan lotion, just to be on the safe side."

"You don't have to be facetious; I worry about you and sometimes you don't duck when you should."

"I'm sorry, Sam. I know you're only thinking of my welfare, and I appreciate it, but I can take care of myself."

"Sure, you can, Gus. That's why you have two holes in your side— from taking care of yourself."

"Point taken, Sam. Now scoot and let me get to work."

"Right, hunk. Don't bring home any mermaids."

Gus chuckled as she went through the door, jingling her keys.

Gus gathered up his hardware with a couple of extra clips, locked the house doors, got into his SUV, and headed for Walmart.

The hat looked ridiculous since he was neither going on safari in Kenya nor taking a trip down the Amazon; however, it was the only one with a brim wide enough to hide his face that didn't have flowers on the hatband. He picked out a fishing rod, tackle box, and lures and took the whole load up to the cashier. Next, he stopped at Wendy's and picked up lunch for later on.

Gus parked in the theatre parking lot and walked across the street to the bridge. There was a sign on the abutment: "NO FISHING FROM BRIDGE." He turned north and walked around the end of the bridge and down a steep bank to come around under the bridge and stepped up on the sea wall. He put a lure on the fishing line and put his lunch in the tackle box. The gun nestled in the small of his back under his belt. He hung the binoculars around his neck and took the tags off his hat and put it on. The camera went into the tackle box. He put on his sunglasses and cast the lure into the water under the bridge. It surprised him that there was a swirl of water near where his lure landed since he didn't really want to catch a fish. The fish would make his charade look more authentic though. He reeled it in and cast closer to the swirl this time. Nothing!

After about twenty minutes he started walking east toward the big cruiser, casting, and reeling it in as he went. He stopped about one hundred yards from the cruiser, set his tackle box down, and concentrated on his technique. He was getting pretty good at casting, placing the lure right where he wanted it each time he cast.

There wasn't much happening at the cruiser or around the house but then it was only 10:15, and they were probably still sleeping after their busy evening.

He cast a few more times and then picked up his tackle box and headed back toward the bridge.

CHAPTER SEVENTEEN

Gus decided to get a more direct view of the rear of the house, so he headed back to his SUV, placed the tackle into the rear, and drove around to the Marine Plaza Apartments along the north side of the river across from the property of Dr. Eduardo Serrano. There were plenty of parking spaces, so he drove to the east end and parked near the water, got out his tackle, and walked to the water's edge. If anyone complained, he was protected by his right to access public waterways. He set his tackle box down, unhooked the plug from the eyelet of the rod, and glanced up from under his hat to see some activity going on in the house across the river. Gus sat down on his tackle box, facing away from the river, and looped the strap of his binoculars around his neck then replaced his hat. Stood up and cast out into the river and retrieved the plug slowly, giving little jerks about every third crank. He didn't want to catch a fish because it would create a commotion that would draw attention to him, and that's the last thing he wanted. But wouldn't you just know it, a fish about three pounds grabbed the plug and took off.

He almost wet his pants from shock. He eventually landed a nice snook slightly less than three pounds. Gus put it on the stringer and dropped it back into the water until he was ready to leave, thinking, "That's supper!"

Gus was so pleased with himself that he forgot to look to see if anyone had noticed from across the river. He peeked out from under the brim and saw that no one appeared to have witnessed a thing. To preclude that happening again, Gus started casting out into open water to avoid the likelihood that he'd draw another snook out from under the docks where they liked the shade.

He walked over to a tree and stood in the shade for a while, cooling off and checking for activity across the river. Nothing was happening, so Gus lifted his binoculars and took a quick look into the house. There didn't seem to be anyone around except for some guy pushing a cart from the house toward the annex as if delivering meals to someone. Gus checked his watch and discovered that it was twelve-thirty, so it probably was someone's lunch. There was a cloth on the cart so he couldn't tell how many there were, but the question was, for whom were they meant?

Since no respectable angler would be caught fishing at high noon, Gus hooked the plug onto the bail of the reel, retrieved the fish and his tackle box, and put them all in the SUV. He wrapped the fish in a piece of plastic he had left over from Home Depot and laid it in the back between the jack and the SUV wall so it wouldn't roll around.

Gus drove back over the bridge and turned into 77th Street, went around the block, and parked facing north on NE 7th Avenue so he could keep an eye on the entrance of the house. He unwrapped the sandwich he'd taken from the tackle box and had his lunch. There was a gentle breeze blowing, so he had opened his windows to take advantage of it, and since he was in the shade of a large rubber tree, he performed his usual stunt and fell asleep.

When the shade moved from over the SUV, it started to heat up, even with the open windows, and Gus awoke bathed in sweat. He looked at his watch and discovered that it was 2:30. For God's sake, he must have slept for over an hour, Gus thought. He glanced over at the driveway of Dr. Eduardo Serrano, and nothing was going on, so Gus fired up the SUV and headed home for a shower and to prepare dinner for Sam.

There was a letter in the mail for Gus from the insurance company that had insured his house. It stated the obvious and went on to say that the investigation had been completed and that the conclusion was that a gas leak had caused the explosion and was therefore considered a no-fault claim. Also, enclosed was a check of $185,000 remuneration and final settlement for the house and its contents. The last sentence stated—"Please sign and date the enclosed receipt form where indicated, indicating that compensation was made in full and that the claim was complete and closed, and then return it in the enclosed envelope."

This didn't quite explain the odor of fertilizer in the house, or the dead dog, or what had triggered the explosion in the first place; but, what the hell, it was more than he'd paid for it. He wasn't going to quibble over details. He laid the letter and check on the counter and prepared to clean the fish.

By the time Sam got home at five thirty, the fish was steaming; the asparagus was ready to sauté, and the rice had been cooking for ten minutes.

"Well, aren't we a busy little chef? What kind of fish are we having, sweetie?"

"Something I caught this morning, snook. You've probably never tasted it, but it's one of the nicest fish in Florida."

"You're right; I've never eaten it before. At least not knowingly. Oh! Look there; you've even set the table and—"

Sam had caught sight of the check on the counter and started reading the letter.

"Why are we eating at home when you've got a windfall like this?"

"Fish is best eaten fresh, dearie," Gus said.

After they'd eaten and were having their coffee, Sam said, "Some fishermen found another corpse in the glades yesterday, or what was left of it. This one didn't even have a shred of clothing on it. No head, no hands and it had been harvested as well. They think he was illegal in his early thirties but had nothing else to identify him, especially after the gators got done with him."

Gus looked at her and said facetiously, "Have you got any bad news to tell me?"

"Oh God, I'm sorry, Gus. I wasn't even thinking. It's just that it was on my mind all day and I just wanted to tell you."

"Don't worry about it, Sam. I'll get over it."

After a long pause, Gus said, "Do you think it's probable that Anita met the same fate?"

"Well, I'd hate to think of her in that light, but I guess anything is possible. I know that it's ridiculous for me to say this but try not to think of that. Just concentrate on finding her."

"I guess you're right, Sam, thanks. Do you feel up to a midnight cruise tonight, Sam?"

"You know I'm up for anything you're up for, Gus. We can stop and get some more coffee to go on the way, and possibly some donuts, eh?"

The little marina, "Bart's Boats," was dark but there was enough light to see the dock and boats, so they walked out to their prize, pulled it up to the dock, and got aboard, being careful not to spill the coffee or drop the donuts into the drink. Gus started the fan in the motor compartment and went below with his bag. There, he took out the Ruger and checked the clips, inserted one and cocked the gun to set one in the chamber, removed it and placed one more bullet in the clip, and replaced it in the weapon. He took out the night goggles and took them up to lie on the console within easy reach. Sam had rearranged the cushions and appeared ready to go.

Gus said, "Want to get the lines, Sam?"

Sam dropped the lines on the deck and headed back to the cabin while Gus shifted into reverse and eased the boat out of the slip. He slipped it into forward and checked the running lights and anchor light, then turned them and the fan off. He eased the boat into the river and adjusted the engine to eleven hundred rpm, so he'd have a four-mile-per-hour forward speed. Bart was right, the motor was in top shape. It ran quietly and had some spunk as he had found out in the bay.

As they rounded the curve approaching the Biscayne Boulevard Bridge, they could see the dock past the bridge where the cruiser was usually docked. It was gone.

Gus was taken aback since he'd become used to seeing the boat attached to the dock that now glared out in the moonlight with its

bleached pilings standing like sentinels along the seawall. He turned to
Sam and said, "Well, this is a whole new barrel of pickles. I'd like to
know what they're doing with it and where it is now."

"Maybe we should have kept an eye on it," Sam said.

"That may not be such a bad idea, Sam. We could bring the big
boat up here and anchor off the south end of North Bay Village if we
can find enough water. From there we can keep an eye on the mouth of
Little River. Right now, I think we should pay attention to the business at hand."

Sam handed Gus the night goggles to Gus and said, "At least we can
see the house better without the boat being there."

"Yeah," Gus said, "and it looks like they're having a party. They
even have the pool lit up and are working that portable bar pretty well.
Move over toward the dock a little, and maybe we can hear what
they're talking about. Set the tachometer to seven hundred, Sam so we
can hear better but don't get too close to the dock."

A heavily accented voice wafted over the dock saying, "I had that
motherfucker up to fifty miles an hour just south of Tamiami until I
saw the biggest fuckin' gator I'd ever seen and figured that if I hit one
of those damn things it would probably kill me. If the collision didn't
kill me, being in the swamp in the dark with that mother sure as hell
would've. I'd have been like one of our castoffs—bait."

Gus could neither hear the other conversant, nor see him, but
pretty well understood what was being said from the reactions of the
one he could see and hear.

"Shit no," he said. "I went further out than I've ever gone before,
and I used a new ramp. Since I got that GPS, I'm not afraid of getting
lost out there anymore."

A moment later: "I stripped him clean. No jewelry, no tattoos, and
no head or hands. I dumped that stuff into Bakers Haulover on an
outgoing tide. It was a clean dump."

"Well, Sam," whispered Gus, "I know what else we should have
bought, a telescopic microphone and recorder."

"We could get one, but the recording wouldn't be evidence since
there's no body, and recording someone without their permission is
illegal," Sam reminded him.

"Don't try to encourage me, Sam. I've made up my mind! Let's get back and do some errands before we turn in."

Sam smiled and said, "You have some errands to do after you turn in as well, so let's hurry."

After they had put the boat back in the slip, Gus handed Sam the key, and they drove to Kings Bay Marina, On the way, Gus explained the plan to Sam.

"I'll take the big boat over to Harbor Island, and you can meet me there with the Grady White. That way I'll be able to anchor in a position where we can see straight up the river. I don't have another hand-held marine radio so just keep your cell phone on so we can find each other. It might be a good idea if you idled down Little River without lights as well, at least until you get into the bay. We don't want them even to hear or see the boat right now."

When they arrived at Kings Bay, Gus leaned over, kissed Sam and said, "I'll see you in about an hour and a half, sweetheart. Stay out of sight."

Gus got out of the car and Sam drove off into the night.

After removing all his alarms, dropping the lines, and getting refueled, Gus was underway into a very dark night.

CHAPTER EIGHTEEN

Carlos was drunk. He didn't get drunk very often because Dr. Cruz was a stickler for protocol and wouldn't put up with an employee who couldn't control himself, or who might talk too much in the wrong company. But Dr. Cruz was gone to Cuba and wouldn't be back for a while. So Carlos decided he owed it to himself to enjoy his freedom, no matter how fleeting. The problem was that he needed a woman and there were none around except for Carlota who belonged to the Dr. and was almost always with him. He felt that he and Carlota had an affinity because of the similarity in names, but she wouldn't talk to him, or even look at him. There were no other women in the compound, so the only way around it was to get a hooker. He didn't like that idea very much either since he'd caught both the clap and crabs from hookers. God knows what else he might get next from a hooker.

Wait a minute! Yes, by God, there was a woman on the compound, and she was locked up in one of the cells. He could get her, take her to his room and give her a bath; use her and then put her back without causing damage to the goods. No one would be the wiser. What a great idea, if he'd been sober, he would have thought of it sooner. The guards were subordinate to him so they would do what he told them.

Carlos went upstairs to the dormitory room of the big house and got one of the guards, Rafael, who was sitting up in bed. Carlos told him to get his gun and follow him. The two of them took a shortcut through the kitchen on the way to the walkway leading to the lock-up.

Rafael knew better than to say anything when they climbed the stairs to the cages and opened the one containing the bitch. He went in, tied her hands behind her back, and then put a blindfold over her eyes and a piece of duct tape over her mouth. Then they led her out and down the stairs.

Carlos asked, "What's the duct tape for?"

"She has a huge mouth as you will see."

Apparently, the little jerk had figured out why she was being taken to the main house, but Carlos said nothing.

"Just put her in the room and come back in two hours, and keep your mouth shut," Carlos said, opening the door to his room.

He removed the blindfold but decided to leave the duct tape on her mouth. It wasn't necessary to talk to her, and she couldn't have anything to say that he wanted to hear. She struggled but was no match for Carlos, so he took her to the bathroom, stood her in the bathtub, untied her hands, and carefully took her clothes off. She was very well built and—from what he could see of her face—beautiful.

He started the water running and adjusted the temperature, then took off his own clothes and laid them with hers on the toilet. He got in the tub, pulled the shower curtain shut, and pulled the shower knob out while she stood at the opposite end of the tub. A little more adjustment on the temperature and he was ready.

"Come around to this end, and I'll wash your hair."

She looked at him and shuffled around him while he steadied her. He turned her to face the shower and pushed her under it. He told her to close her eyes and turned the bottle of shampoo upside down over her head. He washed her hair twice looking for lice or any other foreign items on her scalp. Finding none, he gave her a final rinse and soaped up the washcloth, and started washing her face, tape, and all. As he washed her down, he noticed that she didn't shave under her arms. It didn't matter though because no one else was going to see her but the surgeon.

He soaped up the cloth and got a lot of suds, then stuck it between her legs. She flinched and turned sideways making a grunting sound.

Carlos said, "You may not like this but you sure as hell need it. You smell like a dollar whore, and you're going to damn well get it! Now stop wiggling."

He cleaned the dual ports enthusiastically while she squirmed and moaned, but he didn't give up until she almost glistened. He continued down her legs and had her lean against the wall while he did one foot at a time. Then he went back and gave her crotch another couple of swipes and shoved her under the shower.

Carlos threw back the curtain and stepped out; grabbing a towel to dry himself off, then helped her out over the tub edge and dried her and her hair as well as he could.

She was shivering a little, and her nipples stood up like pencil erasers, so Carlos turned the thermostat up a few degrees. Carlos had had a hard-on since he took her clothes off and the air conditioner, blowing cold air, hadn't affected it at all.

After throwing the bed covers back, Carlos went over to lead her to the bed. She was less than willing, but Carlos was adamant and had no trouble getting her to where he wanted. He pushed her over backward onto the bed and, for the first time, saw the fear in her eyes.

———

Carlos managed to get her clothes and the blindfold on and retied her hands, then poured himself a shot of tequila. He drank it and poured another. No sense asking her if she wanted it because he'd have to take the duct tape off and he didn't have any more tape, so he drank that one too.

He just finished getting dressed when Rafael knocked on the door. They escorted the girl back to the cage, took her blindfold off, and untied her hands. She was struggling to get the tape off as they left.

Carlos was feeling and enjoying the little edge he'd gotten from the tequila, so he poured himself another, and then another and fell asleep on the damp bed.

Rafael, knowing that Carlos would get drunker and would therefore not be a threat, went back to the cage, tied up the girl and blind-folded her again, got some tape from the guard and covered her mouth then took her to the dormitory room. The problem was that they didn't know when to quit and had kept her there too long while they all raped her over and over again. None of them were willing to take her back to the cage for fear of getting caught, and they couldn't leave her there to be discovered by the maid, so they drew straws. Rafael got the short one. His whole demeanor changed at the sight of the straw. He knew that at the very least, he'd get caught and wind up as alligator bait out in the glades. He looked around, desperately looking for a volunteer, and, to a man, they were all drawing their knives.

———

Cordaro, drinking orange juice in the kitchen while waiting for the toast to pop up, caught a glimpse of something quickly passing the kitchen door. He drew his Glock and stepped into the hallway to see Rafael pushing a girl through the outside door.

"Stop! Goddamn it, Stop!"

Rafael pissed his pants and stepped back into the hallway, never letting go of the girl.

"Where the hell do you think you're going with her?"

"Ah, well ah; I'm taking her back to the cage."

"What the hell is she doing out of the cage?" Cordaro screamed at him.

Knowing his life was on the line; Rafael thought fast and said, "Carlos told me to take her back."

"Carlos? Where the hell *was* she?"

"She was in Carlos' room."

The girl, who looked like she was going to collapse, turned her head to look at Rafael through narrow slits but could say nothing.

"Leave the girl with me and go get Carlos. Now!"

Cordaro, who hadn't had a woman in some time, was looking her over and wondering how many times she'd been raped. Not that it mattered a hell of a lot, but he hated sloppy seconds and was not inclined to catch a disease from carelessness. She looked better now than when he'd brought her in and smelled a whole lot better.

He heard a door slam and feet shuffling towards the kitchen, and then Carlos came around through the kitchen door.

"You sent for me?" he asked Cordaro.

"Yeah, what the hell was she doing in your room?" he said, nodding toward the girl.

Carlos knew he couldn't lie his way out of this, and that Rafael had squealed on him. He'd deal with Rafael later, right now — how could he rationalize this situation. He was thinking hard when Cordaro said, "Well?"

Carlos said nervously, "I haven't been able to get out lately and didn't think it would matter if I used her a little. I did give her a bath and washed her hair so she wouldn't smell so bad, and I didn't keep her very long."

"What the hell does that mean; it's six-thirty in the morning. When did you get her?"

"I took Rafael to help with her about nine o'clock last night and took her back about eleven-thirty."

Cordaro looked at Rafael and asked; "Did you go back and get her after that?"

"Well, I figured that if Carlos could have her, I should be able to get some of her myself, so I did go get her."

"Where did you take her?" he asked.

"To the dormitory."

"The dormitory?" Cordero shouted. "Who else had her?" he demanded. "And since you're only now taking her back to the cage, that means you used her all night. Is that right?"

"Yes, sir."

Cordero reached above the door sill and pressed a little white switch.

An alarm sounded in the dormitory that normally would wake everybody up; however, no one was asleep. They'd been talking about the nice piece of tail they'd all had and were too excited to go to sleep.

The alarm meant to get to the main room, armed, as soon as they could, even if they had no clothes on, and many of them were in a state of undress.

Cordero pointed out two of them and told them to get Rafael into one of the cages immediately, or they could join him. He instructed the rest of them that Rafael would be treated as one of the prisoners from now on, no exceptions. He then dismissed them to go about their regular duties.

Carlos started to walk away, but Cordero took his arm and said, "Just a minute, Carlos, I need to talk to you."

When they were all gone, Cordero faced Carlos and said, "Carlos, you know I'm in charge when the Dr. is gone. What you've done is a complete breach of discipline that had repercussions all the way to the bottom. That girl is the property of Dr. Cruz, and you've soiled her. I just hope you've not done any damage to her internally. I can understand your motive, but if the Dr. finds out about it, he will undoubtedly order your demise. You best hope that no one shoots their mouth off because if they do, we're both in trouble; you, as the perpetrator, and me for not reporting it. Just keep this in mind: You owe me one! Don't forget it. Now get your ass out of here."

CHAPTER NINETEEN

Gus followed the channel out to the Intracoastal Waterway and turned north, following the markers. It was a trip where he had to keep his mind on what he was doing since it was so dark. There wasn't much traffic in the channel, but he had to watch out for the idiots who either didn't have or use running or anchor lights on their boats.

It took him an hour and fifteen minutes to come up abreast of Belle Meade Island, which was only about two hundred feet from the Intracoastal. There he turned to starboard, slowed to five miles an hour, and adjusted the backlight on the depth finder. It read four and a half feet. The tide was in, which meant that there was a problem when it went out since he needed at least three feet to stay afloat. As he headed east toward the south end of Harbor Island, the depth gauge indicated a small channel running east and west, probably dredged by the developer for the homeowners on Treasure Island. It was twelve feet deep and about thirty feet wide, with plenty of room to anchor.

Operating the motors, one forward and one in reverse, Gus managed to turn the boat around without bumping anything. He backed up a little, put it in idle, and dropped the rear anchor over the stern, leaving plenty of line, then returned to the cockpit and pulled forward about fifty feet, repeated the procedure to get the bow anchor hooked then backed up about twenty feet, holding the stern line to keep it from fouling the propeller. He removed some of the slack in the line to the stern anchor and then adjusted the slack on the bow anchor and shut the engines off.

There was no sign of Sam, and he was beginning to get worried. He pulled out his cell phone and dialed her number.

After three rings, Sam said. "Hello."

"Where are you, Honey?"

"I'm hiding in the car. I just got here and went to the marina and found the boat on the bottom. It's tied to the dock, but it's underwater."

"They must be right on our heels since we've only been gone for two hours. Don't stay there, Sam. Get out of there and drive to the marina at Pelican Harbor, but make sure you're not being followed. I'll meet you there as soon as I can."

Gus started the engines and reversed his mooring procedure. Pelican Harbor wasn't far away, but he had to go back to the Intracoastal Waterway to get around the causeway and under the 79th Street Bridge.

It didn't take long to idle over to the tiny marina at Pelican Harbor. Sam was waiting on the dock and grabbed the bowline to tie it off, then did the same for the stern line.

Gus said, "We'll sleep on the boat tonight and look for another small boat tomorrow. We're going to need it since all we have is the dingy."

"I made sure that I wasn't followed, but what if I was, and they know where we are?"

"We're going to take shifts on guard duty just to make sure. I'll take the first shift and wake you after two hours, and then you can do the same."

Gus could see the strain in her face and told her, "Don't worry, Sam. I'm going to set up some perimeter alarms and then make a pot of coffee, so just relax, and get some sleep. You're in good hands."

"Oh, I know that, Gus. I'm not worried about me, I'm worried about you, and I'm going to sleep with my gun, just in case."

"OK, Sam. Just don't shoot me when I wake you up, eh?"

Sam smiled and stepped down into the hatch and forward through the V-berth door, which Gus closed to keep out his noise as he looked for the coffee pot and fixings in the galley.

Since Gus's boat was docked at the far end of a long dock, he could set up his monofilament barrier closer to shore. With his little tripwire across the dock, it would provide an early warning of intruders. Gus tied the green low visibility monofilament to a small eyelet he had screwed into the lee side of the piling up on the port side of the dock and ran the monofilament through a small eyelet he had screwed into the adjacent starboard piling and then back to the boat. There he tied the monofilament to the neck of a bottle which he sat on an upturned bucket and placed other bottles beneath. In the event someone did come down that dock, the noise would give Gus approximately eighty feet of advance notice of the intrusion.

Gus opened the door to the starboard locker, fumbled around, and came out with the dark gray 9mm Ruger that Cal had loaned him. He made sure that both clips were loaded and inserted one into the Ruger and performed the same procedure as before, making sure he had at least one extra bullet and laid the gun and extra clip on the counter, then poured himself a cup of coffee. Next, he turned out the galley lights, picked up the coffee, the gun, and the clip, and went up to the flybridge. Here he had a commanding view of the causeway and the whole marina. Nothing was stirring, but then, nothing should be stirring at 1:30 in the morning.

In the still of the night, and with no distractions besides the small waves lapping against the hull, Gus started thinking about how badly his investigation was going and concluded that he was just floundering around and not getting anywhere. He decided that he should stop being pussy-whipped and take assertive, independent action to collect evidence and compile a list of players involved in each scenario and bring the results into a working plan that would shed some light on their activities. Gus thought about Anita, and the guilt washed over him. He knew that he should have worked the problem by himself, even though Sam had been quite helpful, and still was for that matter. He wouldn't have gotten as far as he did if it weren't for Sam.

Gus was still formulating his next moves when the sky started turning a grayish pink. He realized that he'd been thinking all that time instead of watching. Oh, well, Sam needed the sleep, and she had to work today, so nothing was lost. He'd let her sleep till 7:00 and then wake her. He went down to the galley and made a new pot of coffee and got the eggs and bacon out of the fridge. Then he got the frying pan and the toaster out and took the bread out of the freezer. He poured two small glasses of orange juice and put them on the table along with the napkins. Next, he pulled his medicine box out and placed his metformin, omeprazole, Norvasc, losartan, and aspirin next to his place, and sat down. He thought it odd that Sam didn't take pills, but then she was younger than him and probably just hadn't reached that watershed yet.

The toilet flushed, so Gus got up, washed his hands, and put the bacon in the pan.

"You didn't wake me!"

"Well, I was doing some catch-up thinking, and besides, you have to work today, and I thought you could use the sleep."

"Nevertheless, that wasn't our agreement."

Gus looked at her out of the corner of his eye, lifted one eyebrow, and said, "Why don't we have breakfast, then discuss it?"

"You're impossible!"

When Sam took off in the car to go to work, it left Gus with no way to get around. His car was still at Sam's house. Gus needed to make some phone calls anyway, so he checked his phone for Bart's Boats and dialed it.

"Bart's Boats!"

"Bart, this is Gus. I heard that the Grady White had sunk, and I was wondering if you knew of another marina with a boat for rent or sale."

"Maybe I do, or maybe I don't. Depends on how it got sunk. Don't have any ideas, do you?"

Gus said, "Couldn't say, Bart. When we brought it back the night before last, there wasn't a drop of water in her. Last night Sam went over and found it on the bottom."

"Well, the insurance will take care of it, but it's going to be a lot of work to raise her, pump it out, fix it and overhaul the motor."

"I'm sorry, Bart, but again, do you know where I can get another boat?"

After a long pause, Bart, with a slight edge to his voice, said, "There's a marine salvage place across the Bay, over on Indian Creek. Don't know the name or address but I hear they have some boats for rent. Check the phone book."

Gus said, "Thanks, Bart, I'll take a look, and for what it's worth, I am sorry about the boat."

When the cab dropped him off at the house, Gus paid the driver and went in to check out the interior. Nothing was amiss, and all his alarms were still in place, so Gus grabbed the phone book and called the marine salvage yard that Bart had told him about, got his keys, and headed over to Indian Creek.

The entrance to the Indian Creek Marina was down a long sand road, lined with palmettos, that opened up onto a wide flat of exposed coral enclosed by a chain-link fence about eight feet tall. There was a workshop over to the right with a crane on wheels that led to the service dock. Just inside the gate was another small building with a sign that said "OFFICE," and from behind the office, on the water's edge, was another building that ran out to approximately 200 feet to the left. This was no more than an overhang for the approach to the docks. Beyond, Gus assumed, were the docks.

Although he couldn't see it, the fuel dock was on the other side of the service dock.

Gus parked in front of the office and went in. There was a counter dividing the customers from the business with a cash register sitting at the end. There was a craggy old man wearing cowboy boots sitting at a desk with his feet crossed on top of it. He was kind of reminiscent of an old Rowdy Yates, of *Rawhide* days.

"Can I help ya, sonny?"

Gus smiled at being referred to as sonny and said, "You can if you have a boat for rent."

"Ya gotta tell me more than that, sonny. I've got a lot of boats."

"Well," Gus said, "I need a powerboat about twenty to twenty-five feet long with a cuddy cabin and an I/O."

"I've got mostly outboards, but I do have a few I/O's. Let's take a look." He swung his feet around and stood up. He couldn't have been more than five feet, four inches. He turned his head, leaned over toward the desk, and let fly with a gob of tobacco spit that hit a coffee can dead center.

They walked about a third of the way down the building to a twenty-five-foot Bayliner and stepped out on the dock.

"I've only had this one about a month, but I can guarantee it's in great shape, and it runs so quiet that you can carry on a conversation when it's wide open. We just serviced it, and it's ready to go."

Gus said, "Does everything, and I mean everything, such as gauges, instruments, lights, steering, and such, work?"

"It certainly does, sonny! We can take her out for a run if you like so that you can see for yourself."

"I like," Gus said, "But first let's do the math. How much do you want per day?"

"Well, sonny, this is a nice boat, and it's only six years old, so I'll need sixty dollars a day or four hundred a week."

"Do you have anything else?"

"Well yeah, I do, but not as nice as this one, or as clean. I'll tell you what, I'm not making any money with the damn boat sitting at the dock, so I'll let you have it for three hundred and seventy-five a week."

"I'll tell you what," said Gus. "I'll give you three hundred and fifty a week, and I'll buy my gas, but I still want to check it out."

Rowdy sighed and said, "OK, OK. I'll get the key."

The boat handled fine, and everything did check out as he had said; even the motor, which had even more spunk than the Grady White. They went back to the office, Gus paid the three-fifty and got the key and combination to the gate lock, and drove off, with the understanding that he'd be back to get it later.

By now, it was getting on to supper time, so he called Sam at work and told her that he'd gotten a boat, gave her some detail, and then said, "Will you be there much longer, Sam?"

"No, I was just closing up, so I'll meet you at home."

"Sounds like a plan to me; see you at the house."

It only took Gus twenty minutes to get home and, of course, he was the first to arrive. Gus let himself in, grabbed a beer from the refrigerator, sat down on the couch, and started thinking about how to proceed with his investigation. The only real evidence he had was the money and the day planner books that he'd taken from the house in Coral Gables. He went over those books with a fine-tooth comb and could find nothing that tied his wife's disappearance in with the doctor called Cruz. The planners were filled with appointments indicating dates, times, and places. Almost all the entries had a notation that resembled some sort of code; the meaning of which had Gus stumped. He was trying to decipher it when Sam came through the door.

"Hi, lover, what are you up to?" She came over to the couch and peered at his sketch pad. "What are the hen scratches for?"

"I'm trying to figure out this code, or versions thereof, that are in the day planner books and it doesn't look too hopeful. The only thing that looks recognizable is number three, which looks like a type of blood."

"Well, that's something, anyway."

"I just had an epiphany, Sam. I know someone who might be able to do some research on this gibberish and give us some insight."

Gus retrieved his address book and dialed a number.

"Flamingo Clinic, Neil speaking."

CHAPTER TWENTY

Bart got a marine salvage crew in to refloat the Grady White. They brought a barge up the river, with a crane welded on the deck, and attached lines to the bow and stern of the Grady White. They had to be careful because the weight of the water would break it in two if they rushed it. When they got the gunwale above the water, the crew attached hoses to the two-large gas-powered pumps adjacent to the crane. They shoved one into the cabin and held the other on the deck at the stern. The crane lifted the boat until the gunwales were just above the water and then started the pumps. Bart was astonished at the force of the water coming out of the nozzles. When the stern deck came clear, one of the salvage crew hands jumped onto the boat and opened the engine hatch to put the hose into the engine well. They continued pumping until the hoses started sucking air, then shut down the stern pump. They let the cabin pump operate at a slower speed to take care of the sieve effect while continuing to raise the Grady White.

The salvor slipped into the boat and started looking very closely at the deck.

"Hell, Bart, it looks like someone has been using this thing as a target. It appears to be full of bullet holes."

An exasperated look came over Bart's face and he said, "Can you get it out before it sinks again?"

"Oh, sure. We'll just get a trailer over to the ramp and keep pumping until we get it on the trailer and then drag it out. The trailer is on the way."

Bart said, "OK, do what you have to do, but where will you take it to get it fixed?"

"We'll take it to our yard since the repair will be fairly straightforward and not too expensive."

Bart frowned and said, "Like, how expensive, since you'll notice it's not the newest boat around?"

The salvor smiled and said, "I'll call you after we look it over. I have to find out if the bullets damaged the motor or anything critical, or if we have to pull the engine. Since it's a lapstrake boat, we could probably plug the holes with dowels, and that will keep the cost down, for sure. That way we won't have to replace the planking."

"Well, it's not like I have it rented, so there's no hurry, just give me a call, and thanks."

Bart returned to his office mumbling, if it's not one damn thing, it's another! The little tug attached to the barge eased everything over to the ramp while awaiting the trailer.

Bart watched them getting the Grady White onto the trailer but felt no inclination to go out to the ramp. He was hot, tired, sweaty, and depressed and didn't want to talk to anyone.

————

The phone on the wall rang twice, and Neil pulled it off the hook and said, "Flamingo Clinic, Neil speaking."

"Neil, this is Gus Farrell, remember me?"

"Oh, of course, I do. How are you, Gus?"

"I'm doing fine, but I think I need your help again. It's not about me, but I have a little puzzle that I thought you might be able to help me with."

"Sure, what is it?"

After Gus had given him the information, Neil said, "OK, Gus, let me have your phone number, and I'll get back to you as soon as I come up with something."

Gus reached up, took Sam by the wrist, and pulled her down on the couch beside him.

"I want you to look at this and try to be objective about it. Do you see anything that looks familiar to you?"

Sam took the sketch pad and stared at the notation. "I see the 'K' at number eight, and 'K' stands for one thousand."

Gus took the pad and wrote the numbers down in a vertical line. Next to the eight, he wrote 725 thousand

Gus said, "On seven, that looks like military time, and if it is, it would be eight-thirty a.m. Then, if seven is military time, and then combined with six it could be a date/time group which is used in the header of every military message; therefore, it could be September twenty-third at eight-thirty."

"Hey," Sam squealed. "We're actually making progress!"

"Yeah, but I have no idea what the rest of them are. Have you ever seen anything like that?" Pointing to five.

Sam squinted at the letters and said, "Did you ever see those tags on the rear windows of cars? The ones that are oval and about four inches long that have the identifier of the country they represent?"

"Oh yeah," Gus grinned, "I had one of those on my car in Berlin; only mine said 'US.'"

"Exactly. Only, countries have two letters, not three. So, what are three letters used for?"

"Luggage!" Gus burst out. "Every time you fly somewhere, they put tags on the luggage, and they have three big letters on them."

"That's right, Gus. The one for Miami is 'MIA,' but the letters they put on in Miami are to identify the destination airport, like 'MCO' for Orlando."

Gus handed Sam the scratchpad and got up to get his laptop. He brought it back to the couch and turned it on. When the screen came on, he typed Airport/BZE into the Google search bar and hit enter. Bingo! They now knew that the BZE Code meant the Philip S.W. Goldson International Airport, Belize City, Belize. Gus jotted it down next to the number five and said, "Now, what the heck would the number sixty-two be used for?"

"It could stand for someone's age, couldn't it?"

"Well, yes it could, but there's no way to tell until we get to the end of this crossword puzzle, so let's assume that's what it is." He wrote "age" next to the number two. "It could actually mean a lot of things, but for right now age will have to do."

"OK, and if sixty-two is someone's age, then PH could be the 'someone,' right?"

Gus smiled at her and said, "I don't think it's referring to the PH scale since both letters are in capitals, and I don't think it's an acronym since you don't start a sentence or anything else with an acronym, therefore I believe you're right. I don't know how I got so lucky hooking up with the likes of you, smarty." He then wrote initials next to the number one.

———

Neil treated the boy's wound, then gave him a tetanus shot after he had stepped on a rusty nail protruding from a board and was just getting ready to dump the bloody gauze bandages and hypodermic residue off the tray into the red bag when the door slammed open.

There were two Hispanic types standing there dressed in suits. The first one in the door was holding a gun of considerable girth. Neil knew what it was because he'd been around them in the Army and had the 9mm version of the same gun, a SIG Sauer SS 45ACP. Even if it wasn't loaded, it didn't matter because just having the damn thing pointed at you was enough to turn your pants brown.

The mother of Neil's patient fainted. Neil turned to catch her, but it was too far away to get to her before she cracked her head on the tile floor. He continued toward her to lend assistance.

"Get back." The first suit yelled in broken English.

Neil stopped dead in his tracks, stood up straight, and turned to face the gunman.

"What do you want?" Neil asked.

"Shut up and get over against the wall."

"There are no drugs here, just some pills," Neil hissed.

The second suit had moved into the room, pushed Neil's face against the wall, and checked him for weapons. "He's clean," he said to the other suit.

The little boy had hobbled over to his mother, sat down beside her, and was stroking her face. "Wake up, Mommy; Mommy, wake up, Mommy," he sobbed.

Looking at Neil, the first suit yelled: "Shut that damn kid up, now, or I'll shoot him."

Neil scooped up the kid and turned his back on the gunmen to keep his body between the gunman and the boy. The second suit spun him around to face the first and said, "Stand real still!"

———

The day was fading into twilight but was not quite dark enough to need the running lights which were on as the big Regal slipped silently and slowly up the river toward the dock at Dr. Cruz's property. The boat went slightly past the dock and stopped midstream, then very slowly started to turn counterclockwise, with the aid of the thrusters. This was the widest part of the river, or they would never have been able to turn her. When it was pointing downstream, it was forwarded adjacent to the dock, and the thrusters engaged again, easing her gently to the dock. The lines were set fore and aft, and the engines stopped.

One of the dockhands attached the power line to the socket as another hooked up the utility water line and sewage pump. The waste was pumped directly into a sewer line through a connector arising just behind the seawall.

Two maids came down the path pushing a wheeled cart with linens and towels on it. The cart was lifted aboard by the two deckhands and wheeled into the interior by the maids. The captain and his crew, consisting of three other men dressed in white, stepped onto the deck and walked up the path to the house. Another man, dressed in orange coveralls, approached the locker on the dock, opened it with a key, and removed the heavy-duty three-inch hose. He placed one end of the hose into the locker and attached it to a fuel line. He unscrewed a brass cap on the boat deck and placed the other end of the hose into the opening. Next, he returned to the locker and opened a petcock allowing the fuel to enter the boat as he watched the flow meter. He had been instructed on how much fuel he was to pump onboard, and when it reached the specific amount, he closed the valve, bled the line, removed the hose, and stowed it in the locker. He reached over and attached a yellow hose to the bib, located behind the locker, turned on the spigot then went over to the hose reel and pulled the hose to the boat. After removing another brass cover, also on the deck, he stuck the shut-off valve into the opening and filled the potable water tanks. As they were filling, he retrieved a black hose and attached one end to the pump-out station on the dock and the other end to the holding tank on the boat. When all was done, he stowed the hoses where they belonged and secured the locker, then headed for the house.

Ten minutes later, four other men came out from the bowels of the boat, all wearing flowered Cuba Vera shirts and smoking large cigars. They stepped onto the dock one at a time and walked up to the house, passing another man coming down the path pushing another cart full of liquors and mixes, and followed by two other men pushing large carts loaded with food, fruit, snacks, ice, and five-gallon bottles of water.

Within forty-five minutes the turnaround was complete, and the boat was ready for immediate departure. The concerted effort was reminiscent of a NASCAR pit crew. It appeared that the boat and crew were on alert just as much as the Strategic Air Command bomber crews around the world.

———

Gus's eyes roamed down the length of Sam, who lay beside him, and stopped at the bare hip illuminated by the early morning sun streaming through the window and highlighting the creamy unblemished skin. He leaned over and gently kissed Sam's hip as she lay on her side. Sam didn't move, so he gave her a little pinch to activate her and was rewarded by getting his hair pulled, forcing his face into her butt.

Sam rolled over, throwing the bed covers aside, and said, "Maybe you'd like to kiss something a little higher."

"I'd like to kiss everything, no matter what the altitude is," Gus responded.

"Don't let fear hold you back," she smirked.

"Fear? The only thing I'm afraid of is that you'll get out of bed before I can climb your frame."

"Climb, dear boy, climb!"

CHAPTER TWENTY-ONE

They were both greasers, but the first suit had a misplaced sense of fashion. His suit had a sheen to the cloth that reminded Neil of carnival glass with a blue undertone. His shirt front looked like he was trying to emulate Elvis, with the vertical pleats on his chest and double-length cuffs with frills exploding from the ends of the sleeves. Neil was surprised to see black leather shoes on his feet instead of the Nikes he expected. What distinguished him was that he was completely bald, apparently shaved.

The other one had on a light gray cotton suit that appeared to have been slept in and was wearing the sneakers. He either didn't have a familiarity with bathing or had been changing the oil in a lot of cars before he put on the suit. The contrast was striking.

"Put the damn kid down and get on your knees, then lock your hands behind your head."

Neil did as instructed, facing the first suit. The child calmed down when he saw his mother open her eyes. She remained quiet, staring at the suits.

The first suit asked, "What did Gus Farrell call you about?"

"Gus used to be a patient of mine and asked me what the name of the blood pressure medication was that I gave him," Neil lied.

They must have found out the phone number that Gus called, somehow.

"What was it?"

"What was what?" Neil asked.

"The damn blood pressure medication you gave him, stupid."

"Atenolol," Neil said.

"Never heard of it."

Neil looked at him quizzically and said, "Why would you? Are you a doctor, or a pharmacist?"

"Do I look like a fucking doctor?"

"No, you look like a thug!"

Suit One took two steps forward and wrapped the SIG Sauer around Neil's left ear, splitting the top of it. Blood squirted on his suit.

Neil's face was against the tile when he came to, and he opened one eye to see the first suit dropping his pants while the other one held the mother on the floor with her skirt up under her arms. He had a knee on one of her arms while trying to control the other with his free hand and using the other hand to take her bra off. Since they were preoccupied, and Suit One had his back to Neil, it was as good a time as any. Neil jumped up quietly and reached into the drawer in the medicine cabinet, drew out the 9mm Glock, flipped off the safety, and fired as soon as he got it aimed at Suit One. The first bullet went through his right kidney, spinning him around as the second bullet entered just below his left collarbone. The third shot went into the exact middle of Suit Two's forehead as he was reaching for his gun. Suit One's groan behind him was silenced with the fourth shot into his heart.

Neil's legs suddenly felt like rubber and didn't want to support him. He dropped to the floor and leaned back against the wall, totally spent. The boy's mother crawled over to Neil and taking a shred of her skirt, pressed it to his ear to staunch the blood pouring down his neck.

The sirens were faint at first but got much louder as the Homestead police pulled into the community just ahead of the ambulance. Someone must have heard the shots and called 911.

One of the paramedics bandaged Neil's ear while the other checked the bump on the mother's head where it came in contact with the floor. The mother's medic, to keep her mind off of what he was doing and to put her at ease, asked her name and Neil overheard; her name was Marie.

The medics instructed Marie on what to look for in case she had a concussion, told her to see a doctor if any of the symptoms appeared, and then went about the business of returning to Homestead.

The police interviewed Neil, took pictures, and roped off the whole clinic, instructing them both not to cross the line until the Mobile Crime Lab had arrived and finished their investigation.

Neil's expression was one of consternation since the only access to the second floor of the clinic was inside, and that's where Neil was living.

Marie sensed his dilemma and said, "Neil, why don't you come home with us. We live pretty close, and you can stay until they clear out?"

Having noticed the rings on her finger, Neil hesitated and said, "What would your husband think of that idea?"

"I'm a widow, so that's not an issue."

Neil's face expressed his sympathy, and he said, "I'm so sorry, I didn't know."

She replied, "Well actually, he passed a couple of years ago, so it's no problem either way."

"All right, let me get my kit, and I'll be right back, and thanks."

Neil waited until the guard had walked around behind the building, on his pretentious and predictable circuit, and then ran into the clinic. A few minutes later, and after the guard went around back again, Neil came out with an AWOL Bag, containing some underwear, scrubs, and a shaving kit.

Since Marie had driven to the clinic, Neil followed her back to her house in his car. He was impressed with Marie; she had qualities not seen much anymore, for example, warmth, compassion, and tenderness. Even though she was a couple of years older than Neil, there was a distinct possibility that he might get interested.

———

Gus turned on the radio, started the coffee, and performed his morning chores. He could hear Sam rustling around in the bedroom as he was shaving and decided to get out of the bathroom before she came in and had to have a repeat performance. Not that he thought it was a bad idea, but he had to get going. He thought, either I'm crazy as hell, or I'm getting too old for this.

Sam came into the kitchen naked as a jaybird and asked Gus, "Are those eggs for me?"

"Well, yes. They started out to be yours. Do you want them?"

"I do if you don't mind me eating in the buff."

"Why would I mind that? It's something I always thought about but never did."

"Strip off those shorts, bud. I always thought about it too!"

They admired each other through the glass top table as they ate, and Gus found himself rising to the occasion.

Later, just after the nine o'clock news, they left the house and drove over to Indian Creek Marina. The marina was open, so Gus drove up to the dock and got out, giving the keys to Sam. He told Sam to turn back to Pelican Harbor, and he'd meet her on the boat. He was going to bring the Bayliner over to the *Anita*.

"Yes sir, I'll put the coffee on, sir."

At that point, Gus was wondering if maybe he was getting a little too bossy; however, his fears were allayed when Sam reached out, grabbed him by the ears, and planted a big juicy kiss right on his mouth.

The trip took longer than Gus had anticipated since the speed was limited to "no wake" for the full voyage. Gus had to get his thinking in order anyway, and this was a good time to do it. It was fairly obvious that Dr. Cruz had a pretty good size workforce that appeared to be disciplined and on-site. He had to find out how many, and where their stations were so he could lay out a plan. So far, the Zoot suit was the only one he could identify, and he had to get a closer look at the rest of them and the whole layout. There was no way he could disguise himself and sneak in since he was too tall, white, and couldn't speak Spanish. Maybe he could get in as a service employee, such as a plumber, electrician, or lawn service. No, that wouldn't work. If there were something wrong with the plumbing—they'd call the plumber from the phone book. If there were an electrical problem—the same thing, plus they'd notice that immediately and call an electrician. He couldn't just go in and start cutting the grass because they probably had a service already that they would recognize, and he didn't look the part. The only likely thing left that he could think of was a telephone repairman. That would take a lot of preparation, and certainly too much involvement. He would need a truck that looked like a phone repair truck, tools, uniform, and lingo that would look and sound plausible. It would take too much effort to prepare and act out.

Sam, standing on the dock in a provocative pose, patiently waited for Gus to hand her the dock line and said, "Hi, handsome. What took you so long?"

Gus smiled and said, "I'm getting old, and it takes me longer now."

"That wasn't the impression I got this morning, big boy."

"Well, maybe the no-wake zone had something to do with it as well."

"Ok, I'll forgive you. Let's go get some coffee."

Gus stepped onto the dock and put his arm around Sam's waist, and together they walked back to the aft deck of the *Anita*.

"I thought I'd come up with a plan to get into the compound of Dr. Cruz," Gus said over a cup of steaming coffee, "but after thinking it through, I realized that it would take too much effort to implement and wouldn't gain us that much."

After Gus had explained his idea, Sam said, "There was a telephone repairman involved in a robbery two months ago in Miami Shores. He would have fit the bill if you needed him."

"No, it would take too much effort and time, and we don't have enough of either. I'll find another way. But thanks anyway, Sam."

Sam took Gus home first to get his car, then took off for the station to see if she could find anything to help Gus.

Gus took out his cell phone and dialed Neil Hamlet's number. There was no answer, which Gus thought was strange.

Sam found a parking space at the far end of the parking lot and walked to the entrance of the Cutler Ridge Police Station. She opened the door and ran into Lt. Guerry, who was coming out.

"Well, hello Sam, I was just looking for you."

"Oh, hi, Rod, what brings you to these parts?"

"Well, Sam, if you have a few minutes, I'd like to talk to you."

"Sure. Let's go into my office."

Rod turned, and Sam led him to her office door. She invited him to sit, turned and closed the door, then sat down at her desk.

"What's this all about, Rod?"

"Do you remember that guy whose house blew up after his wife disappeared a few months ago?"

"I certainly do; his name is Gus Farrell, why?"

"There was a carcass found in Graves Tract. Do you know where that is?"

"It's just south of the State Road 826, between the Dixie Highway and the Intracoastal Waterway. It's a swampy area with the Oleta River running through the northern end of it. But what are you saying, a 'carcass'?"

"I mean there wasn't enough left of it to call it a body, and most everything was missing. I won't go into detail except to say that there was enough left to get samples. They ran a DNA test on the sample, and it turns out that the DNA matched a sample of the DNA on file for one Mrs. Anita Farrell."

"Oh my God," Sam said.

"It seems the alligators ate most of it, so we were lucky to get a working sample."

Sam looked like she was going to cry and said, "How am I going to explain this to Gus?"

"What do you mean, how are you going to explain this? Have you been working the case?"

"Yes! I've been on it since his house blew up."

"Well, maybe you're too close to it!"

"You might be right, but how can I stop now? We've formed an attachment, and there's no one else that can step in now. Besides, he'd never forgive me for handing this off to someone else."

"You'd better do it soon because the reporters got wind of it and they're like flies on crap. It's probably going to be in the paper in the morning."

"Thanks, Rod. I'll get right on it."

"Listen, Sam, give me a call if you need anything. There might be something I can do."

"Thanks again, Rod, I'll do that," she said as she rose from the chair. She opened the door, and Rod picked up his hat and went out.

"Sure thing, Sam."

Sam sat down and cried.

CHAPTER TWENTY-TWO

Gus had just pulled onto 79th Street, heading for the beach, when his cell phone rang. He had to unbuckle his seat belt to get it out of his pocket, and since Sam would be the only one calling him, he fully expected to get ragged about taking so long.

"Gus, can you meet me somewhere, I've got to talk to you. It's important!"

"All right, where are you?"

"I'm at the office, but I can meet you anywhere."

"OK, do you know where the Libertine Restaurant is in Coconut Grove?"

"Yes, I think I do. It's on Mayfair Lane, isn't it?"

"Yeah. I'll meet you there in half an hour," Gus said.

"OK, bye-bye."

When Coconut Grove started to get populated, people bought land and just built what they wanted, where they wanted. As a result, the houses are so jumbled together that they had to make the streets one way to drive through it. Traffic is always heavy, so you can plan on getting into a few traffic jams whenever you go there. Scantily clad girls on roller skates are everywhere, so it's not difficult to wait.

Gus got lucky and found a spot at the Ritz. It was a short walk to the Libertine, where he found Sam waiting at a window table.

"How did you get here so soon?" Gus asked.

"Well, I am driving a police car!"

"Oh, of course, you are, why didn't I think of that? What's so important?"

As Sam related her conversation with Lt. Guerry, Gus's face became rigid, and the muscles stood out on his jaw. Sam held his hands until she was done, and said, "I'm sorry Gus, to have to break it to you this way. If there is anything I can do, please let me know. I feel like this is my tragedy as well, and I want to be involved in whatever you decide to do."

Gus said, "Well this finalizes it. I know how hard it was for you to tell me, and I want you to know that I do appreciate it."

"I'd do anything for you, Gus, no matter what. You know that."

"Of course I do, hon, but right now I have to formulate a plan that will trap those bastards, and I'm a little baffled as to which direction I should head. First, I'll need to see about the burial of Anita's remains. Do you know where they took her?"

"Yes, Lt. Guerry said they had taken her to the Hartsfield Funeral Parlor in Sunny Isles. I have the phone number for you, Gus."

Sam dug into her purse and handed Gus a card with the logo of the funeral parlor on it.

"Thanks, Sam," he said as he put it into the pocket of his shirt. "I'll call them this afternoon. Now shall we have some lunch while we're here?"

After lunch, Gus, walking at a fast pace, came out of Mayfair Lane and started to cross Florida Avenue He was only half thinking about traffic when as he came out between two cars, he caught a peripheral glimpse of a car swerving toward him. He only just pulled back in time to see a white Oldsmobile tearing around the corner onto Mary Street. Damn, he'd better pull his head out and take a mindset that someone is out to kill him, or he might give them a chance to do it just from stupidity. No chance of catching him, so he headed for the Pelican Harbor Marina.

———

"You stupid worthless piece of shit. So far, you've fucked up everything you've tried! I don't have a clue why the boss keeps you around but if it was up to me, you'd be a donor! Although, you'd probably screw that up as well, by having hepatitis or syphilis or some other damn disease. That's the second time you missed him, so I'll tell you one more time and you better listen. Don't use a car! Use a knife, poison, or a gun, and make damn sure it's fatal, or you'll be wearing an anchor for a pendant." Cordero's nostrils were flared, his ears pulled back to his head, his teeth bared, and the back of his neck a bright red, as he spoke.

Carlos, looking at the floor, thought for sure he'd be on the butcher table if he even made so much as a peep to Cordaro. Cordaro had the means to make it happen and Carlos was well aware of it. He didn't need to pretend that he was scared shitless, he was terrified! In fact, Cordaro was at least a head taller than him and carried at least seventy-five pounds more than Carlos, and none of it was fat.

Carlos could feel the sweat forming in his crack and armpits but didn't dare move for fear of the movement acting as a trigger for Cordaro to punch him in the face. His feet even felt slimy in the new off-white Mephisto golf shoes he'd just bought at Nordstrom's. He was feeling weak in the knees and a little faint, and deathly afraid he was going to start crying. He was trying to remain absolutely still so that Cordaro would finish and go away, and Carlos could sit down before he fell down.

"Get the fuck out of my sight you piece of puke, and get me results, or I'll string you up and skin you like a grape," Cordaro screamed at him, pointing at the door.

Carlos barely made it into the hallway when his knees started to give way. He grabbed the windowsill for support and hauled himself upright, leaned against the wall and took deep breaths for a few minutes until his pulse and blood pressure calmed down, and then headed for his room.

———

Gus got a beer from the cooler and went up to the bridge with the day planners to study them for anything he might have missed earlier. Nothing jumped out; it was just continuations of the somewhat ambiguous notations he'd looked at before.

Gus had finished his beer, laid the planners on the console, and was trying to decide whether to get another beer when the phone rang.

"Hello," Gus said.

"Gus, this is Neil. Sorry for taking so long to get back to you but I had a little interruption."

"What do you mean, Neil?"

Neil related the events at his clinic and told Gus that he was temporarily staying with Marie until the police finished their investigation. He gave her phone number to Gus in case he needed to contact him, and his phone was tied up.

"Christ, Neil. I never even thought about them finding you; you better get out of there before they know what happened to their thugs."

"I can't, Gus. Marie and her son would still be here unprotected. Besides I have a gun, as I told you and they're not exactly stealthy, so I'd see them coming."

"Well, Neil, if you can't leave, at least set up perimeter alarms, so you won't be caught flat-footed. My favorite is the green monofilament fishing line tied to a bottle that will fall into a bunch of other bottles, and then leave the outside lights off."

"Yeah, I intend to take precautions, Gus. Incidentally, I haven't had a chance to investigate the information you gave me yet, but I'll get right on it and call you with whatever I can find out, maybe tomorrow."

"That's great, Neil but don't let it get in the way of taking care of your friends."

"I'll call you as soon as I find out."

Gus laid his cell phone down and went below for another beer.

CHAPTER TWENTY-THREE

He needed a silencer so he'd have to ask Sam if she knew of a gunsmith that could keep his mouth shut. If he thought creatively, what could he come up with that was silent and lethal? Oh, he thought, I'm already using something that fits the description, bow and arrows! Although it fits the parameters of silent and lethal, it's too cumbersome. Bows and arrows don't make noise and they are highly effective, but—crossbow? Of course! That's it, mobile, lightweight, and lethal. It looks like I need to make another visit to see Pimples.

Gus had seen the crossbows hanging on the wall at the Army-Navy store on previous visits but ignored them since they were not relevant. Now they were relevant!

For some reason, "Pimples" liked Gus and was trying his hardest to please him.

"Would you like to see the different types of darts used with the crossbow?"

"Sure, show them all to me."

Pimples almost ran back to the shelves under the wall display of crossbows.

"We have a sale on for the crossbows through Friday so today is a good day to get one."

While Gus was stringing the bows and checking the features of each model, the door opened very quietly and a figure wearing a flowered shirt let himself in and closed the door, making no sound.

Gus had placed a bolt in the holder of the crossbow and aimed at an oar hanging on the opposite wall, feeling the balance and weight of the instrument when a bullet tore into the pocket of his shirt and out the other side, taking part of his left nipple with it.

Without hesitation, Gus swung to the left, aimed, and released the bolt. It seemed to Gus that everything was in slow motion but, it was over in microseconds.

Pimples was hiding behind the counter but had seen everything just before getting there.

Gus grabbed a cleaning rag from the counter, pulled up his shirt, and pressed the rag over his nipple to staunch the blood. He reached for his wallet with the other hand and got out Sam's card, handing it to Pimples. "Give her a call and tell her what just happened, and don't talk to anyone else."

While Pimples was busy calling Sam, Gus went up to the front of the store to see what he had hit. There was a pointed patent leather shoe attached to a leg sticking out from behind the counter holding folding shovels.

Gus kicked the shoe and there was no response. He kicked it again, and then cautiously eased around the corner of the counter. Zoot Suit was lying on his back still holding an automatic, with the bolt from his crossbow sticking straight up out of his forehead just slightly off-center. There was hardly any blood because the bolt that had gone clear through his head was plugging the hole.

Pimples came back and told him that Sam was on the way and that she said for us not to touch anything. Gus thanked him and then told Pimples to shut the door and lock it, which he did.

Gus never realized how sensitive the nipples were until just now. The pain was getting to him, and he asked Pimples if he had a first-aid kit so he could cover it.

Pimples got the kit and Gus smeared some antibiotics on the pad and covered the wound.

The siren was loud, and Gus felt somewhat embarrassed because he was the one who had caused it.

Pimples let Sam in and held the door for the other backup officers as they entered. Sam leaned close and whispered in Gus's ear, "Don't worry, I'm in charge."

She took on the aura of a police officer who's in charge and said, "Could you tell us what happened here, Mr. Farrell?"

"Surely. This lad and I were looking at the crossbows and I suddenly got shot in the chest."

"Oh, I'm sorry Mr. Farrell; I hadn't realized that you were injured. We'll call an ambulance," motioning to one of the other officers to call an ambulance.

"I don't need an ambulance. I put a band-aid on it and it's fine."

"If you're sure, Mr. Farrell."

"Yes, it's fine, you can cancel the ambulance."

Sam motioned the other officer to cancel the request and turned back to Gus.

"Can you continue with what happened, Mr. Farrell?"

"Well, like I said. I had a bolt in the crossbow and was aiming at an oar on the opposite wall. I had cocked it and was getting the feel of it when I got shot in the nipple."

Sam, who was listening intently and looking straight into Gus's eyes, started gritting her teeth to keep from laughing and then had to turn away to keep from laughing in his face, but just couldn't suppress laughing under her breath.

"It's not that damn funny and it hurts like hell. In fact, I don't think I'll ever be able to breastfeed from that one."

Sam burst out laughing and doubled over. The other officer ran over, thinking Gus had hit her, but Sam put up her hand to stop him.

"Please continue, Mr. Farrell."

"Well, my first reaction is to shoot back at anyone shooting at me ever since Vietnam and I just reacted."

"You reacted quite well, Mr. Farrell, you got him almost dead center in the forehead, and that weapon must suit you because the bolt came out the back of his head. Did you have it on the highest setting?"

"Well, yes! There's not much point in using a weapon at half power."

"That's true." Then she motioned to Pimples to come over to corroborate Gus's story.

He did this almost word for word.

Sam looked over at the other officers and asked, "Did you call the meat wagon yet?"

"Yes, they're on the way and so is the coroner."

Out of earshot of the other officers, Sam said, "I'll have to go to the office to write this up and it will take a while, so why don't you go home, and I'll call you when I'm done, then we'll get some dinner, OK?"

"OK," Gus said. "But first, I'm going to get that crossbow."

Pimples grinned from ear to ear.

"Hurry up," Sam said. "This is now a crime scene and I have to close it down and tape it."

Gus grabbed the Ten Point Mag Crossbow w/ scope and thirty Parker carbon bolts, gave Pimples cash and a hefty tip, and then went out the door with Sam.

"I'm going to run this over to the boat first and then I'll see you at home, Sam."

"All right, Gus. Is there anything I can do to help?"

"As a matter of fact, Sam, I need a silencer for the Ruger and you're probably the wrong person to ask about it, but could you get me the name or address of a good machinist who knows how to keep his mouth shut and is willing to make a little extra money?"

"I'll look into it, sweetheart. Now get going so I can go to work."

On his way to the boat, the thought— *"I'm going to kill you first, faggot!"*—came back to him and it was comforting to think that his initial thought had come true.

His nipple had started to bleed again and was soaking through his shirt, so he made a short stop at Doctor's Hospital and got a few stitches and a new bandage.

CHAPTER TWENTY-FOUR

The visit to the hospital took longer than he thought it would, and before he got to the boat, his phone was ringing.

"Hi, hon. Where are you?"

"I'm about halfway to the boat. I needed to get my nipple stitched, and it took longer than I thought."

She couldn't suppress the little snicker, and then said, "Sorry, Gus."

"You'll be sorrier when I bite yours off!"

"Oh, come on, Gus. You wouldn't do that!"

"It's been known to happen," Gus said, laughing.

"Are you referring to personal experience?"

"I'll tell you about it when I see you on the boat, sweetheart."

Gus rummaged through his locker and found a shirt, changed into it, then removed his alarms and went into the galley, pulled a cool one out of the refrigerator, and went up to the flying bridge to catch the breeze. While he was pondering whether the Regal was still docked in Little River, Sam drove up. She got out of the car and waved to Gus as she walked to the dock, smiling. When she got within earshot, Gus said, "Did you come for your punishment?"

Sam said, "You'll see!"

After she had stepped aboard, Gus kissed her, and they both went into the cabin. "Do you need a drink?" Gus asked her.

"I'll just have some iced tea, if you don't mind."

While Gus was getting her drink, Sam asked him, "What's this nipple-biting experience you have to tell me about?"

"Well, Sam, let me give you some background first, and then you'll see what I meant.

"There used to be a strip joint called the Red Barn just beyond NW 37th Avenue on 79th St., and just beyond that was an elevated railroad track running north and south, built up to about three feet above road level in case of flooding. It's probably been there since Flagler built the railroads into Florida.

"Anyway, there was a doctor who was a relative of a friend of mine who was reading his paper one night when someone rang the doorbell. Standing there was a teenager in quite a bit of distress. When the doctor asked what he could do for him, he held out his clenched fist and opened it to reveal a nipple lying in his palm. He stuttered out the story that they'd had an accident and wondered if the doctor could stitch it back on. The doctor told him to bring her in, and he'd see what he could do.

"The doctor managed to salvage the nipple and replaced it with quite a few stitches. When he asked the boy how it happened, he was told that another boy was driving his car and that he'd gotten into the back seat with his girlfriend. When they got to the railroad track on 79th St., the car ultimately left the road and slammed down with such force that he'd bitten off her nipple. The couple both asked him not to call their parents, and he didn't. Now, if you don't mind, I'd like to check your nipples for stitch marks."

Sam laughed and said, "Actually, I was in the front seat."

They both laughed, and Gus planted a big sloppy kiss on her mouth.

Gus said, "Let's fix some dinner on the boat, and then go see if our yacht is still in port. I'll go see what's under the dock, and why don't you start the veggies?"

"Sounds reasonable to me," Sam said.

Gus picked up his Kevlar rod with a Pflueger casting reel from the locker and stepped onto the dock. He had his trusty old red head plug on it, so he walked up to the intersection of another dock, dropped to his knees, and, supporting himself on a piling, leaned over and with the red head only six inches from the rod tip, began swirling the plug in a figure eight under the dock. Within about twenty seconds the water exploded, and the reel began to sing. Gus tightened the star drag and slowed the rush just in time. The fish had darted out the other side of the dock, but Gus stopped him from tangling and hauled him in. Gus had forgotten the net, so he leaned way down and got hold of the leader and hauled it up. Dinner was going to be about three pounds of snook. He got out his cutting board and cleaned the fish on the stern and washed the remains overboard while protecting the fillets from the Pelicans who had missed out on the remains that went into the water.

"Think this is enough?" he said.

"Unless you're a glutton, it is," Sam smiled, "but I'm going to freeze half of it, and it's still more than we need."

"Yeah, I thought it was, too, but I couldn't throw half a fish back."

The sun had set a half-hour earlier, so Sam and Gus loaded their equipment, including the crossbow, into the Bayliner, started the fan, waited five minutes, and started the motor. When Gus was satisfied, Sam loosed the lines, and Gus backed out and headed for the Intracoastal at idle. There was no rush and, even though the tide was in, he wasn't familiar with the bottom in this area. The wind had picked up a little, and there was a slight chop, so Gus advanced the throttle a little to improve the steering.

Gus had the running lights on, as required; however, the Boulevard Bridge lights illuminated the whole area. Gus slowed down to allow a rather large luxury cruiser, heading south on the Intracoastal, to pass because, after all, the cruiser did have the right of way, and to pass in front of it would be bad form and very bad seamanship, so he would have to fight the wake. Surprisingly, there wasn't much of a wake considering the size of the boat and its speed. Thankfully, there was no chop in the wake of cruiser, so Gus slipped in and drafted about thirty yards behind it. Turns out, it was from Dover, Delaware, and aptly named *It's Mine Now*. Getting out over his wake at Little

River did create some bouncing around though. Once clear of the wake, the Bayliner handled relatively smoothly, so Gus cut the lights and glided into the mouth of Little River at about nine hundred RPMs. There was no traffic on the river, so Gus turned over the helm to Sam so he could get the night scope out along with his infrared camera. The camera was an excellent tool in that the night scope would pick out someone in the open but not if they were concealed. The infrared camera would pick up a heat signature from anybody no matter where they were. The combination of the two eliminated surprises.

As they approached the dock where the Regal was moored, they could see that something was going on. Gus checked out the area with the night scope and could make out five people scurrying around the dock, apparently loading something, and three others were moving around between the boat and the house. Although there were light poles in the corners of the yard, they were not on. The only light was the ambient light from the boat, the swimming pool area, and the Boulevard Bridge.

Gus laid down the night scope and picked up the infrared camera to see the area from another perspective. There were two other people in the bushes on either side of the house that hadn't shown up on the scope. He could tell that they were both armed, apparently with the same Uzi machine guns. Something important must be happening.

Gus whispered into Sam's ear, "Lower the RPMs to idle and ease over to the right near the marina. We'll drop anchor and stay here for a while."

Sam looked questioningly at him and said, "Do you think that's wise—so close?"

Gus said, "They're getting ready to do something, and I want to see what it is."

Sam eased the throttle back and turned to starboard while Gus was directing her. When they were within ten feet of the seawall, Gus pumped his hand palm down for her to turn off the key. The momentum carried them to the seawall and Gus grabbed the wall and tied off on a cleat. Sam threw a loop line over another cleat near the stern and tied that off as well.

Sam was smiling and said, "Well now, that's tidy. We didn't have to get the anchor wet."

Gus said, "Don't turn on any lights. I'll just sit here and keep an eye on them. You could go below and get some sleep, since you have to work tomorrow, and I'll wake you if anything happens."

"Like last time, you mean."

"Well, I didn't have to work the next day, and you did."

"I don't think so," Sam said. "I'm not sleepy, and besides, I'm a little hyper right now."

"Good, I like the company."

Sam went down to the cabin and returned with two cold ones and a couple packs of peanut butter crackers to share.

"What do you think they're up to, Gus?"

"I'm not sure, but I believe that they've done some harvesting and are getting ready to make a delivery."

"In the boat?" She asked.

"Don't think so because it would take too long. What we need is a set of wheels because if someone leaves from the front, we need to follow them and that would have to be you since you're a cop. For instance, I can't just get into the airport if that's where they go."

"Well," said Sam. "I could get a taxi and follow them."

"Would you mind?"

"Gus, I told you I'd do anything for you and if that means putting my job on the line, then so be it!"

"Great, Sam. Only it would be better to go back to the marina and get your car, you know, less conspicuous. I don't think they're ready to go just yet and you'd have time. You could park down at the end of 77th Street and keep an eye on the house. In fact, I have a better idea. Come back here and pick me up. We can follow them together. We'll just leave this boat here tonight. You know where the alarms are on the Bertram so be careful when you get the keys."

Gus helped Sam get her stuff together and hoisted her over onto the wharf. She could easily walk over the bridge to the little marina, but at this time of night and being a woman alone; it's almost an invitation to an incident. Sam waved and walked off as Gus reached for his infrared camera to see if he had missed anything.

One man was holding a portable radio in his left hand and motioning to the guards to do his bidding with the right. Several of them were running to get done whatever he wanted, but Gus couldn't tell what that was. Something was going on in front of the house, as well, because two of the guards had come back from in front and motioned that something was ready to the man with the radio.

Damn! Gus thought. I wish we'd both gone to get our cars now. He packed his equipment in his bag and climbed to the wharf and checked the lines, in case they were too tight when the tide went out, and then headed for 79th St.

Sam pulled up beside him and said: "Get in."

Gus stowed his gear in the back and then slid into the front seat and said, "That was fast!"

She smiled. "I had the keys in my pocket."

"OK, let's go around to the front of the house and see what all the excitement is about."

Sam pulled out onto 79th Street and turned left. She drove west to Biscayne Boulevard and made another left over the bridge and then turned into 77th Street and went to the end, around the block, and pulled back out onto 77th Street, facing the Boulevard, and then stopped.

Gus said, "This is great. Now, all we have to do is wait."

Sam laid her hand on Gus's leg, leaned back, and relaxed.

Twelve minutes later, the glow of the gate lights illuminated the area in front of Dr. Cruz's residence.

Gus sat straight up, and Sam started the engine, saying, "Here we go."

A very dark blue, or black, Mercedes sedan with blacked-out windows pulled out of the drive and turned toward the boulevard with Sam following in the dark at a very discreet distance.

"Here we go is right," Gus said.

The Mercedes turned left onto Biscayne Boulevard and headed south at the same speed limit. Sam dropped back two blocks and turned on her lights, maintaining the same rate. It was almost like a casual drive, except that this was anything but casual.

The right turn signal of the Mercedes came on just before 37th

Street and then it stopped at the red light. When the green light came on, the Mercedes turned right, easing around the ramp to enter the 36th Street Expressway, west. Sam was finding it hard to avoid getting too close and being seen, but she didn't have to run a red light to do it.

The only reason for this Expressway was to avoid traffic lights to the airport, and there weren't that many cars on it this time of night, so Sam slowed down even further to just keep them in sight.

The Mercedes stayed in the lane for the Le Lejeune Road exit, so Sam stepped on the gas to close in before he got there. She slowed down when there were about three blocks between them and maintained that distance. The Mercedes swerved to the right and entered the exit for 36th Street and Sam followed. Once through the light, the Mercedes continued to the Red Road light and blinked left. Sam was too far back and got caught by the red light and had to stop. Gus was nervous and was stretching his neck to see where the car was going, but before he said anything, Sam turned on the police lights and eased through the red light. She immediately turned them off, along with all the other lights, and was able to keep the Mercedes in view. The Mercedes continued past the control tower and turned left at the next corner, driving between two hangars.

Gus said, "Let me out before you get to the end of the hangar, I want to see what's going on."

Sam pulled up close to the hangar and stopped. Gus got out and walked over to the corner and looked around.

A beautiful white Learjet 85 sat on the tarmac with both engines idling and the gangway in the down position. Two men in black were wrestling a metal box into the plane while two others, with guns, watched at the gangway. Gus could make out the letters "HU" and "O" on the box, but nothing else. The men in black got on after the box and pulled the door up while the other two guards and the driver got back into the Mercedes and drove around the other end of the hangar.

Gus got back into the car and told Sam to write what he said on her notepad: "N455LJ."

"What's that?" Sam asked.

"That's the tail number of the plane. All we have to do is call operations and find out what their flight plan is, and it will give us their destination."

"Good thinking, Gus. Let's do it."

Sam dialed a number and asked to be patched through to operations. She waited a minute and then said: "Hello, this is Sgt. Samantha Cross of the Cutler Ridge Police Department and I'd like to find the destination of a plane that just took off by the tail number N455LJ. Yes, of course, thank you." Half a minute passed. "Yes, hello. Thank you very much, goodbye."

She looked at Gus and said, "Sao Paulo, Brazil! ETA 0527."

"Sao Paulo!" Gus snorted, "Then it really is an international operation."

Gus said, "Let's get back to that house and see if they come back. Why don't we take 27th Avenue up to 79th Street and see if we can get there first?"

"Whatever you say, boss. We can get there first no matter which way we go. We have a siren and lights, remember?"

"All righty, smarty-pants, do it your way."

Sam left the airport on 36th Street and stayed on it until she turned north on 27th Avenue, turned on the lights and siren and stomped it. She didn't turn them off until they were turning south on Biscayne Boulevard. They parked in the same position they were in before they left and settled in. They waited about thirty-five minutes, and the Mercedes turned in to the driveway.

"Why don't you take a nap, Sam and I'll keep watch."

"OK, Gus. Wake me if anything happens."

"Will do."

It was almost 1:00 when Gus noticed a truck pull into 77th Street towing something. He wiggled Sam's arm, and she sat bolt upright. When the gate lights came on, Gus could see that it was a trailer with an airboat on it. It turned into the drive and disappeared. Then the lights went out.

"That's got to be the disposal unit," Sam said.

CHAPTER TWENTY-FIVE

"I've been thinking, Sam, about being in two places at one time. I believe that what we need is a video camera that overlooks the driveway of Dr. Cruz. That way we could keep an eye on his comings and goings without being there. We could even follow two vehicles if the need arises like it did the last time."

"We have video cameras in the property room, and I could probably borrow one for a while."

"Not a good idea, Sam. I don't want you drawing attention to yourself and arousing curiosity or getting caught; besides, I have plenty of money, so I'll just buy one and install it. I'll see what kind of equipment we have on the truck before I decide what to do. In the meantime, I'll start doing my homework and gathering all the stuff I'll need. In fact, we can mount it in your car instead and leave it at the end of the street."

Sam's left eyebrow lifted, and she said, "And that won't arouse suspicion?"

"Not if you have a luggage carrier on top. Neighbors will think you're visiting somebody on the street, and we can cut a hole in it for the camera and fill it with storage batteries. Since all the action seems to happen at night, we can fake your visit; walk between the houses, get into your vehicle, and take it to recharge the batteries in the daytime."

"You're a pretty smart feller there, Gus. Remind me to reward you."

Gus smiled and said, "You are my reward, sweetheart! Now give me the keys to your car, and I'll run over to Sears and get a topper and some batteries."

"Here they are," Sam said, handing Gus the keys, "And I'll go to work in your car."

"Sounds fair to me," Gus said, leaning over Sam and planting a little kiss on her forehead. Before he could straighten up, he felt his boys being gently cradled in the palm of her hand. She looked him in the eye and said, "I'll need your keys too, you know, and you better bring it back in the same condition it left!"

"You have my word, I swear!"

As soon as Sam left, Gus got dressed and locked up, setting his alarms on the way out. He had to spend at least five minutes adjusting everything in her car before he felt comfortable enough to drive it. Gus had brought his GPS from his car and got busy looking for the nearest Sears store. There was an Auto Center on North Biscayne Boulevard that was only twenty-six blocks away. Gus headed up the Boulevard toward the Auto Center while watching for a video outlet where he could get the camera.

In less than fifteen blocks he spotted one on the west side of the street and had to make a U-turn to get back to it.

Gus got friendly with the clerk and told him someone's been stealing his chickens; said what his plan was and asked for advice on what he would need. The clerk stated that they'd need to pick out the camera so they would know how much current it would draw and how many car batteries it would need for an all-night operation. They would also need a repeater to get the signal from the car to the house, since it was so far away, and then they'd need a receiver at the house for the monitor. He was even able to supply Gus with the mounting hardware for not only the camera but also the muffin fans for ventilation. Next came all the hardware, including wiring, cables, and connectors, etc.

Gus told him to throw in anything else he might need that they hadn't thought of yet and, of course, he did, including a retractable pigtail for the battery charger that would be mounted inside the luggage carrier and a control panel with terminal strips to hook everything up.

Before Gus paid for everything, he elicited a promise from the clerk to help hook everything up if Gus had trouble getting it to work. He was more than willing to agree to anything Gus said after such a great sale.

Gus pulled into the northbound lane on the boulevard and continued to Sears. It was quite the complex, so Gus pulled up to the building that looked like a retail store and went in.

"Can I help you, sir?"

"I'm looking for a car-top carrier, and I believe the Thule Sidekick will do the job. Do you have one in stock?"

"Sure do, sir, if you'll come this way."

Gus followed him to the back of the store and there they were, mounted on the wall.

The clerk pointed out the one Gus asked for, and he was surprised at its size.

Gus related the chicken story to him and told him that he also needed car batteries and mounts to put them in the carrier. Gus then asked him if they could do it for him.

"I don't think that will be a problem, sir. How many batteries will you need?"

"I'll need six or seven, hooked in parallel, and of course, it'll depend on whether you can get them all in there with a battery charger, control panel, pig-tail retractor, and the camera. I will also need to put the camera in the front, so we'll need room for that, and the muffin fans are to be mounted to the bottom half in the front (ingress) and back (egress), on the lower section of the carrier. I also need to mount the control panel inside near the camera. Could you install that equipment as well?"

"No problem, sir. I'll need to keep the car though, and I can have it ready for tomorrow night."

"That's great. All the other stuff is in the car and if you need something extra just add it to the bill. Another thing, make sure the luggage rack can hold the weight of the car-top carrier and is securely anchored to it. Also, would you glue a clear plastic window in front of the camera? If it gets wet, it's a goner. And add a toggle power switch in the battery line and mounted on the bottom of the carrier so I can turn it off?"

"Got it covered, sir. I'd like to get your number though, just in case I run into a problem or need to buy something else."

Gus gave him his number and called a taxi.

Gus took down his security measures, grabbed a cold one from the fridge, and went up to the flying bridge with his binoculars. It was overcast and not at all like Miami is supposed to be. However, it did cut down on the glare, and it didn't happen that often, so what the hey. He got comfortably seated, pulled out his cell phone, and called Sam.

"Hello, sweetheart," Sam said. "Did you get it done?"

"Not hardly, Sam. I just left there, and he said it would be ready tomorrow night. I was thinking about taking the Bayliner up the river to see if the cruiser is still there and to nose around a bit."

"Don't go yet. Things are a little slow here, and I was thinking of coming home, so wait for me. I heard that there was a nice little restaurant near North Shore Hospital on the river, so we could kill two birds with one stone and have dinner there. Sound right?"

"You betcha, sounds great! Hurry home."

Gus continued to keep an eye on Belle Meade Island and the approach to the mouth of Little River, but even at this height, he had to stretch his neck to see over Pelican Harbor, the causeway, and the end of the bridge. He saw his SUV crowning the bridge with Sam behind the wheel, wearing her white police uniform shirt. Within minutes, Sam was walking away from his car in the parking lot and heading for the boat. Sam saw him watching and threw him a kiss. He returned it and held up the beer bottle.

She nodded her head yes, so Gus climbed down to the galley and retrieved another bottle of beer then met her on deck.

"You look like a Cheshire cat," Gus said. "What's tickled you?"

"Hello to you, too, sweetheart. Got some news today; it seems like our parts department is getting sloppy about discarding their leftovers!"

"You mean they found another body?"

"Absolutely; they found the upper half of a male torso that had been harvested."

Gus's eyebrows drooped, and he said, "Who's they?"

"A high school boy, about seventeen, was out in a skiff last night frogging just beyond the Lehigh Radio Towers, and his light picked up the eyes of a pretty good-sized alligator who resented the dinner interruption. Good thing he had his cell with him. He called in and fended off the gator until the Sheriff arrived. It seems that whoever dumped him there dumped the whole body except for the harvested parts. The Sheriff shot the gator, and they found the rest of the torso in its belly."

"Were they able to ID the body?"

"Not yet, but it looks like another 'illegal,' so they probably won't be able to. The water is down, and the deputies were able to follow the track of an airboat back to where it was launched, just west of Mack's Fish Camp off of SR-41. We're canvassing the area for witnesses, and we are bound to come up with something because there's nothing louder than an airboat; especially at night, and especially since an estimated sixty million Americans suffer from insomnia."

Gus smiled and said, "You still feel like eating?"

Sam tweaked his nose and said, "As long as it's not gator, just lead me to it."

"Cops must have cast-iron stomachs," Gus said, as he grabbed the beer bottles and put them in the recycle bin. "The gear is in the boat, but it's too early to go just yet."

"Well, I can kill some time changing out of this uniform. It wouldn't do for a police officer to be seen going up the river with the husband of a woman whose murder she's investigating."

"Ya think? Maybe I'd better help you change."

"I think—that might be helpful! Just let me wash up first."

When Sam called, Gus walked into the V-berth to find her stark naked, waiting.

———

The wind picked up at sundown, and although wave action wasn't bad, it was breaking off the tops and throwing water around.

Gus advised Sam to watch her step on the wet deck and to hang on to something when she boarded. The boat was banging into the dock, so Gus got on first and started the fan then loaded the cooler. Sam loosed the dock lines, leaving a loop around each cleat, and carefully got on board.

Gus started the engine and lit up the running lights. Sam pulled in the lines while Gus backed out of the slip, and they were on the way. He turned the helm over to Sam and got out the tools he'd need for the trip, including the crossbow and several bolts. He placed the Ruger in the glove box after slipping a loaded clip in it then put four more loaded clips next to it.

Sam said, "It looks like you're getting ready for war!"

Gus's retort was, "I would damn well rather be prepared for what I don't know is there, than not be prepared for what is there that I didn't know about! Wouldn't you?"

"Well, since you put it that way, I'm more inclined to agree with you. Just let me say this, I'm glad I'm on your side!"

Gus laughed and said, "Actually, I feel a little underprepared. What I'd like is an Uzi or AK-47."

Sam said, "What I'd like is a SWAT team!"

The North Bay Causeway Bridge acted as a windbreak, and the water calmed down a bit as they passed under it, only to return in full force on the south side. Sam was glad to head into the mouth of the river where the seawalls protected them. Nothing was coming down the river, so Sam turned off the running lights and reduced speed to idle.

Gus was busy setting up the night scope and infrared camera but turned a watchful eye upriver as they approached the yacht. Nothing out of the ordinary was happening, but Gus was curious about what was going on that accounted for all the lights being out, and voiced his thoughts to Sam.

"Maybe they don't have any customers," she said.

CHAPTER TWENTY-SIX

The punch in the face caught Manolo unawares and sent him sprawling over the kitchen chair and onto the floor where two of his broken teeth lay.

Getting up on his hands and knees, Manolo whimpered, "Honest, Mr. Cordaro, I didn't know that Carlos was dead until this morning!"

"What took you so damn long to tell me? Did you think it wasn't important that one of my men was murdered, or by whom?"

"No sir, Mr. Cordaro, it's just that I was put to work on guard duty right after I found out and didn't get a chance to see you until now."

"Well, get your ass out of sight and tell the others to stay out of sight. The cops will probably be here nosing around in a little while, and I don't want them to see any of you."

The kitchen staff got busy clearing the dinner table and cleaning up when the phone rang.

Cordaro barked, "I'll get it."

He answered the phone to hear the gate guard say that the cops were here and wanted to speak to someone in authority from the house.

"Tell them I'll be right up."

Cordaro hated cops but to preserve a good relationship with them he put on his good-neighbor facade and approached the gate saying, "What can I do for you gentlemen?"

The beefy cop stood behind the headlights of his cruiser while the thin Sergeant approached and asked if a Mr. Carlos Aguilera lived at this address.

"Yes, he does. He's one of my employees. Is he in trouble?"

"Not anymore," the cop replied in an indolent drawl. "He was killed during the commission of a robbery, and the body was taken to the county morgue at Jackson Memorial Hospital. Could I impose on you to come down to identify the body?"

"Certainly," Cordaro replied. "Would it be all right to come in the morning?"

"Anytime within the next three days will be all right. He's not going anywhere."

"Thank you for letting me know, Officer." With that, Cordaro turned on his heel and headed for the house.

Cordaro felt no sense of loss over Carlos, but he was one of the few who could speak English and had a driver's license, so his death left him a little shorthanded. He'd have to recruit some others and get them trained and in a hurry.

————

"All this preparation and nothing is happening," Gus said quietly to the back of Sam's head. "Do you still want to go to that restaurant near North Shore Hospital?"

"Inactivity doesn't make me any less hungry, big boy, but if you want to call it off, it's all right with me."

"Not what I meant," Gus grunted.

Sam smiled and turned to look at Gus. "I guess we could find something else to do instead, but I am getting hungry."

The river was a little shallow, but by lifting the I/O a bit, they could get over the sand bars without tearing the prop off.

The restaurant had an outdoor patio with a pergola over it, and wisteria intertwined with the slats and gardenias growing around the edges. The perfume was a little overbearing, but with candles on the tables, it had a romantic Italian flair that Sam liked. The food was above average, and the drinks were well made, so they rated it a keeper.

They had to use the lights getting back but turned them off going past the cruiser. Gus scanned the yard with the infrared camera but found nothing unusual.

"It's too quiet," Gus said.

"Maybe they're in mourning for Zoot Suit," Sam laughed.

The wind had died down and made the crossing back over the Intracoastal a breeze. After they had docked, Gus checked the alarms and turned on the lights in the cabin.

"Would you like a cup of coffee, Gus?" Sam said.

"Sounds like an excellent idea."

———

Gus awoke to the sounds of sizzling eggs and the smell of coffee. He rolled over and looked up through the galley door to see Sam standing at the stove in just her underpants with a frying pan in one hand and the spatula in the other.

"You'd better get a bathrobe on; I don't want my toys blemished with hot grease!"

"You might be right. I didn't think about it until just now. So, you can see what a great cook I am, right?" She grabbed a purple house dress from the galley chair and slipped it on before resuming the cooking.

"There, I've put your toys away for safekeeping. Would you like to eat these eggs or wear them?"

"Be right there."

Sam took a shower and got dressed while Gus washed the dishes and cleaned up the galley and made the bed. Sam came up on deck and came over to Gus, who watched her come and got weak in the knees with her perfume preceding her and the glow of her skin and her hair blowing in the breeze. It was all he could do to remain upright, and yet it was at this very moment that Gus knew, without a doubt, that he loved her.

"You look like you're having a heart attack, Gus. Are you all right, sweetie?"

"No! That is, I'm not having a heart attack, but I just realized that I love you with all my heart and never want to lose you!"

"I feel the same way, Gus, and you don't have to worry about losing me because I'm sticking to you like glue from now on, period!"

Gus took her in his arms and kissed her full on the mouth for what seemed like an eternity.

Sam said, "I hate to leave, Gus but I have to. I'll give you a call as soon as I get a chance."

"I know, honey, and I have to go pick up your SUV, so we better get moving."

Sam gave Gus another kiss and stepped over onto the dock, waved, and headed for his SUV.

Gus grabbed the phone and called Sears to see if the car was ready yet; found out it was, then called a taxi.

"Everything is ready, Mr. Farrell, except for the house receiver and monitor. I put the small monitor in the cab, and since you can't adjust the camera, you'll have to position the car to change the view. I have the camera pointing straight ahead."

"That'll be fine; I think I can take it from here. Let's run it through its paces."

Gus reached up and flipped the battery switch, mounted just behind the support strut of the luggage rack over the driver's door. The monitor in the cab came to life, and he could see the other end of the garage entirely. Gus started the car and backed up in a turn while watching the image follow on the monitor.

"Couldn't ask for anything better," he said. "How often do I need to service the batteries?"

"You don't! They're gel batteries and don't need water. They last about the same as wet-cell, so when the system goes dead—you need new ones; in about three years."

Gus smiled and said, "Now I have to go set up the receiving end at the house. Thanks for all your help; handing the clerk two hundred-dollar bills and saying, "Split this with anyone who helped you."

He paid the bill, drove back to the marina, and parked facing the boat near the power outlets running along the dock. He got out and pulled the power cord from the luggage carrier over to the dock, made a loop around the piling, and plugged it in. Gus reached up and flipped the power switch on the Thule. He started the SUV, and the monitor in the cab immediately lit up to show an extremely clear picture of the boat. He took the monitor, antenna, and receiver, along with the mounting hardware and cables, from the back of the SUV, over to the boat, pushed them onto the deck, and disconnected the alarms.

Gus mounted the receiver and monitor on the dash in the cabin and ran the antenna cable out the window up to the flybridge where he mounted the antenna to the dashboard. Down in the cabin, he plugged the receiver and monitor into the power take-offs and flipped on the power switches. It worked! The same bright image had appeared on the screen.

When Sam got home, he drove her SUV, and she drove his over to 76th Street and went to the end, NE 8th Avenue, turned left, and left again on 77th. He reached up to the power switch on the carrier and flipped it on. The monitor came to life with a picture of the street and the entrance to Dr. Cruz's driveway bright and clear. Gus pulled off the road on the left to get the camera pointed at a better angle and stopped. There was a slight tilt equal to the shoulder, but that didn't matter, so he turned off the monitor, got out, and locked the door.

"Let's see what we're getting on the other end, Sam," Gus said as he crawled into the cab with her.

"Yes, Sir," Sam said and started to giggle like a schoolgirl, as she pulled out. "You know, this is the first time I've ever spied on anybody before," she said.

"Me too," Gus laughed. "It would be kind of fun if it weren't so serious, don't you think?"

"There's no reason why we can't enjoy ourselves until we drop the hammer on them. Is there?"

"None whatsoever, sweetheart."

Neither one of them could wait to get into the cabin to see what the monitor was telling them and almost forgot the alarms.

"Look at this," Sam said as she flipped on the monitor and the receiver. The image of the driveway was perfect.

"Couldn't have done a better job myself," Gus said, squeezing her shoulders. "Now we have to set up a watch, but it's too early yet. Why don't I take the first one starting at 10:00, and you get some sleep?"

I know how good you are at waking me up, so I'll take the first watch, and you get some sleep, instead."

While they were bantering, Gus's phone rang. He fished it out of his pocket and said, "Hello."

"Hi, Gus, this is Neil."

"Boy, am I glad to hear from you. Are you all right?"

"I'm all right, Gus. I just got back into the clinic yesterday and managed to get hold of that doctor friend of mine to find out what the numbers meant."

"Terrific, Neil. What do they mean?"

"The number 'B1073-3751' that you gave me is an insurance code that stands for a heart transplant."

Gus smiled and said, "That certainly simplifies the whole entry in the planner. We had everything figured out except that, we think, and this gives us a clue for what we needed. Thanks, Neil. Are you two OK?"

"We're doing all right, Gus; thanks for asking. I'm going to ask Marie out on a date. We seem to have a lot in common, and she's not hard to look at. Plus, she's a really sweet girl."

"I'm glad to hear that, Neil. You need someone beside patients in your life. When this is all over, we're coming down to see you."

"Great, Gus that gives me something to look forward to. If you need anything else, give me a call."

"Will do, Neil. Thanks again." Gus said as he hung up.

CHAPTER TWENTY-SEVEN

Gus went below and took off his shoes, lay down on the V-berth, pulled a throw rug over himself, and was fast asleep as soon as his eyes closed.

Sam poured herself a cup of coffee, pulled out the day planners, and with the new information began to compile a list from each entry in the planners, allowing for a full year to date. She was sitting in front of the monitor, keeping one eye out for any movement, and remained that way for two hours.

"Get up, sport," she mumbled in his ear and then stuck her tongue into it. "I made you some ham and eggs."

Gus rolled over and stuck his finger in the ear and wiped it out.

"You've got cold spit!"

"But the rest of me is nice and warm, isn't it?"

"You can say that again. Now let me get my shoes."

When Gus came into the cabin, Sam told him to take a look at the spreadsheet she had made out showing all the pay planner entries for the previous year.

"I'm impressed, Sam. This points out all of what he's been up to for a while. What we need now is to find out what all the other medical procedure numbers are, and we have a complete record."

Sam looked at him out of the corner of her eye and said, "We have enough information right now to hang him, if we can get the evidence to back this up."

Gus said, "In that case, I need to get one more item I didn't think we'd need, a digital video recorder that we can attach to our spy equipment. Then we'd have a record of his comings and goings. We would also have to get another hand-held video camera for when we're on the road."

Sam said, "Sounds like a good idea. You'll have some nice quiet time to think out your plans while I get some shuteye."

Sam started down the stairs to the V-berth, stopped, turned around, came back up and planted a big juicy kiss on Gus's forehead, and said, "Now I can sleep!"

Gus started thinking. There's not much point in staying up past 2:00 because I don't think anything is going to happen that early in the morning anyway. My time would be better spent getting some rest and then getting started on that DVR and video camera tomorrow morning.

He began looking through the spreadsheet to see what Sam had come up with, when about twenty minutes into his perusal, he caught a quick movement on the monitor out of the corner of his eye. He turned his full attention to the monitor, but no further movement was detected. It was probably shift change at the gatehouse, and one of the guards had checked the street. This was exactly the reason for getting a DVR: so he could back up and see what he'd missed.

Further scrutiny of the spreadsheet only left Gus with a feeling of futility since he didn't have the answers he needed to know exactly what the procedures were. The thought struck him like a hammer; make a list of the methods, e-mail it to Neil and have his doctor friend identify the codes. It took him twenty-five minutes to copy the codes into a Word file and save it. Next, he created an e-mail and attached the file then saved it as a draft. He didn't have Neil's e-mail address, so he'd have to call him in the morning and get it.

Gus turned off the lights and equipment and crawled in beside Sam without waking her.

In the morning, Sam was surprised to find Gus lying beside her but didn't question his reasoning or actions because she trusted him completely, and besides, this was his show, and she'd go along with what he did, no matter what. She stretched her neck over and kissed him on the cheek.

"Good morning, sweetheart."

"Good morning, little girl. Who are you?"

"I'm your main squeeze. Don't you remember paying me all those bucks for my services?"

"Oh, yeah. You were worth every penny, and then some." Gus smiled, running his hand over her breast. Shall we romp in the hay for a while, or do you have to get up?"

"I have a job and so do you, remember the DVR and video-cam, and then there's the car we have to pick up to recharge the batteries, and then I have to get to work! So, what do you want to eat, besides me?"

The breakfast was just that—fast, and taking their coffee with them, they sealed the boat and drove over to the SUV. Sam dropped him off on 76th Street and headed off to work while Gus walked through a yard to the van on 77th Street and drove it back to the marina. He plugged the battery charger into the outlet on the dock and returned to the boat.

"Flamingo Medical Clinic; Neil."

"Hi Neil, this is Gus again. Have you got a minute?"

"Sure, Gus. What's up?"

Gus explained what he'd done, expressing his idea about Neil's doctor friend, and then asked Neil for his e-mail address.

"I'll send the file right now, Neil. If you don't get it, give me a call, and thanks."

Gus hit the send button and closed down the equipment, got some more money, and locked up the boat. He drove to the same video store he'd bought the other stuff from and purchased a VCR, video camera, and cables.

It was a tight fit, but Gus managed to get the VCR into what space was left on the dash. He connected the cables to the receiver and the VCR, turned it on, and pushed the record button. Of course, nothing happened because the video camera in the van wasn't on, but the red light on the front panel came on as though it was recording anyway, and that was a good indication that it worked. Next, he unpacked the new video camera and connected a cable between the camera and the VCR, turned it on, and aimed it at the van. He let it run while he recorded it and then stopped it, backed it up, and watched what he'd just recorded. The picture from the new camera was much better than the picture he got from the van, but the van picture, even though it was a little fuzzy, was still good quality.

"All set!" he said out loud and then shut down the equipment.

Gus put a small pot of water on to boil, fished a hot dog out of the reefer, and threw the hot dog into the water. He found a bun, some mustard, and the last beer he had and put them on the table. When the water boiled, he got the tongs out of the drawer, grabbed the hot dog, and placed it neatly onto the mustard in the bun. A few chips and lunch was finished.

With lunch out of the way, Gus locked up the boat and took the van over to the house. He wanted to retrieve the rest of the day planners to see if there was a difference in the event recordings. He pulled into the driveway and plugged the battery charger into a weatherproof outlet on the side of the house.

The house needed airing out. It smelled a little musty, so Gus went around opening windows and doors to let that great Miami breeze flow through. Along with the breeze came the gardenia's sweet, pungent odor to add a little ambiance.

Gus pulled the dining room table aside and rolled up the rug, then pulled up the ring to open the trap door.

The odor hit him like a sledgehammer. Since Gus was already on his knees, it was like a force that pushed him over on his side and rolled him away. He was retching, scurrying to get away from the hole. Finally, he jumped up to his feet. He went to the kitchen and got a flashlight out of a drawer and brought it back to the hole with a tea towel over his nose.

There was someone in the hole, and he had an arrow through his throat.

Gus pulled out his cell phone and dialed Sam.

"Cutler Ridge Police. Sgt. Cross."

"Sam, we have a problem! Can you come to the house right now?"

"I'll be right there, Gus."

Within twenty minutes Sam pulled up in the driveway and went into the house.

"Oh my God, Gus. What is that odor?"

"It's a dead body in the hole," Gus replied.

Sam borrowed Gus's flashlight and looked into the hole. "Looks as though your booby trap worked. There must have been someone with him; otherwise, the table wouldn't have been replaced."

"That's what I thought, and they probably thought that discretion was the better part of valor as well. That's why he's still there! No one wants to crawl into a booby-trapped hole like the tunnel rats did in Vietnam."

"That's all well and good, but how are we going to get him out of there?"

"Well, Sam, that's the one thing I didn't think about—how to get back into the hole again with a body in the way and another live booby trap."

"There is a way," Sam said. "When they built these houses, they left an entry hole for the plumbers in the back wall that's big enough to get through. A slab of plywood covers it. Come on, I'll show you."

They walked around the house, and sure enough, there was a hole in the concrete blocks about one and a half feet high by two feet wide, painted the same color as the foundation.

"I'll get a screwdriver, and then we'll see what we've got."

It didn't look inviting. It was black inside with cobwebs around the entrance, and God only knew how many scorpions or snakes.

Gus said, "I'm not going in there without a flashlight. Would you get one and a pair of dikes?"

"Be right back, Gus."

Gus got up and walked over to the kumquat tree and retrieved a limb from underneath.

Sam was coming around the corner of the house, and Gus waved the limb saying, "My sword! Just in case!"

Gus wiped the cobwebs away from the hole and then beat on the ground a few times to scare away the animals he might encounter. He stuck the flashlight into the hole and then his head and looked around the full one hundred and eighty degrees. Nothing dangerous was apparent, so he crawled in on his belly to the remaining bow and released the trigger. The first trap had worked just as he planned. The body was wrapped in wire and fishhooks.

It took Gus the better part of an hour just to get the wiring and fishhooks off the body and frequent trips to the entry hole for fresh air. He tied a rope around the ankles and pulled the arrow out of his neck, then crawled to the access hole and squeezed out taking the rope and bag of day planners and money with him. Sam was waiting for him.

"We'd better wait until dark before we get him out of there, or we'll have a swarm of cops all over us. In the meantime, I'm taking a shower. You don't have a body bag on you, do you, Sam?"

"As a matter of fact, I do have one in the patrol car, but we can't use that. It's made specifically for patrol cars and would be recognized by any cop. We need to find something like a furniture pad or blanket to wrap him in."

"OK, I'll run over to Henniker's Freight and pick up a furniture pad and—what do I use to get rid of the odor?"

"The police and coroner use a product called NNZ (odor eliminator) and you should be able to get it at Henniker's as well. It's perfect for its intended purpose!"

"I'll get in the shower first. Don't want to stink up the car, and then I'll, or we'll, take a run over there. Be right out."

They got back to the house at 10:30, after having stopped for dinner along the way, and even though they'd left the windows open, the sweet stink of death permeated the whole house. Taking one of the pads, Gus went around to the back of the house and crawled through the opening in the back. Gus had paid for four furniture pads which he told the clerk he'd collect on his way out after paying for them. The clerk was taking care of another customer when Gus left with the NNZ and five furniture pads. This way he could account for the four pads on the receipt if he were questioned about them.

Gus laid the pad out flat and rolled the body onto the edge of the pad and rolled him up in it. He dragged him to the opening and crawled out then pulled him out with the rope.

"Sam, would you turn the car around and back to the back edge of the house? I'm stinking again and don't want to have that odor in the car."

Sam looked a little piqued and asked, "What are we going to do with him?"

"Bakers Haulover has a nice ring to it. There are a few rocks there as well that we can use for ballast. We'll just take a couple of pieces of rope to tie the ends after we add the rocks."

Sam said, "I'm glad he wasn't any taller, we're almost out of pad."

They opened all the windows, waited until the tide started to go out, and arrived at the perfect time. It took both of them to lift the body out and fling it into the outrushing tidal surge. The rocks they put in the ends would keep him from floating and allow the tide to carry him out further before it sank. They sprayed the inside of the car with NNZ, drove north for half a mile, and went swimming with their clothes on.

CHAPTER TWENTY-EIGHT

Gus found an old window screen and propped it over the crawl space opening at the back of the house, to keep out everything but the fresh air, then placed a floor fan over the hole in the dining room blowing down into the hole. He sprayed NNZ in front of the blades and around the periphery of the opening. The bag of day planners and money got a fair dose of the spray as well.

Sam had put on a pot of coffee, while Gus sprayed around the house. Then they took a shower together and scrubbed each other until they were pink. They dried off and went out on the lanai to have coffee and discuss the events of the evening.

Gus said, "Well I hope nothing happened on 77th Street tonight because we sure missed it if it did!"

"Even if it did happen tonight, we'll have plenty more opportunities, but now we're better equipped to handle it. Don't you agree?"

"You're right about that, Sam, but what bothers me is the fact that they were in the house not long ago, and what's his face didn't come back out. That means they know there's something hidden here and it's probably the day planners. Whoever was with him was too scared to find out. This house is now a target, and we'll have to take this bag back to the *Anita* and keep it under wraps, so they don't find it. It's the only real evidence we have. In fact, it might be a good idea to get a safety deposit box to keep it in. They already know about the *Anita*, they just don't know where it is, *maybe*."

Sam said, "All good ideas, Gus, but now we need to get some sleep. Then we can take care of all that in the morning. Give that bag another spray."

Despite the coffee the night before and his churning thoughts keeping him awake, Gus woke early and decided to make breakfast. The fan was still running, and the odor had subsided quite a bit, so it was bearable to be in the kitchen. He carried the breakfast stuff to the coffee table on the lanai, where it was even less odoriferous, then started cooking.

The smell of the coffee wafted into Sam's nostrils and started the juices flowing. There was no way she could stay in bed now, she thought. It was fairly warm, so Sam just walked out of the bathroom to the lanai naked.

"You had better get something on, Sam, or I won't be able to function!"

"It looks like you're 'functioning' now," she said.

"I meant in any other capacity."

"I'll slip on a housecoat just for you, sweetie."

After breakfast, Gus got cleaned up and dressed while Sam cleared the dishes. Then she took her turn while Gus put the bag in his car and gave it another all-around spray. He came back into the house and put the four furniture pads in the bottom of the linen closet along with the receipt.

By then Sam was ready, so they partially closed the windows, sprayed all over the house, and locked the doors.

Sam headed off to work and since it was too early for the bank, Gus decided to visit the *Anita* to make sure nothing was going on. Nothing was! He plugged in the van and went aboard the boat and turned the computer and video equipment on.

Gus drove to his bank, rented a large safety deposit box for the bag, and after stocking up on money headed out to the Army/Navy store to see Pimples.

After waiting for Pimples to serve a kid looking for a hammock,

Gus said, "I have a particularly important mission and need your undi-
vided attention and confidence. Do you think you can do that for me?"

"You have my word, Mr. Farrell."

"OK, well here's the skinny. I need some C4 and thought you might
know someone that has some for sale. Oh, and by the way," Gus said,
"ask him if he has any blasting caps as well."

Pimples smiled and said, "Will do!"

Gus drove away trying to think of a way to set the damn thing off
without going up with it. Until he had the C4, he wouldn't know what it
would take to detonate it, but other bombs were set off with cell phones;
maybe he could rig it for a phone. He should be able to work it out, after
all, he didn't spend forty years in electronics and not learn something. As
he thought about it, he remembered that you could use external speakers
with a cell phone, and to do that you need a voltage to operate the speakers. On impulse, Gus changed course and headed for the Radio Shack on
Biscayne Boulevard to see if they had cheap telephones.

Gus stopped at a gun shop on NE 79th Street and picked up two
more boxes of Black Talons (for the effect of one-shot-stopping) to add
to his bags of booty, including the telephone, and batteries.

He was going over in his mind how to construct the bomb. He got
to the point where he needed to know how to attach the C4 to the
hull when it finally hit him. The hull was fiberglass—magnets were out
because they wouldn't stick to that! Velcro! That was the answer.

Somehow, attaching the C4 to the hull didn't seem too problematic
since he could get plenty of Velcro and it would stick to anything.
After all, the C4 didn't need to be underwater — just out of sight and
the curvature of the hull would take care of that.

Gus pulled onto the wharf, plugged in the battery charger in the
luggage carrier, and headed over to the *Anita*.

He was busily transcribing the medical procedure codes when the
phone rang.

"Mr. Farrell. This is Freddy, and I've got some good news for you.
The items you requested will be available here tomorrow morning
around 10:00."

"Thanks, Freddy. I'll be over to get them."

After several hours, Sam came through the door and kissed Gus on the forehead, saying, "There's another body in the morgue, Gus. It seems some Seminoles were fishing and found what was left of it in about a foot and a half of water three-quarters of a mile from Ingraham Highway on Pine Island. There wasn't much left of it, but the skin was dark, so they'll probably never be able to identify it."

"Jesus, Sam, when will it stop? I've got to close them down, and quick."

Sam put her arm around Gus's shoulder and said, "You're doing everything you can, as fast as you can, Gus. Don't forget the police are also working on this."

"Yeah, and we see how far they've gotten," Gus sneered.

Sam leaned over and bit the top of Gus's ear, saying, "Don't be so snitty, old man. They didn't find a bundle of money or a horde of people to investigate around the clock as if they had no other cases either."

Gus ran his hand up between her legs saying, "You haven't given me much time to 'investigate' either." They both laughed.

Gus washed the dinner dishes while Sam got changed into dark clothing, then Gus changed in preparation for taking the van over to 77th Street. It was already dark, and Gus was a little fidgety in his hurry to get going. He turned on the receiver and video recorder before they set the security traps and then hurried up the dock.

He parked the van on 77th Street in the usual spot, aimed the camera, turned on the video transmitter, locked the van, jumped into Sam's car, and headed for McDonald's for take-out coffee. They arrived back on the *Anita* forty-five minutes after they left.

No sooner had they cleared the traps and gotten into the cabin than they saw activity on the monitor. The lights around the guard post had been turned out but the lights of a vehicle on the way out lit up the guard shack and its occupants to show two guards in the shack and one standing off to the side in the shadows.

"Must be a small army in there, eh," Gus said in a whisper.

Sam looked at him and said, "Why are you whispering?"

"I didn't want them to hear us. Heh, heh."

"Do you think we can get over there in time to follow them?" Sam asked.

"Well, we better try, otherwise that equipment is worthless," Gus said as he flipped off the lights and started setting the traps. They raced to Sam's car and squealed the tires as they turned to get on the causeway with Sam at the wheel.

They were too late. The lights were back on, and the vehicle was gone.

Gus said, "Maybe too late here, but I'll bet they're going to the airport like last time, so turn this thing around and let's get going."

She turned around and left by 76th Street to get onto the Boulevard headed south. They switched over to the 36th Street Expressway and headed to the airport. Sam flipped on the lights and siren to clear the traffic and pushed the patrol car up to eighty. At the airport, Sam slowed down to get into normal traffic and turned the lights and siren off.

"Same hangar?" Sam asked.

Gus shook his head yes and whispered, "I doubt that they have another plane."

Sam parked in the same place as last time and turned the lights off. In a matter of minutes, the Mercedes came around the other end of the hangar and pulled up to the same plane as before.

It was almost like watching the same movie over again. The same people were there except neither pilot was visible. He knew they were in there though because the people outside were talking to someone inside.

Gus wrote down the tail number and handed it to Sam. "Call operations to see if they've filed a flight plan, will you?"

Sam pulled out her little black book, looked up the number, and dialed.

"Airport Operations Control Center. Chuck Henley, how may I help you?"

"This is Sgt. Samantha Cross of the Cutler Ridge Police Department, and I just witnessed a Learjet 85 take-off from the Miami Airport. I was wondering if tail number N455LJ has filed a flight plan."

"Just a moment, Sergeant, I'll take a look."

After a lengthy pause, "Yes ma'am. The pilot, Mr. Barry Ingram, filed a flight plan with that tail number from Miami International Airport to Sao Paulo, Brazil leaving at 23:00 and arriving at 7:48 tomorrow morning."

"Thanks very much, Chuck, I'll be sure to ask for you next time I need a favor."

"You're very welcome, Sgt. Cross, whenever you need anything."

"One more thing, Chuck. Can you find out who the plane is registered to?"

"Just a second, ma'am, OK? It's registered to a Dr. Angelo Cruz of Miami."

"Well," blurted Sam, "that's interesting. Thanks again, Chuck."

"Anytime, ma'am, bye-bye."

Sam hung up and looked at Gus. "Now we're getting somewhere."

Gus smiled. "Looks like it's time to hire a private detective to find out just where that cargo is headed and why."

"I can help with that. We have a source that works for the cops when we're undermanned and need help. He's very discreet and not expensive. Should I contact him for you?"

"Yes and find out when he can start and if he has a passport."

CHAPTER TWENTY-NINE

The detective didn't fit the picture of what one would have thought a detective would look like. He was short, balding, had a slight stoop in his shoulders, and wore horn-rimmed glasses.

"Good morning, are you Mr. Gus Farrell?"

Gus had been watching the replay of the last night's video and was startled by the intrusion.

"Yes, and you are?"

"Frank Morgan, the detective. Sgt. Cross said you might need my help."

"Well, come in and make yourself comfortable. Would you like some coffee or a drink?"

"I'll take some coffee; it's a little early for a drink, but thanks for the offer."

Gus got a clean cup, poured it full, and handed it to Frank.

"So, what can I do for you, Gus?"

"I don't know what Sam has told you, but we have an investigation going and got a little stretched out. Do you have a passport?"

"As a matter of fact, I still have a valid passport," he replied.

"OK," Gus said. "Let me give you a synopsis of our investigation, and you can base your charges on that. Let's start at the beginning."

An hour and fifteen minutes later, Gus said. "That brings you up to the present. Now, what I'd like for you to do is find out where that plane is going, who's on it, where they're going with the cargo and who the recipient is. Then I'd like to know how they intend to use it, with as much detail in your report as you can manage."

Frank looked at Gus and said, "I can do that for you, and as for the charges, I usually charge five hundred a day and expenses."

"That sounds fair to me, and when can you get on board?"

"Right away, if that's what you want."

Gus smiled, and said, "That's great, and I'll give you a week in advance to get you started."

"I'm on," Frank said.

"Good, and now I'd like to show you around. Have you got the time?"

"I'm all yours for as long as it takes."

Gus spent the next two and a half hours showing Frank around, including the house and grounds on 77th Street, and the van with the camera.

Back at the *Anita*, Gus said, "Please feel free to call me at any time if you see anything suspicious or that you think I should know about."

"Right, and I'll be talking to you soon." He got into an old pickup truck and drove off.

Gus went back to his monitor and called Sam while watching the activities on the screen.

"Hello, Gus. What are you up to?"

"I just had a meeting with your friend and have hired him to do some leg work for me, starting with the plane."

"That's great, and I'm sure he'll do a good job for you. He's very competent. Oh Gus, while I have you on the phone, they've discovered another body. Two young boys in a homemade boat found a girl about a mile and a half southwest of Route 27, on SR 997, near Thompson Park. She had been harvested, and the alligators had also found her."

Gus grunted and said, "Looks like we may have some more activity at the airport again, doesn't it?"

"Most probably, since it was a relatively recent kill."

"OK. Well, I've hired your detective, and I'll let him know about this latest development. Who's handling the case?"

"Didn't find out but I'll give them a call and then let you know."

"Thanks, sweetie-pie. Talk to you later."

Gus picked up his phone and dialed Frank.

"Hello."

"Frank, this is Gus. Sam just told me that another body was found." Gus gave him the details as far as he knew them, then said, "Probably handled by the Hialeah PD. But we don't know who the investigator is yet."

"Thanks, Gus. I'll get right on it and get back to you."

Gus went back to the videotape and continued to monitor a higher speed version.

He was just barely awake when something caught his eye. Gus tapped the switch to stop the recording and backed it up to see what he'd missed.

Good thing he had bought the recorder with a time display on it because when he got to the point of interest, it said 2:08, and the lights at the guardhouse had just come on. After a few minutes, the guard came out, looked around, and then went back into the driveway. Soon after that, the big Mercedes drove out and turned right, headed for the airport no doubt.

Gus had started a journal to keep track of the activity at the house. He retrieved the journal and made an entry then put the recorder on the higher speed and watched to the end. Even though Gus was looking at the recording, the monitor was displaying the driveway in real-time, and nothing was happening there either. He picked up his cell and called Frank.

"Hi, Gus, what's up."

"Plenty. The Mercedes left last night at 2:08 and I'm pretty sure that the Learjet was headed to Sao Paulo shortly after that. So, drop what you're doing and get a flight down there as soon as you can and find out where that cargo is going. They're flying a white Learjet 85 with tail number N455LJ. You probably won't get there before they do but stay and find out all you can and take pictures. Give me a call when you've got something. If you need more money, let me know how to get it to you."

"OK, Gus, I'm on my way, talk to you later."

Since most of the activity at the Cruz house occurred in either the very early morning or late morning, the afternoon was the best time to charge the batteries in the van. He called a taxi and had him drop him off on 76th Street, to avoid being seen, and walked to 8th Avenue and around the corner to the van. It was undisturbed, so Gus got in, backed up, and drove around the corner to 8th Avenue and turned on 76th Street to Biscayne Blvd.

There was an open power outlet at the marina, so Gus pulled up, pulled out the extension cord, plugged it into the outlet, and walked over to the *Anita*.

———

Juan Cordaro was beginning to get antsy about the new product. He would have to go out and locate some more illegals soon to keep the larder full. There were currently only three left, and they were in a blood group that wasn't called for very often. A field trip was called for. He sipped his coffee and began planning the details of his next excursion.

———

Sam parked near the van and walked over to the *Anita*. When she opened the cabin door, Gus was sitting at the monitor with a beer in one hand and the mouse in the other, sound asleep. She carefully took the beer to keep him from spilling it and kissed him on the cheek.

"Oh, hi honey. I guess I'll have to watch this tape over again."

Sam smiled (thinking of how late he'd worked the day before) and said, "You're excused, honey. Are you awake yet?"

"I think so, why?"

"Because I found out who the investigator is that's assigned to the case out on Route 997, near Thompson Park. It's Stew Cardin out of the Hialeah office."

"I've heard of him, and what I've heard was complimentary. He's supposed to be good at what he does and has only one unsolved case, so far."

"Yes, but no one could have solved that one. It was a pair of man's legs, from the knees down, that had washed up on the beach. It seems they had been bitten off, obviously by something very, very large. Although they got the DNA, there was nothing to compare it with, and no one was reported missing."

Gus grimaced and said, "Sounds gruesome."

"It was, have you heard from Frank yet?"

"No, not yet, but then he won't be in Sao Paulo yet; unless he got really lucky."

"You're probably right, so what do you want to do now?"

Gus stretched and said, "Are you hungry yet?"

"Famished, let's go."

They decided on a Cuban restaurant in Little River. It was off the beaten track, tucked in an alley behind the local movie theater. As they looked for a parking spot, they came across a wide area in the alley that had a sign on the wall, Serrano Clinic, reserved parking. Since there were no cars parked there at this time of night, Gus pulled into one of them and looked at the sign for the parking space. It said, "Reserved for Dr. A. Cruz."

Gus could hardly contain himself. "This is too good to be true, Sam."

"What is, sweetheart?" Sam replied.

"Look in front of you. This is the clinic I've been looking for. Dr. Cruz! "

"Oh, for God's sake, Gus. We find it by accident when you couldn't find it with a thorough search."

"Doesn't that beat all?" Gus snickered.

Sam smiled and said, "Now that you've found it, what are you going to do with it?"

"The first thing I'm going to do is have dinner, and then maybe we'll take a stroll around to the front and see what the address is. You OK with that?"

"Sounds reasonable to me, let's go."

The restaurant wasn't that good, so they didn't linger, just got up and left. The clinic was on the other side of the block, so they walked around through the alley and turned onto the street where it was facing. The name, "Serrano Clinic," was engraved on a brass plate mounted on the side of the only door to the building. Above the door was the number 830583, and they were on NE 83rd Court.

Gus got out his notepad and jotted down the address. It wouldn't be hard to remember the location since it was right in front of the Florida East Coast Railway, with the river on the other side of the tracks.

"This is very handy; we can bring the Bayliner up the river and search the clinic later."

"That's illegal, Gus!"

"So is killing people for their parts!"

"You do have a point there, sweetie."

They arrived back at the *Anita* just after ten o'clock. Gus removed the booby traps and went to the port side to check on the Bayliner. It was still there and hadn't been touched as far as he could see.

He went into the cabin where Sam was straightening up and asked her where the night scopes were.

"The last time I saw them, they were in the port cabinet, top shelf. Do you want me to get them?"

"Sure, if you don't mind, and I'll get the spook suits out. I know where they are."

He went out to the bow and lifted the smallest seat on the starboard side storage seats. He got out all the black clothes that were stored there plus the black stretch caps and shoes. Once completely dressed, they were invisible in the dark.

Gus asked, "Are you ready yet, Sam?"

"You betcha, honey, let's go."

"OK," Gus said, "now all we need is a camera team, and it'll look like we're in the movies."

Gus went up on deck and set the traps, and then they both left for the cars and headed over to their particular parking spot. Gus arranged the van for the best view and then got into Sam's car for the return trip to the *Anita*.

Again, they had to fiddle with the traps, then went into the cabin and hauled their equipment over to the rail. They stored the clothes and equipment on the Bayliner, then Gus went forward and checked the alarms on the *Anita*. Gus climbed onboard the Bayliner and started the fan and then the engine. He turned on the running lights, checked the meters, and made sure all was running right. Sam dropped the lines into the boat and climbed aboard. Gus backed the boat out of the slip and turned to starboard. As they crossed under the 79th Street Bridge, Gus turned off the running lights, and Sam began putting on her spook clothes. When she finished, Sam took the wheel while Gus got dressed, then got out the night goggles, checked if they worked, put them on, and adjusted the straps.

"Guess we're all set, Sam."

CHAPTER THIRTY

As luck would have it, there was only a sliver of the moon, so they didn't have to be especially careful about being seen. As Gus's father used to say, "It's darker than the inside of a black cow."

Sam was busy looking for a place to tie off on the sea wall, and Gus was careful not to bang into it because there was extraordinarily little ambient light. Gus put on his night goggles to make sure he could see where the wall was and when he did, the world lit up.

"Hey, Sam, put on your night goggles, I'll wait."

Sam knew where she had put them but had to feel around to find them. Finally, she did and put them on, turned them on, and said, "Wow. It's so much nicer when you can see where you're going. Eventually, Sam found a steel pole sticking up from the water alongside the seawall and dropped the bowline over it and tied off the boat, then hustled to the stern, threw the anchor over the wall, and tied it loose enough to keep it near the wall, but not banging into it.

"Now," she said, "good luck finding it when we come back."

Gus said, "That won't be a problem, I marked an X on the side of the boat."

Sam giggled and started throwing the gear up on the seawall while

Gus stopped the engine and helped her. When they were satisfied that they had everything, including flashlights, Gus helped Sam climb over onto the wall and then followed.

The weeds were tall between the railroad tracks and the street in front of the clinic, but they didn't feel the need to hide in them since there was no one around and they needed to make better use of their time. Gus got to the road first and looked around for passersby, just in case. No one appeared, so he walked across the street and up to the door of the clinic. He waited for Sam to arrive because she had the lock picks needed to gain entry. Sam went right to work, and the door swung open to a short hallway with two doors on either side and a single door at the end of the hall.

"You're a real professional," Gus said. "Now, let's see where the office is. You take the left side, and I'll get this side." Their search disclosed several storage rooms, with one custodian's room with mops, buckets, and cleaning material. They met at the locked door at the end of the hallway.

Sam whipped out her lock picks and went to work. It was taking a little longer than the last one and Sam said, "This one is different, but I'll get it."

The door swung open, and they stepped into a much larger room with offices around the sides and a reception desk in the middle.

Gus said, "Let's go around together," so they started around clockwise to check all the rooms.

Gus said, "There's nothing spectacular here, just examining rooms and offices." Then they got to the third room and hit the jackpot. It was full of filing cabinets; three rows of six cabinets each. Gus started on the right row, and Sam took the left. They were full of medical records of patients who'd had transplants, both in the United States and South America. Gus laid out a few records on a worktable and started taking pictures of them. They were both taking pictures for about an hour and a half.

Finally, Gus said, "Let's check out the other rooms."

There was a door at the back of the large room, so they opened that one and found a small transition room with a table, chair, and palm tree. The door to the left opened into a stock room, which curiously enough was lined with organ transport coolers, and the door to the right opened onto a scrub room. One of the two doors in the scrub room led to a full-blown operating room with overhead lights and all the equipment to perform any operation. The other door led to a preparation area, and it too had another door. The other door led to a stark room with two sets of bunk beds, a toilet and sink along the back wall and a small TV set on a stand. The doors were steel, and there were no windows. Gus took more pictures and relieved himself in the toilet.

Gus kept taking more pictures of all the rooms and then the loading dock. The one next to the OR was what looked like a holding area, literally, with tie-down straps on gurneys and a medicine cabinet full of tranquilizers and pain killers, hypodermic syringes, and other paraphernalia required in a real OR. While Gus was checking all the rooms and taking pictures, there was one thing he noticed that was conspicuously absent, licenses that are required to be displayed in all businesses and diplomas or awards. In fact, all the walls were bare.

Gus opened another door at the back of the preparation room, and it led to a hallway that led back to a small loading dock, opening on the alley they had been in, and to the right of that was a gas incinerator. Obviously for the disposal of mistakes.

They went back into the larger room and continued checking the side chambers. The room, accessed at the end of a small hallway near the front door was bigger and appeared to be a break room with coffee pots, a sink, wall cabinets, overstuffed chairs, and a telephone. Gus took one picture of the room and left for the next room. The other side of the large room was obviously for show and only contained desks, a chair, and some decorations.

Gus said, "I think we got it all, Sam. What do you say we get out of here?"

"That's an excellent idea, because the sun will come up soon, and we don't need to be here when it does."

"Right, but can you make those lock picks work in reverse because we need to make this place look secure when we leave."

"No, but I can lock it from inside, and no one would know the difference."

Gus said, "Before we go, I'm going to grab one of those organ transport coolers, just in case."

Coming back with the cooler, he said, "Let's go,"

They double-checked to make sure they had all their gear and slipped out the front door. It always seems further to go somewhere than it does coming back, and they were on the boat in no time. The tide was coming back in, so the boat was higher in the water and easier to board. They kept the night vision goggles on until they were well away from the area and then Gus switched the lights on, removed his goggles, then said, "We're just a couple of fishermen going out early."

They rode in silence until they reached the *Anita*. Sam tied off to the nearest cleat at the bow and then again at the stern. They piled their equipment on the dock and rigged a spring line. Sam went up on the deck of the *Anita*, and Gus handed the stuff over to her. Together, they put it away and went to the cabin. Sam put a pot of coffee on, and Gus got out the cameras to upload the pictures to the computer. He rigged the cable to his camera first and started the upload.

"I'm not so sure who we should go to with this, Sam. If we go to the police, we take a chance that they've been paid off and the same applies to the district attorney. Maybe we would be better off going straight to the FBI."

Sam scowled and said, "We're not even sure that they're not involved any more than the local police either."

"That's true," replied Gus, "we'd be better off keeping it to ourselves, besides, if we involve the FBI, they'll know who's involved with the destruction of Cruz's compounds and we won't have alibis. I think I'll go out and get some big thumb drives for transporting the data."

Gus went back out to the electronics store, where he bought the recorder and picked up four thirty-five gig thumb drives. When he got back, Sam had a big breakfast on the table for him.

"That looks good, Sam. Just let me change the cameras, and we'll eat."

He took her camera and hooked the cable to it and started the upload.

"Now I have to set up the monitor and download the computer to the thumb drives." Gus got everything started and went up on deck to hide the alarms, came back down, changed drives, and restarted the download.

CHAPTER THIRTY-ONE

Gus was watching the recording from the van that he'd started before and thought that his decision to keep everything to himself was the best way out of a bad situation. Besides, he would have no defense against his involvement.

Sam interrupted his train of thought by saying, "Gus, how long are we going to investigate these murderers?"

Gus looked at Sam with renewed appreciation and said, "You're right, Sam. There's not much left to do since we have all the evidence we need and people are still dying, we need to stop them ourselves, and there's no need to wait; we need to assemble a team. What we still need is a report from Frank Morgan. I need to know how extensive the operation in Brazil is." Gus pulled out his cell phone and dialed Frank.

"Hello, Gus."

"Hi, Frank. What have you got for me so far?"

"Well, I just sent you a package of what I found, and it's quite an operation down here. I have to pay for everything I get so send me another couple thousand to pay for the details I haven't got yet."

"OK, Frank but are you being careful? You could be putting yourself at risk with all those questions."

"As careful as I can be, I guess. You should be getting the package tomorrow, and I'll send you the details of what I'm looking for as soon as I get the money."

"Thanks, Frank and be careful."

Gus hung up and turned to Sam. "I have to go wire Frank some money. Would you like to come with me and then we'll have lunch somewhere?"

The closest Western Union was over on Miami Avenue and after the transfer they looked for a little hole-in-the-wall that served Philly cheesesteak sandwiches and split one, washing it down with beer.

As they were getting into the car, Sam asked: "Where will the package from Frank come?"

"To the marina office, and they distribute it to whoever, but I don't think it would be here yet. We could check when we get back. Right now, it's a good time to charge the batteries, what do you think?"

"Fine, I'll drop you off at the van."

Gus parked at the marina, plugged in the charger, and walked toward the *Anita*, all the while thinking where he could move the *Anita* to avoid being found. They were well established right here, but it shouldn't be all that much of an effort to go somewhere else. While he walked into the cabin, he was thinking about where he'd left the yellow pages. He looked up, and Sam was standing there naked as a jaybird.

"Whoa, what's all this?"

Sam smiled and said, "Well, as you know, it's Sunday which means a day of rest, and since we've been on the go all week, I thought it would be a beautiful day to just *rest*."

"I never thought of it as 'rest' before, but I'm all for it. If I fall asleep, wake me up."

"I can pretty well guarantee you won't fall asleep for a while, honey," Sam said smiling. Gus forgot all about checking for the package from Frank, or the yellow pages.

———

Another beautiful day in paradise, Gus thought as the breeze picked up and the sun slowly crept up his bare chest. Sam was nowhere around, but he could hear her softly moving things around in the galley.

"Who's in the galley?" Gus said.

"The chief cook and bottle washer, and if you want to eat what I've got, you'll have to come to where it is."

"I'd certainly like to eat what you've got, sweetie. I'm on the way!"

There was a bowl of fruit, a plate of bacon, eggs, and toast with jam and butter, and a plate of home fries on the table, all steaming hot with a cup of black coffee.

Gus said, "While I was in bed, I thought I was already in paradise. How wrong was I?"

When they were both dressed and ready to go, Sam got into her car and headed for work. Gus took the van over to set it up for more viewing and called a cab to get back to the marina.

Gus found the yellow pages and checked it for marinas where it was convenient to the areas where he was working.

Sea Isle Marina looked like the spot where you could, like the saying goes, "Hide in plain sight." He called the marina to check on the availability of slips and was told that there were a couple that could handle his boat.

"I'll be down to talk to you when I get a chance," Gus said.

"That's fine Mr. Farrell, just ask for Jeff when you get here."

The marina had a lot going for it. It was closer to the airport, closer to Cutler Ridge, where Sam worked, and it was hidden from the majority of people by the high-rise condominiums, hotels, and apartment buildings along the shore.

Gus waited for Sam to get home from work and then they both went to the marina to check it out.

"This is really nice, Gus, and look there," pointing at the hotel, "a restaurant."

"Let's move the boats first, and then have dinner there."

"Exactly," Sam said, "but first we have to go sign for the two slips."

They went to the office and signed for the slips and then Sam drove Gus up to the Pelican Harbor Marina where they both removed the mooring lines and launched the *Anita*. Gus started the engines and headed for the channel, while Sam drove back to the Sea Isle Marina.

It wasn't as long as Sam thought it would be for Gus to come into view. She got out of the car and walked over to the outward slip where Gus was headed and helped Gus moor the *Anita*.

Gus set the alarms, jumped down to the dock, and they both drove back up to the Pelican Harbor Marina. They repeated the same procedure as was done to the *Anita*, only this time with the Bayliner which they moored to the inside slip directly across from the *Anita*.

When they finished, Gus walked across the dock to the *Anita* to check the alarms. He noticed a man in a small boat at the end of the dock who seemed to be interested in everything they were doing. Without saying anything, Gus made a mental note and they walked over to the restaurant.

CHAPTER THIRTY-TWO

Before turning in, Gus turned out all the lights and checked the spy boat at the other end of the marina. Sure enough, he was smoking. Gus set the alarm for 2:00 and crawled in beside Sam, who was lightly snoring.

The alarm didn't wake Sam, so Gus slipped out of the bunk quietly, went up into the cabin, and got into his wetsuit. He pulled his cap on and tied a crescent wrench to his wrist, slipped it into the sleeve, grabbed his flippers, and stepped over the gunwale. He walked about halfway to the end of the dock and slipped quietly into the water. Using only his flippers, he quietly swam to the boat containing the spy, who wasn't smoking, but was breathing rather loudly, and carefully took the line off the cleat on the dock at the bow, then swam around to the stern and disconnected the stern line from the dock. Being careful not to bump the dock, he quietly eased the boat into clear water and pointed it toward the bay. He checked the direction and started pushing the boat toward the bay. After about a half-hour, he again checked the direction and pushed for another fifteen minutes, until he could feel the tide pushing against the hull toward the south. Gus took a deep breath and gently pulled himself under the stern and felt around for the drain plug. Finding it, he took the wrench out of his sleeve, set the opening to fit the plug, and very carefully unscrewed the plug and dropped it into the deep. Time for air! He came up and checked direction, It was headed slightly southeast and beginning to move a little faster with the outgoing tide. Gus pushed as hard as he could without making noise and let it go, then swam back to the dock. Gus thought to himself, isn't he going to get a surprise, as he slipped back into the bunk.

———

The sun was up when Sam came down from the galley, where she was getting breakfast, and excitedly woke Gus to tell him that the spy boat was gone. Gus smiled, and it was then she noticed that his sheets were damp. "You didn't...."

"Who, me?" Gus snickered.

Neither one of them mentioned the late-night escapade during breakfast, but both were thinking about it.

Finally, Sam said, "Just because you got rid of one of them, it doesn't mean that there aren't others watching."

"I know, Sam, but at least they didn't see anything happening."

After Sam went to work, Gus got busy correlating the events in the ledgers to the documentation from Brazil and his recordings, to create a timeline of events for each occurrence. Once he established a work-flow, it was relatively easy to complete a timeline for each procedure. He had just completed the fourth one from four years back when his phone rang.

"Gus. Sam here. Another body was found this morning tangled up in some mangroves near the mouth of the Miami River. Right around the corner from you. Guess the disposal crew was too lazy to go further into the glades and dumped it where it could be affected by the tides. "

"What are the particulars-of-the-body, Sam?"

"Just your everyday, run-of-the-mill dead male without his organs. From what I can gather, he was about five feet six, swarthy, approximately one hundred sixty pounds, before the harvest of course, and was covered in tattoos, mostly the MS13 genre. That's the reason for the flippant attitude."

"You have every right to be flip, Sam, this killing is getting a little old, and we have to formulate a plan to stop it. Why don't you meet me at Morrison's for dinner and then we'll go to the house and work on it?"

"Good idea, Gus. I'll meet you over there at five-fifteen."

Gus got the boxes out from under the bunk and packed up everything he'd been working on, taped them, and stored them in his car. He got the drawings he'd made, rearranged the bunk, stowed all the stuff he'd been working with but wouldn't need tonight, set the alarms, and drove over to Morrison's. Sam was already there and after they ate, they drove to the house separately.

Gus opened the front door and said, "Smells like someone died in here."

"Maybe this isn't such a good idea, Gus. I have a weak stomach."

"We have to do it sometime," and he set about turning on the fans and air conditioner, then sprayed the rooms with NNZ, then moved the table and rug, opened the trap door, and sprayed almost another can down the hole. "It's almost bearable now. Why don't we move out to the lanai and work there?"

"OK, Gus, and I'll put on a pot of coffee."

They worked until ten o'clock, then repacked everything back in the boxes and put them in Gus's car. They closed the house but kept the trap door open so there'd be a flow of air from the fans through the access hole, then cracked the back window slightly to provide fresh air. They drove back to the *Anita* separately and parked side by side, unloaded the boxes and stowed them under the bunk. They were both tired, so they just brushed their teeth and went to bed.

Something was tickling his nose, and when he opened his eyes, there was Sam wagging her hair over his face.

She asked, "How would you like your eggs, this morning?"

"Cooked," Gus said.

"Then you better get up because they're cooking now." When she turned to go, Gus could see that she was naked again, except for the apron.

After Sam went to work, Gus started looking for house cleaning services in the phone book. He found one, at a decent price, and told them where the house was, and that he'd meet them there. He drove over to the house and went in to turn the fans off, cover up the trap-door, and reset the rug, table, and chairs. Then he opened all the windows.

When the cleaners arrived, Gus told them that a raccoon had accessed the crawlspace while they were gone and had died in there. He told them to thoroughly clean all the surfaces including the carpets and windows, cabinets, and ceilings. When asked about the price, they gave him a quote of eight hundred and fifty dollars. Since there were four of them, it seemed reasonable. Gus accepted the price, and they told him that it would be done by five o'clock the next day. Gus gave them the key and his phone number and told them to give him a call when they were done, and he would come over to inspect it and give them a check.

When Gus got back to the marina, he went directly to the office and asked the clerk who had signed up for the slip where the spy boat was docked. The clerk told him that a man named Manolo Gutierrez had signed for it a day and a half ago.

Gus thanked him and went back to the *Anita*.

As Gus walked up to the *Anita*, he could see that his security measures had been removed and the cabin door was open. He slipped off his sneakers and cocked the Ruger he'd pulled from his belt. Very cautiously he moved into the cabin to find it a mess. The monitor was smashed, and the recorder had been thrown on the deck but, nothing was where it should have been. It didn't look like there had been a theft because the recordings were still in their box under the cabinet and there didn't appear to be anything missing at all. Either they had been looking for something they hadn't found, or it was an act of revenge.

Gus went down to the galley, which was intact, and then into the berth area, which again had been torn apart as if looking for some-thing. The storage area under the berth had been missed, so all their data was still there. Obviously, changing marinas was a waste of time. He started the cleanup. As Gus cleaned, he was mulling over the direction this whole investigation was taking. They had gleaned an enormous amount of information; at least enough to put them all behind bars, so what was the point of continuing to collect more information that wouldn't improve the outcome. It was time for action.

CHAPTER THIRTY-THREE

When Sam got back to the *Anita* after work, she was a little shocked to find every horizontal space in the cabin loaded with a crossbow, darts, bows and arrows, wetsuits, flippers, night vision masks, guns, etc., etc.; in fact, everything they had collected to wage war against the scumbags they had been investigating.

Gus looked up from his cache and said, "Hi, honey. Don't look so surprised, you knew this was coming, and it's time to act before they get any closer to us. Find out if any of your friends would like to join us, and I'll get Frank back here to help out."

"Good idea, Gus, and you're right; it *is* time to stop these murders. I know several officers that are sick and tired of this slaughter and are frustrated that they don't have any leads. I'll get hold of them and tell them about the evidence we have that proves who the perpetrators are and their involvement. I'm pretty sure they'll want to be in on the takedown."

"Great, Sam, and I'll call Frank back in to get his take on the new evidence he's collected since my last call, and also to be here to help on the final event after I get the van and bring it back."

When Gus finally got hold of Frank, he was eating supper. Gus told him to mail what he had and get on a plane to Miami as soon as possible.

Frank hung up and called his airline to make reservations for the following morning. He then went to a Pack-N-Ship to buy boxes, tape, labels, and a marker. He took them back to his apartment and started packing the information, pictures, maps, and comments he'd written explaining, in English, what he was sending. In the morning Frank hailed a cab and went to the post office, filled out the customs forms, and mailed his boxes He had a couple of hours before his flight, so he thought he'd kill them at the airport, having breakfast. He again hailed a cab from in front of the Metropolitan Cathedral and told him the name of the airline. They headed out to join up with the Avenida Tiradentes. As the cabbie pulled out on the main road, a freight truck hit them from behind, pushing them across the road into the path of a city bus, killing both the cabbie and Frank instantly.

The boxes from Frank didn't arrive until four days after he'd sent them, so Gus and Sam weren't aware of the tragedy Frank had suffered, and there was no one there who could let them know.

While Gus was correlating the information from the day books with the worksheets from Dr. Cruz's office, the phone rang. "Mr. Farrell?"

"Yes."

"This is Ted Ralston of the Pelican Harbor Marina, and there are a bunch of boxes here for you from Brazil. Do you want to come to pick them up?"

"Absolutely," Gus replied. "Can I come over now?"

"Yup, just get here before five."

Gus arrived at 3:30 and backed up as close as possible to the office.

"Are you Mr. Farrell?"

Gus nodded his head, and in response, Ted said, "Your boxes are there near the door," pointing at the entrance Gus had just come through.

———

After wrestling the boxes down to the table in the galley, Gus went topside and replaced the alarms in case someone decided to make an unannounced visit while he was going through the boxes. Most of the information was pictures of people working in the hospital and the buildings themselves. The pictures of the people had the information printed on the back, e.g., which building they worked in and what their job was. There was lots of other information, including copies of receipts for medical furniture, tools, linen, and uniforms; applications for business licenses, tax forms, and utility statements; and best of all, payment receipts from patients.

There was so much information that it would have to be categorized. Tearing through it now would confuse anyone who had an inkling of what they should be trying to find. Since Sam was the expert in evidence, he would grab a beer and wait for her.

About halfway through his beer, Gus started to get antsy. Knowing the approximate time Sam would be getting home, he decided to start supper. He pulled out a package of four pork chops, a can of asparagus, a jar of applesauce, and a box of scalloped potatoes. He put the frying pan on the burner and plopped the pork chops in at about medium heat. He was getting the bowl for the potatoes when he heard the car door slam. Good timing, he thought.

It took just over four hours for them to get through all the items in the boxes. Each item was categorized according to importance, location, and time frame. They were then stacked in neat piles, indexed, banded, and laid out in sequential order over any horizontal space available until fourteen stacks were decorating the cabin.

"Are you ready for dessert yet?" Sam asked.

"I was ready after dinner!" Gus replied.

"Well, sweetheart, you get the ice cream, and I'll put the coffee on."

"Sounds like a deal, baby."

In short order, Gus was coming into the cabin with two medium bowls of green ice cream. "I'm glad you like pistachio as much as I do. Otherwise, I'd have to eat both of these." Sam gave him a look through her eyebrows and poured the coffee.

———

Breakfast was easy, fresh fruit, oatmeal, toast, and coffee.

Sam broke the ice with the comment, "Now that we've done the FBI's work for them, do you think we should share the information with them as well?"

Gus laughed and said, "There's something else we'd be better off doing than pissing off the FBI. We need a file of each category and a copy of everything."

"I love you, Gus, but I think you have someone in mind for that job, and I don't think she's very far away at the moment."

"You're right, Sam, but then I started to think, and I believe I've come up with something."

"I need to hear this Gus, so don't hesitate, let's have it."

"Okay, rather then put this whole thing on ourselves, we need to form a consortium of willing police officers, detectives, lawyers, DA's, and anybody who is fed up with this rash of murders. You've mentioned quite a few names of people involved in the investigation of these murders, people who have had to deal with the consequences of them. Mind you; this will be completely *illegal* since we'll be keeping the courts out of this, so we'll have to be fast in accomplishing it, and thorough in its completion. How does it sound so far?"

"Great, but how do you intend to form this consortium?"

"I need you to make a list of the type of people I mentioned and then introduce them to me. I'll interview each of them and assign one of the categories to them to read and make copies and a file of each. Each file, in turn, will be read by all members of the consortium. This way, there will be no question of what those bastards have been doing to their victims and we'll all be up to date."

"It sounds as though you've given this quite a bit of thought, Gus, so count me in, and I'll start on the list right away. However, I'm not sure I can get fourteen volunteers, so we might have to double-up on a few of them. I plan to take on a few of them myself."

Sam figured that with all the different sizes and configurations of data contained in the folders, it would be easier to buy a printer that could handle all the information rather than take it to a print shop. She suggested this to Gus, and he was totally in favor.

Together they cleaned up the dinner dishes, set the alarms, and headed to one of the large warehouse stores that carried a large inventory of printers. Along with the printer, they picked up three sets of ink cartridges and four reams of paper.

Making the files took until after lunch the following day. Each folder was numbered with a large felt marker and banded with rubber bands. They stacked them on the galley table and went out for a late lunch. During lunch, Gus asked Sam, "I've been thinking, Sam, why don't we set up a meeting with the folks on your list. That way we can do the introductions, hand out the files, and get a feel of their reactions and even possibly find out if they know of anyone else, we could recruit."

"Great idea, Gus. I'll start making calls this afternoon."

The meeting was set for the following Sunday at 2:00 aboard the *Anita*. Directions were given and participants were requested to keep silent on their activities for the sake of security. The first to arrive was Ben Harden and he wasn't alone. He had recruited two other cops who wanted to wipe out the murderers once and for all. The biggest was Will Tucker and the red-headed one was Lenny Hart. Introductions were made and they both got a beer from the cooler. Chuck Addison arrived shortly after with another detective named Martin Pochciol. After they all arrived and made themselves as comfortable as possible. Gus took the floor.

"Hello to all of you, thank you for coming. My name is Gus Farrell, and this is Samantha Cross from the Cutler Ridge Police Department. The reason we felt the need to form a consortium is that we have an ongoing problem which all of you are aware of, in that people are being murdered, their organs harvested and then their bodies disposed of in the swamps or desert, depending on what state you're in. The harvested organs are sold to whoever can afford them. My wife was one of their victims! I couldn't let this keep happening, so I started investigating over a year ago. The results of that investigation are in these files. What I would like to do—and keep in mind that this is completely illegal because we're keeping it out of the courts—is go after these scumbags and eliminate them from everywhere they operate. To do this, I will need expertise from wherever I can get it to form an invasion force to attack them, free their prisoners, destroy their facilities, and burn them down. Not only are they operating in this country, but they also have a hospital in Sao Paulo, where most of the organ implants are performed. I hired Frank Morgan to investigate the Brazil operation and he sent boxes of evidence. We haven't heard from him since, but I'm pretty sure he'll show up. In the meantime, we had to take him off our list since he's not physically here."

Holding up the file packets drawing for packet assignment, Gus said, "There are fourteen packets, and my job is to make sure that all of you have a couple of packets to look through until you have seen them all. After you have read them, we'll get together again in approximately two weeks for the final meeting. Please keep track of the ones you've read to make sure you've seen them all. Also, please bring all the ammunition, firepower, explosives, etc., that you can muster. We have quite a bit already but can always use more."

With this, Gus got the packets and started handing them out while Sam recorded who got them. Gus then said, "Please read them as soon as possible and get them back to me so I can reassign them. Does anyone have a problem with Sunday afternoon two weeks from now?" No hands went up, so Gus said, "All right, see you after you read the packets. Also, if you know of anyone interested in eliminating these murderers, and if you trust them, bring them to the next meeting, along with any weapons they can provide. If you do find others who would like to participate, please stress the secrecy of this operation. All right, ladies, and gentlemen, we'll see you here in two weeks."

———

The following weeks were a blur, with Gus making the transfers of the packets, trying to find ammunition, transportation, and vehicles; all the while planning the assault. With the help of Sam, he tried to figure out who had military experience and leadership abilities that he could put in charge of the squads leading the attacks. Passports would have to be acquired for the squad going to Sao Paulo, and details of their targets, such as addresses, maps, etc. There was such a myriad of details that Gus was near to having a breakdown.

There was nothing for it but to just start. He made lists for everything he could think of and then handed them to Sam for any thoughts she might have. There were a few small details, but the big one he hadn't thought of was the pilots. "Who was going to fly the plane?" Sam said, "Or we could just take a commercial flight."

"No, we can't, Sam. How will we get the armament there?"

"Well, certainly not on the plane. Don't forget there's a customs inspection at the other end."

"Damn," Gus said. "We'll have to buy the armament in Sao Paulo."

"From whom?" Sam replied.

Gus thought for a little while then said, "Let me make a phone call, and then maybe I can answer your question."

The phone call was to Pimples, and the question was, "Freddy, this is Gus and I have a question for you. Is your organization operated on an international basis?"

"Yep, we operate all over South America, Africa, Europe, and some parts of Asia. Why?"

"If I were to need some armaments in Sao Paulo, would I be able to get them without too much trouble?"

"One of our biggest caches is in Sao Paolo. If you know what you need now, I can arrange to have them there for you. When are you going down?"

"Within a couple of weeks, I hope. I'll make a list and drop it off to you in a day or two, so you'll have time to fill it. And thanks."

Hanging up, Gus turned to Sam and said, "Sam, do you still have the information on the flight plan of that Learjet and the pilot who filed it?"

"Pretty sure I do, Gus. Hold on and I'll get it for you." Looking through her notebook, she eventually came up with the information: Tail number N455LJ; filed by Barry Ingram (Pilot), with the Airport Operations Control Center Supervisor, Chuck Henley, from Miami to Sao Paulo, Brazil.

"Wonderful, Sam, I could kiss you! We now have a pilot, even if he doesn't know it yet. Now I have to hire him."

Gus dialed the number for the Dade County Professional Pilots Association.

"DCPPA, how may I help you?"

"Hello, my name is Gustav Dutz and I need a pilot for a private Learjet from Miami to Sao Paulo in approximately two weeks, preferably someone who has made the trip before more than once."

"All right, Mr. Dutz. My name is Gustavo Gonzales and we have a couple of pilots that fit your requirements, so we shouldn't have a problem. When would you require the service?"

"Not for a couple of weeks. Would that be OK?"

"Oh yes, Mr. Dutz, that would be fine."

"Good, and I'll be getting back in about a week to set up final details."

"Very well, Mr. Dutz. I'll be looking for your call."

Gus hung up and redialed the number for Freddy.

"Hello, Fred speaking."

"Fred, this is Gus and I need to ask you a question."

"Shoot."

"After you collect all the stuff we talked about, when could you have it ready in Sao Paulo?"

"It will take a week to find it all in Rio then I'll have to stage it and transport it to Sao by truck, so I'd say just shy of two weeks. We have an outlet in Rio, and we could have it ready two weeks after I get your list."

"OK Freddy, also, can you tell them to meet us at the airport in Sao Paulo when we arrive? We'll need transport to the work site in Sao. I have the list almost complete and will bring it over tomorrow, so the time starts the day after the meeting, Okay?"

"Sure, Gus. I'll have the transport loaded with your order and they'll meet us at the plane if you tell me where to meet us at the airport."

"I'll get that info for you when I bring you the list tomorrow. And what do you mean "they'll pick 'us' up?"

"Well, Gus, that's because I'm going with you so there won't be any screw-ups."

This was a total surprise to Gus, and he said so.

"Freddy, this excursion is going to be extremely dangerous, and I don't think you should involve yourself in something like this! You could get killed, or at best, arrested."

"Either I go, or you go without armament."

"Looks like I can't talk you out of it, so if you're that determined you'll have to get a passport. I'll bring the info on how to get it."

Freddy smirked and said, "Just bring a lot of money when you come, I have a passport."

Gus laughed and said, "See you tomorrow."

CHAPTER THIRTY-FOUR

The next two weeks were a flurry of activity, with both Gus and Sam planning, arranging, managing, sorting, assigning. and notifying those who were to participate in squads with assignments and locations where they would be best suited.

During his haste to cover the details, and ensure that all the logistics were in place, there was one especially important item he had overlooked: bullet-proof vests. Gus picked up his phone and fast-dialed Freddy.

"Freddy here."

"Freddy, this is Gus, can you get a dozen bullet-proof vests for me right away?"

"As a matter of fact, I have about two dozen of them in stock, so I'll set aside the sizes you want and put a hold on them."

"Good, do that until we decide where the jumping-off point will be. Bring a few X-large and the rest of them can be large sizes. Don't forget to come to the meeting at 2:00 on Sunday at Sam's house, and I'll be over this afternoon with the list and location to meet us at the airport in Sao Paulo

"OK, see you Sunday, if you tell me where Sam's house is located."

"Good thinking, Freddy. We also moved the boat and haven't told anybody where that is yet either." Gus went on to explain its new location and hung up, then began contacting everyone on his list with directions on how to get to Sam's house and the *Anita*.

Gus got a tablet and pencil, sat down at the galley table, and started forming up the teams for the attack:

Team One: Attack and destroy the Sao Paulo clinic.
Gus Farrell (Leader)
Freddy Larson (Logistics)
Martin Pochciol (Pilot)
Stan Groves (Linguist-Speaks Portuguese)
Team Two: Attack and destroy Dr. Cruz's office in Little River.
Samantha Cross (Leader)
Rodney Guerry (Armorer)
Ben Harden
Team Three: Destroy compound (and yacht) at 624 NE 77th St.; release prisoners.
Chuck Addison
Will Tucker
Lenny Hart
Neil Hamlet

With that finished, Gus made copies for the meeting and stowed them in a cabinet, then started thinking about the actual date of the attack. There was a lot to consider, so getting everything to come together at the right time was a real ballbuster. A lot hinged on the equipment availability and location. For one thing, the *Anita* was not the place for staging an attack, so the only alternative was Sam's house. There was plenty of room there and everything could be delivered there without attracting too much attention. Now, the problem was getting Sam to agree, even though he had already decided to use Sam's house for the meeting place on Sunday.

"Of course, we can use the house, Gus," Sam said when he told her.

"Great," Gus said, "now I have to get three panel trucks for our transportation, so I'll talk to you at home, sweetheart."

Getting the trucks wasn't as hard as he thought it would be, except for the date he'd need them. He told the rental agency the approximate day and gave him a hundred-dollar deposit by credit card to hold them. Next, he called Freddy and asked how the collection was going.

Freddy said, "Not to worry, everything's going swimmingly, and I only have a few things that haven't come in yet, but they'll arrive on time."

"Can you give me a more precise time when you'll be ready, Freddy?"

"Yes, we'll be ready the Friday after the Sunday meeting."

"Great, now I can plan for it. Thanks, Freddie. I also want you to write down an address where you can store them until we're ready. On second thought, Freddy, I'll come over now and bring the list, the location of the hanger in Sao Paulo, and the address to make deliveries here."

"That's even better. I'll be at Henson's until you get here."

Gus said, "Good, see you shortly."

There were only three more days until the meeting, so Gus called everybody to alert them of the meeting and told them to bring any weapons and ammunition they could find to Sam's house and then gave them her address.

Next, Gus drove over to the electronics store and got six sets of walkie-talkies that had the longest range, and extra batteries for them, went over to Henson's to drop off the information for Freddy, and then went back to the marina. Sam was waiting for him, and they went over to the hotel restaurant for dinner.

The next day was just as busy as all the days before. It was now time for him to alert the pilot about the trip, so he called and arranged for the flight, giving him the location of the plane, time of the flight, tail number, etc. They told Gus the pilot's name was Ted Harrigan. He didn't know it yet, but Ted was going to have a co-pilot by the name of Martin Pochciol.

Gus set aside $200,000 to assure the silence of the new pilot, then with hardly any difficulty, found his name in the DCPPA directory, which had an entry for each pilot, including his professional credentials, i.e.: training, hours flown per aircraft, etc. family names: Carol, and children: Marci and Benjamin, and address, including his phone number, and other details, like his police record, military status, etc. Gus printed it off and placed it with the passports, medical records, extra money, and all the paperwork he thought he might need.

As an afterthought, Gus called Martin Pochciol to ask him an important question.

"Martin, this is Gus and I need to know something. We will not have keys to the aircraft, and I was wondering if there is any way to start the engines without them?"

"Not to worry, Gus. I worked for a repossession company for a while, and I can start any aircraft with or without keys."

"Great," Gus said, "that's a load off my mind. Thanks, Martin, one other thing, can you arrange to refuel the plane in Rio before we leave Miami?"

"Sure, Gus. I'll get right on it."

"OK," Gus said, "I'll see you at the meeting then, and thanks again."

Gus had the table set up on the stern and dinner laid out ready to eat when Sam got home. She was surprised that Gus had taken the time to do all this, especially since he'd been so busy, so she rewarded him with a big juicy kiss. "You're my favorite boyfriend, you know!"

"Favorite, hell! I'd better be your *only* boyfriend, or you'll have to find a way back on board!"

"I don't feel like taking a swim, so I'll just keep you as my *only* boyfriend, sweetheart."

"That's better, so eat before that expensive swordfish gets cold."

Time was closing in on the meeting date, so Gus and Sam started going over the lists they had compiled making sure that all the bases had been covered, all the i's had been dotted and all the t's had been crossed. They gave each other a kind of smug look when they found nothing wrong, either with their grammar or with their actions. They were right to be satisfied with their accomplishments, after all; it had been much harder than they had envisioned.

Gus had planned to have the jet refueled early Friday morning to reduce the possibility of anyone from the Murder Squad catching them doing it. He also told all the participants to deliver any firearms, ammunition, or armaments to Sam's house before the meeting in case there were any nosy people around the marina, and to try to arrive separately to avoid curiosity.

Since there were items to be done in order, he decided to make an itinerary, so he wouldn't forget anything. For this, he asked Sam for input. After all, two heads are better than one. They put their heads together and wrote the itinerary. Surprisingly, it turned out to be pretty long, including refueling the plane that Gus had thought of earlier. They made copies of it to hand out at the meeting. Gus then called Freddy and asked him for fifteen each duffel bags and ammo bags, and to deliver them to Sam's house, along with the bullet-proof vests.

On Meeting day, Gus had checked around the marina in the morning to make sure there were no unwanted visitors hanging around and found nothing. In fact, even the water was without ripples, no dogs barking nor birds chirping. Perfect, the teams were told to straggle in separately to avoid attention, and that's just what they were doing. Gus had the coffee going and Sam had baked a blueberry coffee cake for the entourage. By 10:30 they were all there, talking quietly.

At 10:45, Gus started the meeting. "Good morning, could I have your attention, please? What we're going to do this weekend will shock a lot of people and save a lot of lives. You mustn't feel remorse for this, because the people we're going to take out have police records as long as you can imagine, including murder, dismemberment, rape, etc. They certainly have no remorse or sympathy for their victims, and we're going to put a stop to it. Bulletproof vests, duffel bags, and ammo bags have been delivered to Sam's house and will be ready for pick-up when we meet there on Friday.

"There are three teams, so we'll need three vans to get to our assignments, and I need three people to pick up the vans on Friday afternoon at 1400." Two hands went up, so Gus said "Good, and I'll be the other one." Gus explained where the rental office was and said he'd meet them there and drive them back to Sam's house to park separately. The flying time from Miami to Rio is just over eight hours and thirty minutes, so Team One will meet at Sam's house at 1600 on Friday and be at the plane for takeoff at 1800. We want a coordinated attack at 0400 Saturday. Teams Two and Three need to make a dry run preceding the date of the attack to get the location and layout in preparation for the attack Saturday morning. Please, learn as much about your target as possible so you won't be caught short, we can't lose anybody!

"We are one man short, and we don't know why. His name is Frank Morgan, and he is a detective that I sent to Sao Paulo to investigate the medical facility owned by Dr. Angelo Cruz. We got his information but haven't heard from him since. It is his information that is contained in the packets you've been reading. Keep an eye out for him. The packets are the direct result of his investigation into these murdering bastards, so don't feel sympathy or remorse for what we're about to do. The longer they live, the more dead bodies there will be turning up. Destroy not only them but all their facilities so they can't ever be used again. Are there any questions?"

There was a bit of murmuring, but no one actually asked anything, which meant all the bases had been covered and they felt confident about their missions.

Gus said, "One more thing. For security reasons, I've picked up lightweight hooded jackets and masks for you to wear during the raids. Please get them and use them. They're in the dining room. As another precaution, get a couple of pairs of rubber gloves, also in the dining room, and keep them on you at all times. We don't want your finger-prints all over everything. There's one more 'One more thing': we have walkie-talkies for each of you which are set on channel 18. Try to use them sparingly, but not until the mission, although you may test them."

"That's all I have at the moment, so if you think of anything later, call me on your cell phone. Meeting's over. See you all at 1600, here at Sam's house on Friday."

CHAPTER THIRTY-FIVE

The rental agency had all three vans lined up and ready to go, so it was just a matter of Gus paying for them and picking up the keys. They were all black, as requested, so Gus handed out the keys and they headed for Sam's house.

When they arrived in Sam's neighborhood, two of them parked a half-block apart and one parked around the corner to prevent as much suspicion as possible, Of course, three shiny new vans still looked suspicious, but it couldn't be helped.

Sam arrived a little late, but, in her infinite wisdom had collected box meals for everyone, including fish and chips, sandwiches, salads, and an assortment of drinks (sans alcohol). There was plenty for everybody, so they ate first, cleared away the trash, and got down to sorting out the material to be used by each team. They packed their assortment into the vans, one at a time, after everyone set their watches, they all shook hands and promised to return to Sam's house when they were able to, and the coast was clear.

Team One arrived at the airport a little early, in order for Martin to start the engines without the keys. He had found a key that would fit in the ignition of the plane so it wouldn't look suspicious and then started both engines by hot-wiring them.

Ted Harrigan, arriving on time, looked a little surprised when both engines were running already. Gus walked over to Ted, introduced himself, and said "Is the plane fueled?"

"Yes," he said, "they fueled it early this morning. I'll check the plane and then it's ready."

"OK," Gus said, "but first let me introduce your co-pilot, Martin Pochciol."

Ted gave Gus a quick look but said nothing.

Martin said, "Let's get some gear on board, and then we can go."

While Gus took the van over to the side of the hangar and parked as close as he could get, Ted had seated himself in the left chair and was checking the instruments.

When they were all on board, Martin closed the door and took his seat in the cockpit.

After getting clearances, they took off, heading southeast.

Gus had no intention of telling Ted anything until they landed in Sao Paulo. He had no way of knowing how Ted would react when he found out what their mission was. Once in Sao Paulo, Ted would have become an accomplice and $200,000 richer.

The flight was long and easy, and with a slight tailwind, they arrived in Sao Paulo, at 2:15. After the plane shut down, Freddy got off and went to locate the vans for the trip into Sao Paulo,

While Freddy was off looking for his vans, Gus approached Ted and said, "Ted, can I talk to you for a minute?"

"Sure, what's up?"

"I wanted to let you in on the purpose of our mission."

"Mission! What do you mean by that?"

Gus patiently explained what Dr. Cruz was doing, how Gus's wife had been caught up in it, and how they were going to stop it by eliminating the whole operation.

"For your part in this, we want you to have $200,000," showing him the bag, "to forget what you've seen and heard for the rest of your life."

"What makes you think I'd go along with this?"

"Because we know where you live, we know your wife, Carol, and the kids, Marci, and Benjamin, and if you don't go along with this, remember by the time this is over, we will all be murderers, and you'll be an accomplice! But, if you keep your mouth shut, you'll be $200,000 richer, and no one will ever know you were even involved."

He stared at Gus with burning eyes for a long minute, and then said, "If you harm even a hair on any of my family, I'll make it a personal vendetta to find and kill you, even if it takes forever!"

"You won't have to because you're going to keep your mouth shut. That's all that's required of you. However, you may want to get a new passport. You can wait here at the aircraft because your co-pilot has arranged for refueling the plane."

While they were talking, three sets of lights were coming up the road towards the hangar, then turned in towards the plane.

Freddy got out of the SUV and yelled, "Found them!"

There was the SUV, a van, and a box truck. They loaded their luggage into the van and then got into the SUV for the trip into Sao Paulo. Freddy was driving and had a map of the city where he pointed out the location of the target to Gus. The twenty-five-kilometer trip took longer than expected, but they had time to reconnoiter prior to the raid, and since Gus had studied this facility in particular, thanks to Frank's drawings and maps, he was familiar with the layout.

They pulled into the alley at the rear of the building and unloaded their gear, then got the weapons from the box truck, spread out, and prepared to assault the top floor first, then work their way down from there. Gus checked his watch and found they had a few more minutes to wait, so he had them check their weapons and ammunition again, then put on their masks, and turn on their walkie-talkies, which is how they would receive the attack command, and spread out in preparation.

———

At exactly 4:00, EST, the attack began on all three facilities. The only unmanned target was the doctor's office in Little River. Since no one was allowed to live apart from their work, the staff in the other locations were housed within their workplaces, including Dr. Cruz. Therefore, all the staff would be available during the attack.

Since Brazil was in the Atlantic time zone, it was already 6:00 local time, and the sky was getting a little lighter. They had agreed to stick to the Eastern time zone so there would be no confusion, and everyone's watch was set to EST.

Hand grenades were the first weapon used. Each door was opened, and two grenades, one fragmentation, and one incendiary grenade were tossed in as they progressed down the hall. If anyone opened their door and came into the hall, after the grenades, they were to be immediately shot. After they had opened all the doors on the top floor, they dropped down to the next floor, where the staff was housed, and repeated the process until all the floors were on fire. No one survived, or came into the hallway, after the initial attack.

The team regrouped at the vehicles and moved them away from the burning building, then fired four RPGs (rocket-propelled grenades) into the main floor and spaced the full length of the building. It was collapsing as they drove away toward the airport.

Chuck Addison had already picked up the Bayliner at the Sea Isle Marina and loaded it on the north side of Treasure Island with his team's required munitions. He and Will Tucker would take the Bayliner up Little River and tie off out of the line of fire across from the Yacht.

Meanwhile, Neil and Lenny would take their van over to NE 7th Court where they could see the guard shack of Cruz's compound. They talked between themselves and decided that Lenny would drive the van through the gate and Neil would go on foot to take out the guard with the crossbow, shoot an RPG into the mansion, reload, and keep firing RPGs until someone showed up, then use fragmentation and incendiary grenades to wipe out anyone still alive in the mansion. The blockhouse, to the right of the gate, would be taken out with grenades until the prisoners could be found and released, then incendiaries would be used to destroy the building.

After the yacht was destroyed, Chuck and Will would drive across the river to assist Neil and Lenny in destroying the blockhouse and mansion, load the prisoners into the boat, and head for Treasure Island, after making sure no one escaped from the compound. Neil and Lenny would drive the van over to Treasure Island, load the prisoners into the van and drive it to Sam's house. Chuck and Will would then return the Bayliner to the dock at Sea Island Marina and then drive their cars to Sam's house.

Sam's team arrived at the doctor's office the same way they'd approached it the last time. Sam had memorized the office configuration and had a pretty good idea how many file cabinets there were, and where, so she had brought enough incendiaries, and more, to do the job. They went to the rear of the office building and set the incinerator on fire by carefully placing the incendiaries in the most vulnerable locations, with one fragmentation grenade on the gas meter, connected to a timer, then worked their way to the front door, destroying each room as they went. Once outside, Rodney and Ben both fired RPGs into the building, which was already blazing, and watched the building blow apart. After the clinic had become a blazing inferno, they walked over to the river, where they had parked the van, and returned to Sam's house.

Ted was quiet all the way back to Miami, although you could see on his face that he was not unhappy about the money after Gus personally delivered it to him. He figured, what the hell, nobody knew he was involved in the "mission," so how could anybody pin anything on him; and as for the money, well, he would have no trouble figuring out what to do with it.

Team one was the last to arrive at Sam's house and the first thing on the agenda was to clean and return the trucks to the rental agency. With the trucks returned, each drove their own cars to Sam's house.

When all were present, Gus collected them on the lanai, and told them, "Gentlemen, and ladies, I want to personally thank each and every one of you for your efforts to rid Miami of the scourge that has plagued not only this city but others as well for years. Not one word of what we did must ever pass your lips to anyone. Just rest assured that what we have done was a donation to the city and has to remain anonymous forever. Thank you again, and now it's time to disband and return to your lives. I guess you could call this 'The Final Cut.'"

The prisoners, two men and one woman, who didn't understand English, were huddled in the corner of the lanai. They were told, in very poor Spanish, that they should get back across the border and to never mention what had happened, because their names were known, and would wind up dead if they ever spoke of what they'd seen. They were taken to the bus station in Miami and given one hundred dollars each and told to disappear.

After everyone had gone, Sam looked at Gus and said, "Am I disbanded as well, Gus?"

"Oh yes, you are. In fact, I would like to re-band you with this," and he held out a one-and-a-half-carat diamond engagement ring.

"Are you serious, Gus?"

"Never more serious in my life. Now get your paperwork completed to retire, and then we're going off to see the world together."

ABOUT THE AUTHOR

Thomas Ulmer is a former Miami, Florida, resident who retired as a United States Air Force Master Sergeant. He was a radio technician for five years, then served as a Crypto Technician for another fifteen years. During his tenure in the USAF, he became one of the youngest technicians to operate the largest computer at that time in history. Its purpose was to test the Detroit Air Defense Sector radar units. After retirement, he began a second career with the National Security Agency. He currently lives with his wife, Janice, in Summerfield, Florida.